THE SPY PRINCESS

C.2

THE SPY PRINCESS

SHERWOOD SMITH

VIKING
An Imprint of Penguin Group (USA) Inc.

VIKING
Published by the Penguin Group
Penguin Young Readers Group, 345 Hudson Street, New York, New York 10014, U.S.A.
Penguin Group (Canada), 90 Eglinton Avenue East, Suite 700, Toronto, Ontario, Canada M4P 2Y3
(a division of Pearson Penguin Canada Inc.)
Penguin Books Ltd, 80 Strand, London WC2R 0RL, England
Penguin Ireland, 25 St Stephen's Green, Dublin 2, Ireland (a division of Penguin Books Ltd)
Penguin Group (Australia), 250 Camberwell Road, Camberwell, Victoria 3124, Australia (a division
of Pearson Australia Group Pty Ltd)
Penguin Books India Pvt Ltd, 11 Community Centre, Panchsheel Park, New Delhi – 110 017, India
Penguin Group (NZ), 67 Apollo Drive, Rosedale, Auckland 0632, New Zealand (a division of
Pearson New Zealand Ltd.)
Penguin Books (South Africa) (Pty) Ltd, 24 Sturdee Avenue, Rosebank, Johannesburg 2196, South
Africa

Penguin Books Ltd, Registered Offices: 80 Strand, London WC2R 0RL, England

First published in the United States of America by Viking,
a division of Penguin Young Readers Group, 2012

10 9 8 7 6 5 4 3 2 1

Text and map copyright © Sherwood Smith, 2012
All rights reserved

LIBRARY OF CONGRESS CATALOGING-IN-PUBLICATION DATA IS AVAILABLE
ISBN 978-0-670-06341-3

Printed in U.S.A.   Set in Agfa Wile Roman Std   Book and map design by Kate Renner

To the memory of that attic room overlooking Lake Arrowhead,
the summer I turned fifteen

THE SPY PRINCESS

PART I

Friends

If you visit my old home, Selenna House, the first thing you see is the wrecked gate. Weeds grow all around. The broad drive, once so smooth, is pitted with holes.

Then you come to the fountain, which still spouts four streams of water, for the magic spell on it will probably last another hundred years. You think, Whose idea of art is this, flying babies and cats and other sentimental footle? Well, let me tell you, that fountain hides secrets.

But you don't know that, so you look at the house. Its forty tall windows—twenty-four upstairs, sixteen downstairs—are now mostly broken, like a big grin with missing teeth. Soot blackens the walls, and if you go inside, you see the dangling chain where the great silver and crystal chandelier once hung, and the grand stairways on either side of the hall that sweep upward to a landing littered with animal nests and ashes and broken bits of furniture. A row of rooms opens off it.

The door at the end? That led to my rooms.

It's cleaner downstairs, because the last tenants swept the floor before they were swept by slam justice.

Oh, I'm sure you've heard about that, and maybe some of what you heard is what actually happened.

I am here to tell you the real truth, because I—Lilah Selenna—was there.

one

I glanced at my time-candle. It hadn't burned down any farther since I last checked. If only the sun would hurry! Because a person's first adventure *had* to begin at midnight. Wasn't it that way in all the best records?

One of my windows overlooked the cedar-lined drive that led to the high, guarded gates. Beyond those gates was Riveredge Village. The only glimpses I ever got of Riveredge were as our carriage, surrounded by armed guards, rolled through on the way to the royal city. The houses were falling apart. The boys and girls my age—dirty, ragged, and sullen—stared at the carriage, and I stared back. Of late the stares were more angry than sullen.

Once a girl yelled something at me. One of my father's outriders veered his horse just enough to club her with the hilt of his sword. "That girl—" I exclaimed.

"Worthless, Lilah," my father snapped. "Sit properly. Remember your manners."

I sneaked a peek at my older brother Peitar, whose thin, tired face didn't change, except for one quick glance in my direction, which I knew was a warning.

I didn't want warnings, I wanted answers. "She sounded mad. Is she mad at us, Father? At me? Why?"

"No reason, child. They are merely lazy and disobedient."

"But—"

My father, His Highness Oscarbidal Selenna, Prince of Selenna, pursed his mouth in disapproval. "That filthy rabble is not a matter for your concern." His courtly drawl had shortened in irritation. "Your duty is to learn to be a proper lady."

I gave up on my father. I'd ask Peitar. And if he disappointed me, as happened more often these days, I'd find out on my own.

Not that Peitar treated me like Father did. Far from it. But Peitar was moodier than ever. I assumed his lame leg pained him, because he stayed in his rooms reading and writing not just all day but far into the night.

Once I managed to get him alone after supper. His answer? "Politics, Lilah. Let that subject lie while you can. I am very much afraid . . ." He looked away. "There's little we can do at present." Then he fell into one of his abstract moods.

I decided I had to find my answers on my own. Since I was confined at home, and expected to waste my time thinking about ruffles and hair ribbons, I needed a disguise.

I got my idea from Lasthavais Dei the Wanderer. Ever since I'd discovered her amazing life, I'd been glad of those long, tedious lessons learning Sartoran, even though it was no longer spoken at court.

Lasva had written, *The best disguise is to assume a role that no one would expect. From man to woman, or woman to man—though these are not always possible for all people, and are very hard to maintain. The next easiest is to change status, but again it is hard to maintain, for it is not only our clothes but our manners and mode of speech that divide us from the other tiers of society. Be observant, my young sisters reading my words! And pay attention to detail. . . .*

So I'd disguise myself as a village boy.

My father didn't like servants—even stable boys—to wear stained or ragged clothes. If something got ruined it went to the rag pile, which I had made part of my daily walk, resulting in a shirt one day and some knee pants another. I'd had to wait longest for the cap.

Last year, the noble boys had all worn soft cloth caps. When the fad passed, those caps were handed down to the servants. Peitar's, worn by his favorite among the stable boys, had found its way to the rags just the day before.

Now it was tucked under my mattress, and I was ready to go exploring.

JUST BEFORE THE midnight bells, I got out of bed, drew my curtains, and lit a single candle.

First, I yanked a brush through my reddish-brown mane. It always looked messy and made me hot, and I longed to cut it all off—except noble ladies had long hair, and that was that. I braided it tightly and wound it around my head, tucking the ends under. I'd practiced many times and had finally gotten it to stay.

Then I pulled out the cap and the clothes, which were wrinkled and dirty from their stay on the rag pile. The tunic fit fine, but the knee pants were much too big. I tied them on with one of Peitar's old sashes. Last, I fitted the cap over my braid.

Then I looked in the mirror and laughed.

It is easiest for the young to disguise, Princess Lasva had said. *Those without adult contours have more freedom of choice.* It was true!

The boy in the mirror would not have raised a second glance. True, my slanted eyes and bony face now seemed more foxlike than ever, but these were common enough features in Sarendan. I'd borrowed the name of a former stable hand, now in the Blue Guard: Larei.

The one problem was my clean skin. *Remember the details!* My first appointment would be with the dirt in the garden.

It was time to go.

My palms were sweaty. I wiped them on my knee pants, opened the curtains and the window, and shinned down the argan tree, fast from long habit. Then I eased through the ferny border near my brother's windows.

As soon as I was out of sight of the house, I dug my fingers into the clean-smelling loam, then rubbed it over my neck, face, arms, and legs. Since I was little, I'd run barefoot through the garden. My feet were tough.

I let my eyes adjust to the darkness. Above me, the clouds glowed like a ceiling of silver cotton, rendering the garden and house as silhouettes. The brightest light came from the windows of the guardhouses at either side of the big gates, far to the south.

Then I looked around, giddy with triumph. The one good thing I'd inherited with my slanted Selenna eyes was night vision. I ran toward the wall between the guardhouses, then stopped in dismay. It was a lot higher than I'd remembered.

I found an oak with one great branch that extended beyond the wall. I was about to hoist myself up when a taunting voice startled me.

"What's the matter? Are you turning into a hatchling?" I could just make out the speaker, a scrawny boy. "Too cowardly to stay and have fun?"

"Got lost." I could tell from the way he spoke that he was a villager, and I tried to talk the way he did.

"They're all over there. Except the hatchlings. Went home. Are you one?"

I wasn't about to admit where home was. "I'll stay."

"Right, then. Come along." He stepped closer. "You don't sound like anyone I know. Who told you about the run?" His face was narrow, with eyes slightly less slanted than my own. "Like that cap," he added. "Nacky. Swipe it from a noble?"

"Yup."

He gave a nod of approval as we walked. "How old are you?"

"Twelve and seven months. You?"

"Twelve this season. You count the months, like the nobles?" When I shrugged defensively, he added, "Or is it your mother counts?"

"No mother," I said. "Father couldn't care less. Only the—" I remembered that villagers didn't have governesses or servants.

"The . . . ?"

"Never mind!" I snapped, afraid of being discovered.

The boy flung up his hands. "You sure do get riled! What's your name?"

"Larei. You?"

"Bren." He scowled. "I'm named for a noble, so if you hear t'other name and use it I'll smash you a good one. Sometimes my cousin says it when she's mad."

The stable boys talked to each other like that. It meant that the speaker was upset about the thing in the threat. "What's the name? I won't use it," I added, "but so I know."

"Sharadan." Wondering why Bren's mother had picked the name of a court family, I only nodded. "Anyway, Breneos is my dad's name. He said I could use it, too. Ma's snobbishness might get me into trouble."

I wasn't sure what he meant, but I was glad that he was so talkative. "So you hate the family in the palace?" I asked.

Bren laughed. "Where you been?"

"In my house. Sick. Long time—most of my life."

"So that's why I don't know you, and your dad is, what,

one of the farmhands, lives out east o' the village?" After I shrugged, he said, "Want the whole story?"

At last! And I didn't even have to figure out how to ask!

He let out a happy sigh. "Derek said we ought to recruit, and I never thought I'd get the chance. See, Riveredge used to be a good market town. Used to be lots of 'em in Selenna. But King Dirty Hands wanted more taxes, on top of the prince's, so a lot of the guilds and merchants moved. Now all that's left are people who work for Prince Greedy—or don't have skills enough to get away. And Prince Greedy still collects taxes, even with the drought going on now two years. Derek says the taxes are supposed to be against times like this, so there'll be food, and money for the Blue Guard, and renewing the magic spells—like our cleaning frames and the wands to get rid of animal droppings. Well, the taxes go straight to the prince's belly. Or to his brats, Lady Fluffbrain and Lord Cripple. Or get wasted on his fancy wigs. And the rest go to the king, who's got a gigantic army, even though there's no danger from outside."

Lady Fluffbrain? Heat prickled my face. "What about defending ourselves against the evil warriors of Norsunder?"

Bren snorted. "Everyone talks about them, but they never come."

"They hold Sartor," I said.

Bren snorted even louder. "They won't come here. Nobody's crossed those mountains in generations. King Dirty Hands is building that army to use against *us*, Derek says.

Because people are tired of being hungry. In some villages, where the spells have run out and haven't been renewed, things are dirty and falling apart. It causes disease—everyone knows that. We're tired of a king who doesn't do anything but collect taxes and make ready for war. No one helps us." He laughed. "So here we are, to help ourselves. Slam justice, that's what it's called!"

I forced a laugh as well, wondering what they were there to help themselves to. Then he pointed at a plum tree. "I didn't believe it until I saw it myself. They really do grow food as *ornament* here," he said with loathing. "And in Riveredge people sleep hungry at night!"

He plucked viciously at the plums, cramming one in his mouth and flinging others against the nearby trees.

I thought that it would make more sense to carry some back to the hungry people, but again I was afraid to speak.

Crashing bushes and the light thud of footsteps were followed by a girl's voice. "Bren?"

"Here! With Larei."

"Larei? Who's that?" The girl appeared, two boys with her. "Phew, it's hard to get about in this dark. We found an orange tree, right near the stream. A stream! All for no one, and we only have the one well left for the whole village!" She hefted an apron full of oranges.

Bren began adding plums to her pile as the girl continued, "Where are the others? Went hatchling on us, huh?

Just like I thought! Well, we saw someone lurking round the house, and we yelled 'Down with tyranny!' and ran. Fun! Where you been?" Her voice was wonderful, high and clear, like a singer's.

"Here, talkin' to Larei."

"Never saw you before," she said, coming close to me. She was small and thin, the shape of her face like Bren's.

"I never saw *you* before," I said, deciding that it was better to bluff.

The others laughed.

"Larei lives out on one o' the east farms," Bren said. "Larei, that's my cousin Deon."

"She's the one who met Derek first," Bren added. "And those are my brothers, Tam and Tim."

The younger boys bobbed their heads.

"I'd like to meet Derek," I said.

"Is he coming to the village?" Bren asked his cousin.

"Tomorrow night. If the scummers don't get him first." Deon jerked her chin in the direction of the walls, where the guards patrolled.

Bren turned eagerly my way. "We meet him at the bridge, when the moon comes out. If it's cloudy, we wait for the next night, unless he says. Can't see if the Selenna scummers are sneakin' up on us if it's too dark."

"Don't need to overwork the gallows." Deon was grim. "They already get more customers than most traders, these days."

I tried to sound casual. "Don't suppose you tried to talk to the noble brats?"

"Try seeing if they'll talk to *us*," Deon scoffed. "Only time their precious highnesses breathe our air is when they ride by in their fancy carriage on their way to the capital to visit the king."

"Better them than me," Tim said in a low voice.

All the others agreed—and I did, too. I mean, *I* knew what my uncle was like!

"Be at the bridge at moonrise day after tomorrow." Bren thumped me on the shoulder. "You'll meet Derek then, and he can tell you lots more. And maybe we'll hear some *real* news."

"I'll try to be there. If I can get away from my dad. 'Bye."

I ran southward, glancing back once. Sure enough, Bren was following, and I heard the others blundering along behind him. They wanted to see where I lived.

I laughed to myself. I knew the gardens too well for that to be a problem and soon lost them.

Once I'd climbed to my room, I stashed my disguise under the mattress, jumped through the cleaning frame, pulled on my nightgown, and threw myself into bed. The most I'd dared hope for was a walk around the village to see the buildings up close. I hadn't thought to meet anyone at all, much less someone my age.

This adventure was going to be easy.

two

I was sound asleep the next morning when my governess came in.

Lizana was middle-aged and stout, and very, very smart. She'd been my mother's maid and had taken care of me since I was born. I woke up to find her eyeing me suspiciously. Usually I was the first one awake.

"I think I have a fever," I mumbled. I meant to sneak out as Larei again, and the last thing I wanted was bed checks!

Lizana's eyebrows rose. She was used to sickness. Peitar was sick all too often.

"I'll get the medicine." At the doorway, she turned back. "Now, you lie there and rest. His Highness wishes to talk to you."

Within a very short time shoes clacked on the landing, and my father came in.

I tried to see him the way the villagers did: a heavy man wearing a purple velvet suit with lace at throat and wrists and an old-fashioned wig of long, curling red hair. His features were pinched with irritation. He pulled over one of my dainty chairs and sat down carefully, then examined the gold-edged buckles on his shoes with approval.

Lizana reappeared with a tray, and His Highness lifted

his nose. "Be gone. You know I dislike servants hovering when I talk to my children." My father spoke in the court drawl that had been popular for years—until my uncle came to the throne.

Uncle Darian never drawled. Nor did he wear wigs.

Lizana set the tray down and left.

"Lilah, child, this illness is most inconvenient," my father began. "I was going to tell you at breakfast today that in two weeks we depart for Miraleste."

To the capital! That meant the royal palace—and my uncle, the king. My stomach knotted. "Why?"

Father's brow furrowed. "You are a good child most of the time, Lilah, but this inquisitiveness is most unbecoming. You must curb the habit. Well-bred children are polite and obedient. Suffice it to say that we make the journey for your benefit."

"Yes, Father," I said in my well-practiced Polite and Obedient Voice, though I burned with indignation—and with questions that I knew would not be answered. As usual.

"Good child." He rose, adjusting the satin edges of his cuffs. "Sleep well."

As soon as he had clacked down the stairs, I hopped out of bed and inspected the tray. Broth and medicine: from the smell a bitter, nasty willow-bark decoction, suitable for fever and ache. I dumped the medicine out the window. I hoped it wouldn't poison the trees.

The broth I drank as I wondered why we had to go to the capital—and why *I* should benefit. The dread was even stronger than the questions.

Next came the uneven rhythm of Peitar's step. That was a surprise. He entered, leaning heavily on his crutch as he always did after climbing the long stairway. His face seemed more drawn than ever, set in an expression of hard-won patience.

From where I sat I could see us framed in my mirror, in some ways so alike—the slanted eyes and sharp chin and angled cheekbones—and in some so different. I was built more like my father. Peitar was just over medium height, dark-haired, and light in build. Like our mother had been. Like Uncle Darian.

I shuddered and did my best to look sick.

"You don't have to feign illness. You're as healthy as I am."

"You aren't healthy—"

"So everyone tells me," he retorted. "I'm crippled, not sick. Though I admit I use that when I have to."

"I hate it when you sound like Uncle."

"I saw you sneak past my window last night, Lilah," he said mildly.

I sat upright. "You know?" Peitar's smile made him look younger—more like his nineteen years. Yet the smile didn't quite reach his eyes. "Are you going to tell?"

He shook his head, still smiling. "Ah, little sister, how I've wished to do the same! What did you find?"

"I met some villagers sneaking around, and—" I stopped short. "Wait, *you* want to explore, too?"

"I kept that to myself until I saw you last night. We're too good at hiding our real selves, I suppose." He paused, as if making up his mind about something. "But we've been fooling one another when, perhaps, we should be working together."

"Working together? How? On what?"

"First tell me what you found out, and what you think of it."

I have loved my brother ever since I was tiny—all the more intensely after our mother died when I was two. He was the one who had given me books to read after Father had forbidden Lizana to continue my lessons. He'd done it with her unspoken approval, too, telling me all the details about Lasva Dei and the adventurers I admired, and he also practiced Sartoran with me when Lizana was busy. I trusted him more than anyone—but then he'd stopped answering my questions.

I told him about meeting Bren, what he had said, and what I had answered. Peitar listened, and when he didn't look angry or shocked, I finished, "So I ran back here, and I was trying to figure out a way to get over the wall before moonrise tomorrow, and meet this Derek person."

"I wonder . . ." Peitar's hand tightened on his crutch. "I wonder if you ought to meet Derek. The problem is, it's

almost impossible to separate him from dangerous circumstances, even just to talk."

More surprises. "Dangerous? Wait, wait! You *know*
Derek?"

"Yes."

My insides felt as if someone had dumped me out the
window along with the medicine. "Tell me! I want to know
what's going on."

"I've known Derek for years. Ever since we were—oh,
not much older than you are now. Lilah, he wants to raise
Sarendan in revolution." *Revolution?*

"Why? How?"

Peitar's forehead puckered with worry. "He wants to
right the wrongs he sees about him. We both do. He thinks
the way is through violence, and I'm not so sure. But then
I sit here in safety."

"Safety!" I repeated in scorn.

Peitar's lips twisted. "To those outside the family, it
seems our lives are nothing but plenty and bliss. The plenty
I will grant, but the bliss—well, you know as well as I.
Derek doesn't know, nor do his followers, what life is like
here, or in Miraleste, for us."

"Can't you just tell him?"

"It's not that simple." He looked distracted, and I wondered if he was going to get lost inside his head as he often
did. Then he blinked. "As for how, those children in the vil-

lage are to be a part of it, just as countless ordinary people in towns and villages all over the country will be a part. On a given signal they will attack the local authorities. Like us." Peitar indicated himself, me, and then downstairs, where Father sat in his rooms.

"Attack? But people might get hurt!" I exclaimed.

"Yes. Yet too many think it's a game. Not all. But some think it's impossible that any real harm could happen to them, because their intentions are good."

"What can we do to fix things?" When he hesitated, I said, "Not telling me doesn't stop me from worrying. Nobody answers my questions. That's one of the reasons why I dressed as Larei, to find out! And why are we going to Miraleste, anyway? Father said it was to benefit me. What did he mean?"

"Lilah, I think it's to arrange a marriage for you."

"Ugh!" I exclaimed. "You're not betrothed, so why should I get stuck with it?"

"I'm not because . . . more politics." Peitar looked away. "Though I might be forced into it, if . . . oh, if things don't change." He met my eyes. "If it helps, you and your intended will decide when the marriage actually takes place. So if you want, it could be ten years. Or twenty, if you're deft— you will probably have the higher rank, so you'll have more say. You just need to be diplomatic."

"But I'll still be betrothed. Some fun if he's a snob, and

most of those court boys are snobs. And what if Uncle says I have to live with the boy's family? At least if he joins ours, I can stick him in the farthest room and pretend he isn't here."

Peitar grinned. "None of that has to be decided now." He struggled to his feet. "Maybe you *should* go into town—but go during the day, if you think your disguise will hold. Far too many of those children are roaming around with nothing to do and little to eat. Talk to them. Listen to them. I'll invent a cover for you. The threat of contagion ought to keep Father away. Just come back as soon as you've met Derek. We'll talk tomorrow morning."

He left. I stared after him, in wonder.

three

Next morning, Lizana brought a bigger breakfast than usual. "Eat everything," was all she said.

Had Peitar talked to her? And *that* would mean that she also knew about Derek and revolution, wouldn't it?

I'd worry about that later. Right now, what worried me was the fact that I was going to try my disguise in daylight, among people who hated me and my family.

I pulled out the Larei clothes and inspected them. Bren and Deon hadn't recognized me. *If I don't try, I'll hate myself forever.*

I rebraided my hair, dressed carefully, and after I shinnied down the tree, dirtied myself everywhere, even underneath the tunic's laces. Then I raced through the garden, made sure the sentries couldn't see me, and got myself over the wall.

Outside Selenna House the weeds grew untended, and the wild olive trees were picked clean. I set out for Riveredge, using the shrubbery along the stream as cover. I was glad I was used to going barefoot, because the ground was stony and full of weed-stickers. I passed abandoned houses, the roof-thatch gone along with the doors. Some of the stone walls had been taken apart and hauled away.

Soon the occupied part of the village was in sight.

My father's carriage always followed Prince Street, the once-grand main road, which cut through the town square. The houses there were in the best condition, though much repaired. The rest of Riveredge looked terrible.

On the few remaining fences, somebody had scrawled *Unity!* and *Down with Tyranny!* Then I stopped short. Decorating one wall was a skillful drawing of my father, Peitar— and me.

The fat, fox-faced girl with the long hair had her nose turned up and her mouth turned down. Next to her stood a larger, fatter man wearing a gigantic wig, his mouth turned down, too. The one that upset me was the crooked figure, more crooked in the sketch than in real life.

I burned with anger. It wasn't Peitar's fault our father had forced him onto the back of a warhorse when my brother was seven—of course he'd get thrown!

Even when I was small, I somehow understood that the accident never would have happened if Uncle Darian hadn't insisted Peitar was spoiled, that he needed to get trained and tough. My uncle had banished all the mages from the kingdom, in case any were conspiring against him; that meant the healer mages were gone, too. Uncle Darian always said a strong man healed on his own.

So Peitar's shattered knee was never treated correctly. That was when he'd started reading in earnest—Lizana had told me about the first year, when pain kept him awake at night, and he set out to read every single book in our library.

Whoever made that drawing had no idea.

I gave the wall a last glare and walked on. I passed a few more houses and reached a rickety bridge just as a swarm of boys and girls arrived from the other direction.

"There he is!" Bren! My heartbeat quickened again. "Larei! Here!"

He was perched on the wooden rail. In the daylight, I saw that his patched tunic had long ago lost its laces, and that he, too, wore knee pants, cast-offs from the fashion of the generation before. The others were as ragged and dirty. I sauntered warily toward them.

"We were calling the hatchlings hatchlings." Bren flapped his arms at me. "Said they were chased off. I say they lie. Did you see anyone t'other night?"

A small girl with filthy blonde hair whined in look-at-me injury, "I *saw* the *cripple* and they won't *believe* me. He said I should run away before the guards got me. So I *did*."

"Now why would he do that?" Deon asked sarcastically. "I think you made it up. His Crookedness would call the guards on you and laugh as they dragged you to the guardhouse."

"Doesn't make sense," another boy exclaimed. "Why should Crook-Leg send you off?" As he said it, he made a gesture with two fingers, one straight and one bent.

"He did! He did!" The little girl hopped from one foot to the other, shrieking as the others continued to scoff.

I didn't dare tell them that Peitar would be likely to do just that. But the girl crouched down in a ball on the other side of the bridge, her arms wrapped around her legs as she sobbed, all showing off forgotten. "He did," she cried. "Crook-Leg sent me away."

I couldn't stay silent anymore.

"I say it could've happened." Everyone turned my way. "It's a big place. Who knows—maybe some of them are on our side."

"Oh, sure, and they just haven't had a chance to come over here and help us," Deon sneered.

"Well, maybe Prince Redwig would have 'em killed." Bren spread his hands. "I know! We'll ask Derek."

Deon tilted her head. "Fair enough."

The little girl gave a hiccup, her crying over.

"So let's have some fun," someone said.

I was worried, for I didn't know any games, but the rules were easy to figure out.

As we played, I discovered that they all knew one another, but they weren't old friends. In fact, judging from things I overheard—and some exchanged looks—the village children had kept to separate groups until recently. The ones who worked on the Selenna farms were distrusted by the trade families, and villagers scowled at farmers.

I asked Bren about it when we were hiding in an empty trough. He told me that Derek had insisted they make friends, because he wanted them to work together.

"For what?"

"Derek says we need to be unified. Learn everything nobles do. He even made us practice reading and writing! You'll see."

By late morning, I was hungry and thirsty, despite my big breakfast. People ran down to the river to drink. So did I. I had a feeling that there wasn't going to be any food.

When the midday bells tolled, everyone stopped, looking grim as they began picking up rocks and stuffing them in pockets or wrapping them in worn aprons or skirts.

"Hurry up," Bren said to me. At my puzzled expression, he added, "Slam justice! Get those rocks, fast!" and smacked me on the shoulder. I staggered, bit back a protest, and loaded up until he gave a short, sharp whistle. "Come on. You're with us."

We joined some boys loping along a street winding between shabby houses, then over a low wall and up onto the roof of a stone building. It was no harder than climbing a tree. I looked down—straight into the guardhouse courtyard.

Bren whispered, "We can't stop 'em from that." He pointed at the main street, where two families slowly departed, the adults harnessed to old carts piled with possessions. "They can't pay the taxes."

"Where will they go?" I whispered back.

"I don't know." Bren made a face, then indicated the adjacent rooftop, where Deon stood with a group of girls. They each held something—some had stones, but others had metal pans or trays. "At least we might be able to stop *this*."

Below, several people marched out. I gulped when I recognized my father behind an honor guard, all of whom carried spears. He wore his pale gray velvet judgment robe, trimmed with blue silk braiding, the Selenna colors. He looked hot and sweaty and in a very bad mood.

Then came more guards, leading a disheveled man in bloodstained clothing.

At the other end of the courtyard was a gallows.

My mouth dried, and I clutched the rocks tightly.

Again, Bren whistled.

Everyone on the roof began throwing stones at the guards, except for the girls with the pans. They aimed them so the sunlight reflected into the men's faces, dazzling them.

"Get those brats!" my father roared.

I flung my rocks as hard as I could. Not one hit the targets. The boys began jumping down from the roof.

"Run," Bren said, tugging me. "Unless you want to get caught! Down with tyranny!" he shrieked, and leaped awkwardly after his friends, his arms windmilling.

I landed hard, my ankles twinging, and followed Bren between houses, under an ancient, warped fence, and across scrubby vegetable gardens. Finally, we collapsed onto a grassy bank near the slow-moving river, laughing breathlessly.

"Did ya see that one with the purple nose?"

"I got three of 'em!"

Bren poked me. "You're sure bad with a rock, Larei. Couldn't hit a fence at two paces."

"I was sick for a long time, remember?"

"Oh, that's right." As Deon and the girls flopped down nearby, Bren asked, "Did they get him away?"

"Yes," she said, grinning. "The big girls hobbled the guards' horses. I heard Prince Greedy cursing just before I hopped the stable fence."

Everyone cheered, sending the birds perched on a roof pole flapping skyward. I listened to the excited chatter as they either bragged or praised each other. We had been the decoys for some adults rescuing the condemned man, who was one of Derek's followers.

Then everyone raced down to the river and jumped in, clothes and all. The cool water felt delicious, though I had to be careful my cap did not come loose or even get wet.

After a time we climbed out and lay on the bank, some talking—mostly about food—until a patrol rode along, imposing in their fine blue battle tunics and shiny weapons.

"You brats." The leader reined in his horse. It was the captain of the day guard, uncle to one of the stable boys.

"Any of you near the guardhouse today?"

"No, sir," a little boy said. Everyone else shook their heads.

"Liars," another Blue Guard snarled. "We ought to hang 'em all."

"We will," the leader said, scowling as he mopped his brow. "If we catch you worthless rats anywhere near there."

Catcalls and scorn were the result—when the patrol was well out of hearing.

Bren shook his head. "Don't strut too much. Remember what Derek said. Most of the Blue Guards here are the stupid, lazy ones, or the ones whose families work for Prince Greedy. The smart ones get taken into the king's army. If they send *them* here, we'll catch it hot."

"Aw, quit nagging," another boy said, and the rest made rude noises.

After another game, the sun began to sink beyond the distant mountains. The shadows melted together, hiding the ugliness of the houses and the hungry, underfed look of my companions. The smells of supper drifted on the air, mostly corn mash fried with wild olives. The gang gradually left, until finally it was only Bren, Deon, the twins, and me.

By now I had figured out that Bren and Deon were the leaders. Though I was ravenous, I wanted to meet Derek. If they could endure hunger, then so could I.

We walked through the village. The twins took turns skipping rocks down the dusty path until we reached the bridge. Bren hitched himself onto the creaking rail.

"I don't know how many more times the roof plan will work," Deon said finally.

"Probably none." Bren shrugged. "That's what Derek said, 'Surprise only works once.'"

"It might be one of our parents next."

Bren said nothing.

Tim poked Deon. "Sing for us."

"Something good, not mushy," Tam added.

She drew in a deep breath, and launched into an exciting ballad. She had a good voice and brought the story to life. Her next song I liked even better. She'd taken the melody to a soppy love song and put new words to it, all about Derek's adventures. She sang several more songs, mostly ones she'd made up.

I leaned back, enjoying the soft night air, the songs, the success of my disguise. I had—for the first time—friends. They didn't pretend to like me because my father was a prince and my uncle the king, like the young courtiers in Miraleste. In fact, if they'd known that, they would have hated me. Still, I wished that this moment would never end.

But it did. Deon finished the last song, and Bren pointed at the moon, which hung low over the rooftops.

We listened. Water chuckled over stones in the river below; one of the twins fidgeted, making the bridge creak. I could hear Deon's quick breathing.

Then came the sound of hoofbeats.

four

The rider dismounted at the foot of the bridge and handed the reins to Tim and Tam.

Derek was difficult to see in the darkness, until he looked up and moonlight illuminated his face. He was about Peitar's size, and he walked soft and wary. He had light brown eyes, a short nose, a mobile mouth. His dark hair was ragged, as if it had been cut with a knife.

"Deon." He had a fine voice. "Timrei, Tameos, Milord Sharadan—"

"Hey!" Bren protested, and the tension vanished.

"I was wondering if you'd notice." Derek laughed. "Remember last time?"

"I couldn't help falling asleep! We'd been on watch for days."

Derek laughed again, joined by the others. "I know. I can't help teasing you—you're so easy to get a squawk out of."

"Hmph," Bren mumbled, embarrassed.

"Another recruit?" The brown eyes turned my way. "Name?"

"Larei," I said, self-consciously pitching my voice low.

"You'll be a good asset." The way Derek said that, I got

the feeling he knew who I was. He must have talked to Peitar.

Bren gave me a questioning look. That good feeling I'd had earlier, the sense that I'd found some friends, had vanished. I remembered Lord Cripple and Lady Fluffbrain and Prince Greedy. I was afraid that if they found out who I really was, this time the stones would be thrown at *me*.

Derek seemed to notice the renewed tension, for his tone changed. "Listen. To business, for I have to be quick. The guards are on the prowl, and I have much to discuss with Number One before I can leave the area."

"They're prowling because they're mad. At us," Deon said proudly. "Did you hear about the rescue?"

"I spoke with Selenna Leader just a while ago," Derek responded in a tone of approval. "Good job. But that won't work again. I'll tell the adults, too."

"Better the grown-ups don't get caught in the first place," Deon said sourly.

"Sometimes that's harder than it seems." Unlike Deon, Derek sounded mild. "We're all taking risks these days. We must."

I was still thinking about something Derek had said. My family name, Selenna, also belonged to the principality. Maybe "Selenna Leader" was a kind of regional leader. Obviously an enemy of my father's. Or—could it be my brother?

I looked up at Derek. "Is your leader—" It was out before I thought.

"No," Derek snapped.

Bren looked from one of us to the other.

"We haven't met," I said.

"Remember what I told you." Derek lifted a hand as Bren groaned, looking from Derek to me and back again. Deon crossed her arms and glared. "You'll find things out when you need to know them, and until then, don't go looking. It will only add to your danger, and you'll be in enough before long. We've moved up the date of our strike for freedom."

I could feel the others' excitement.

"I want you to find a way to spy at the estate," Derek said to me. "Tim. You and your brother are to continue as messengers for Selenna Leader."

"Right," Tim said, and from the grass came Tam's voice, "Messenger it is."

"Deon. Bren. You two are going to have the toughest jobs of all." Deon grinned, straightening proudly. Bren hunched, all elbows and shoulder blades. "Bren, you first. You're going to have to make friends at the guardhouse."

"What? We can't betray the cause by being friends with *them*."

"I already told Selenna Leader. We desperately need someone on hand to hear their talk and report anything important. And Deon: if your mother still wants to send you to your aunt to work at the royal palace in Miraleste,

don't refuse anymore. I have to have eyes and ears there—
ones I can trust."

Deon's frown vanished. "You don't mean to *work* for
those court scummers. You mean to spy."

"That's exactly what I mean. While you are working."

She danced around. "A spy! A palace spy! I'll go tell Ma
I changed my mind."

"And that's all for this time," Derek said.

"Tell us a story," Bren demanded. "About one of your
adventures."

The others drew close, and Derek mused for a moment.
"I had a real close call up at Obrin," he finally said. "I was
meeting Obrin Leader, and she nearly got nabbed because
her horse went lame. So it was raining, and there we
were . . ."

As the tale spun out, I began to wonder if Derek spent
all of his time running from Uncle Darian's considerable
army. And I noticed the parts that he emphasized. Not his
own deeds, but the people who worked together to keep
their information secret, to protect each other. He made
it sound so exciting—hidden codes, everyone with secret
jobs, all loyal to the cause. By the end, Deon, Bren, and his
brothers were grinning, breathing fast. Me, too.

Derek said, "I'll be back when I can. I'll want full
reports. The kingdom is counting on you, not just me. So
do your jobs, and remember to keep practicing your reading and writing." He clapped Bren on the shoulder, brushed

his hand over Deon's head, and flicked Tim's ear. He sent a smile my way, then took the reins of his horse from Tam.

As soon as he rode off, Bren yawned. "I'm desperate hungry. Even boiled beans will taste good." But he gave me a funny look.

I ran off, looking back frequently. No one followed.

NEXT MORNING, I took a bath and came out to the welcome smells of hot oatcakes and eggs. As I ate I thought about what had happened—and that's when the Idea struck me. I would write everything down.

But how? I couldn't ask Father for paper, much less a blank book. He'd demand to know why, as paper was expensive. I could ask Peitar, who wrote a lot of letters—but it was clear to me now that he needed every sheet. Writing letters was as important to him as being able to escape out into the garden was for me.

Well, maybe it was a bad idea. Derek had talked about the importance of keeping secrets, and if I wrote everything down, what happened if the wrong person read it?

Books . . . my eye strayed to the shelf above my ladylike desk, which mostly held old lesson books. Then my eye was caught by the gleam of gilt—the binding of a volume I'd never opened.

On my last Name Day, my bossy Great-Aunt Tislah had sent me a set of court fashion drawings as a hint about what a young lady in my position ought to concern herself with. The right-hand pages of the small, thin book were illustrated, with the name of the court and the particular fashion lettered below. The left-hand pages were blank.

Blank pages! And who would ever think to check a fashion book? Not even Father's nosy, disapproving valet. If he did . . . supposing I used some code words? No one would know what it was about. They'd think I was talking about clothing and court.

I opened to the first drawing, smoothed the page opposite, and dipped my pen. Using my tiniest handwriting, I put in everything I could think of, from the way my father admired his new shoe buckles while dropping hints about my future to Peitar's tense forehead when he was thinking, Deon's quick movements, Bren's way of turning into knots and angles when he was worried. At first I made up code words, but by the time I finished half a page, I realized I wasn't using them. So I started abbreviating and drawing tiny pictures as symbols. Just as I finished, there was a knock at the door. I hurriedly put the book in a drawer.

Peitar entered and smiled absently at me. "How was your day in Riveredge?"

"We saved somebody from hanging! And we saw Derek, and he said I'm to be spying here."

"That's to get you in and out, in case Bren or one of the others spots you."

"So you *did* know! Are you Selenna Leader?" I asked.

Peitar made a curious grimace. "No. He calls me Number One. Selenna Leader is someone else, someone in Riveredge."

I tried so hard not to yell my voice squeaked. "*You* are Number One?"

His cheeks reddened. "Does that seem so impossible?"

"No! It's just that I thought—well, isn't part of revolution a lot of sneaking around? Like in Derek's stories."

"I cannot sneak, it's true," he said almost apologetically. "So I have to get my information in other ways, and I must use it to outthink the—the enemy."

"Enemy," I whispered. "It's so strange. Being Number One means you're even more important than these leader people."

Peitar moved to my window seat. "In a way. We'll see. What do you think of Derek?"

"He tells good stories," I said, suspicious that he was trying to distract me. "I want to know more about what it means to be Number One."

After too long a pause, he said, "I don't want to tell you that. I am uneasy enough telling you this much, but I confess I'm glad to have an ally."

"I'm not a baby! Do you think I'd blab it to Father? Or anyone else?"

"You would under torture." His face was grim. "And don't think our uncle would hesitate."

"Oh, I believe *that*. So why do the village boys and girls get to know more than I do?"

"That's just it—they don't. They only know their portion of the plan." Peitar paused. "It was a promise I extracted from Derek. He's been fomenting revolution ever since I first met him, when we were boys. He's used to risk—he and his brother, Bernal, both. He wants to give the young a chance to participate as much as the adults. But I don't think they really understand the risks, or the cost. So I made Derek promise to tell them only as much as they need to know. That way, should things go wrong, it might buy their lives."

"You say you've known him since you were boys, so that means that *you* were a boy when you started being Number One, right?"

Peitar glanced at my time-candle, then struggled to his feet. "Lilah. The point is, I am just trying to keep you safe."

"Which is why you're suddenly too busy to answer questions?"

"As long as you act like that, I'm reluctant to tell you anything," he retorted, and swung out the door, crutch *thock*ing on the polished wooden floor.

I fumed. *Something* was going on. Then a thought struck me. Why would he glance at the candle? Because he had an appointment?

I returned the fashion book to the shelf, capped the ink bottle, then raced out, silent on bare feet. No one in sight.

I ran downstairs and crossed the great hall, just in time to see Peitar walk out into the garden.

He skirted a neatly clipped hedge and made his way to the front of the house, where he stopped at the fountain and glanced around, though the lower windows were curtained.

I'd never seen Peitar act sneaky before. He leaned against the rim of the fountain and reached toward one of the cherubs, the one with the harp. His hand turned. He bent farther—shifted—and disappeared.

five

A secret passage!
I dashed outside to the fountain. Now it was my turn to check over my shoulder. But if I wanted to find out what was going on, I'd have to take the risk.

Peitar had fiddled with the little cherub with the harp. I patted the cold marble face, then pressed, poked, and tweaked its little round nose. Something gave slightly.

When I tweaked more firmly, one of the shallow pools moved silently beneath the central statue, sending ripples through the water. A wedge-shaped gap opened, just large enough to slip through. I had to see where it went.

I clambered down the stairway, and when I trod on the seventh step, the marble rumbled, closing over my head, leaving me in cool darkness.

My eyes adjusted as I descended. Cleverly placed slits in the fountain let in air and a dusty, bluish light. I reached a floor of hard-packed dirt and looked around. I was in a small circular room lined with a jumble of chests and dully gleaming carved objects.

A treasure room? A *second* treasure room—we had one in the house, but it was empty. I could explore later. Right now I was more interested in where Peitar had gone.

There were passages on either side, and from one came the rise and fall of voices. I followed the sound, walking down an incline. Something moist brushed my face—tree roots. Then the tunnel turned sharply—light glowed on the rough walls—and the voices were clearer.

". . . from where?" That was Derek!

"Yes," Peitar said. "No one pays attention to the rag pile."

"Then she suspected us. How did we slip up?"

They were talking about *me*!

Peitar said, "Lilah came up with her plans for investigating the village on her own. She had no ideas about revolution. I'm sure of it."

"She did show surprise last night, but I have been lied to before." Derek sounded tired.

"Well, I've put her off again." Peitar sighed. "Just now. So, to business. Why have you moved up the date for your uprising?"

"*My* uprising," Derek repeated, sounding displeased. "*You* keep quoting the wisdom of the greats. Wasn't it your favorite, Adamas Dei of the Black Sword, who said, 'A ruler can only govern by the consent of the governed—'"

"'—and when the interests of the governed are replaced by the ruler's own interests, that ruler has become a tyrant.' Yes," my brother replied calmly. "But right after that he said, 'This is why education is a necessity, so that the governed may enlighten the ruler.' He never advocated violent overthrow. Derek, I will help, as I promised. But I will tell

you again and again, until the very end, that I think violence is the wrong approach."

"I see no other solution. The nobles will not give up
their privileges without bloodshed. To think otherwise is
to dream, safe in this big house—ah, Peitar, don't give me
that look! We both know that your father's valet spies on
you, and there are your own tensions with the king. But
you've never starved, or been forced to sleep out in the winter cold, or felt the desperation that drives people to murder
just to feed their families!"

"We've been over this ground before," Peitar said. "Has
something new occurred?"

"Two reports from the capital. From the palace, as it
happens. Neither of these contacts knows the other, but
their reports came on the same day—and concerned the
same events."

"About my family's trip to Miraleste?"

"Yes," Derek answered. "One overheard a command to
the city captain for garrison space for incoming regiments
next month. The other intercepted a written command to
one of Irad's minor moons—"

"Moons?" Peitar sounded like he was smiling.

"Tasenja was the name."

Tasenja? I didn't know any Tasenjas, but many nobles didn't
bring their children to court until they were Peitar's age.

"Ah," Peitar said. "A northern family, not powerful, but
dedicated, and wealthy. Go on."

"He was ordered to produce his son for a betrothal."

Peitar's voice dropped; I could barely hear him, so I crept closer. "A betrothal? How does this relate to the uprising?"

"Because there's apparently to be a big military review as part of the festivities," Derek said. "Don't you see? It's an excuse to cram Miraleste with warriors, who can squash any signs of unrest."

"I . . . see. Yes, I think you are right. My uncle would certainly never exert himself for a series of social events. He hates balls and parties even worse than I. So, what must I do?"

"First, find out if your fox-faced little sister likes the prospect of a big party—"

I snorted. Then remembered I wasn't even supposed to be hearing the conversation.

"Fox is right." Peitar laughed. "And I believe she just flushed a pair of rabbits."

I backed hastily out of the tunnel, used to Peitar's inability to maneuver. But I had forgotten about Derek. Strong hands clamped down on my shoulders, and he marched me to where Peitar sat in a low chair, his bad leg extended before him. A single candle on a small carved table lit his rueful smile.

Peitar said, "You know what would have happened to you if you'd been a spy?"

My temper flared. "You and your 'safety'! Being *so* condescending and making me more curious with every word!

It's your fault, not mine, that you're so easy to follow! And what crime did I commit anyway, besides the terrible offense of being young? Which *you* were when you met Derek."

"You're right. Ah, I did slip up that time, didn't I?" His tone was bitter, aimed not at me but at himself.

My anger vanished. "It's all right. I followed you on purpose. And I made sure no one followed me. Or saw me, since I'm supposed to be sick."

Peitar rubbed his eyes. "If only I could get down the garden entrance! This fountain one is far too open."

Derek was silent during this exchange, elbows on knees, gaze unwavering.

He said, "Peitar, you're just going to have to use the garden, however long it takes you. As for Lilah . . ." He paused.

The pause lengthened into a silence. I finally dared another glance, to see Derek staring at the candle like the flame was in another world. "Black wool and ambition." He clapped his hands on his knees. "You remind me of an adventurous kid I met on my travels."

"Kid?"

"Her word for everybody under adult age. My point is, people of *any* age must choose freedom for themselves and cooperate in their own government! People of any age have worthy skills as well as loyalties."

Kid, I thought. *I like that!*

Peitar asked slowly, "Cooperate in their own government with no example of how to go about it? Derek—"

Derek waved his hand. "Never mind! We'll discuss it another time. What I'm trying to say is, I learned never to underestimate kids."

Peitar grimaced faintly. I could tell he hated the idea of kids in revolutions.

"I think we ought to figure her in our plans—and it might just help." Derek turned to me. Now I understood why Bren, Deon, and the others so admired him. "Lilah. Do you want to be part of changing life for the better for everyone? Even if it might mean giving up your high rank and all your fine things?"

"Yes! Who cares about fancy dresses and going to court? I sure don't!"

"Are you going to tell Bren and the others who you are?"

I thought about what the village kids had said about nobles—especially the Selenna family. "No."

"Good. Probably safest. But be careful. Bren has a very sharp eye, and he finds things out. It's why I put him at the garrison. Peitar, I'll do my best to be back within a week. There are some questions I must answer for myself."

He rose from his chair and left, swift and silent.

I snuffed the candle and followed Peitar through the room under the fountain to the other tunnel, which was longer, mossier, and danker.

When we reached the end, we found Derek climbing stone steps carved so steeply into the rough wall that they were almost a ladder. He pushed at something, and greenish light shafted down as he hoisted himself out. My brother slowly and painfully negotiated the first few steps, then handed his crutch up and continued climbing, his breathing harsh. As soon as Peitar was in reach, Derek gripped his hand.

Derek strained to haul him out. *I can't do that,* I thought. *I'm not even strong enough to pull up someone my own size, much less Peitar. How am I really going to help?*

"Lilah." Peitar's voice was hoarse. "Quick."

I lost no time in scrambling up the ladder. Derek had already disappeared. As soon as I was out, Peitar used his crutch to lever something that closed with a muffled thump: a trapdoor. "Learn this place," he murmured.

We were inside a circle of tangled, thorny shrubbery. The trapdoor was hidden by the moss and ferns beside a distinctively shaped stone. Tucked under the stone was a twine handle to pull open the door.

"Hoo," I breathed, as he struggled to his feet. "I *love* this!"

"Now for the brambles," he warned. I pushed ahead, holding aside the worst branches. The shrubbery seemed solid when I looked back, and within a few paces I recognized where we were in the garden.

"We'll part here. I'll go the front way. If you have occasion to use this tunnel again, never use the same route to and from it."

"Are all the servants spies, besides Father's valet? Not

Lizana, I know," I asked, looking around carefully.

"All Father's personal servants share his views," my brother said. "I don't know that I'd call them spies. But if they see something they know he wouldn't like, they would consider it their duty to report it, and I find I cannot quarrel with that in theory, however much I regret it in practice."

I sighed. Typical Peitar, always thinking of everyone else first.

"Lizana isn't certain about one or two of the new kitchen help. The few servants left from Mother's day will turn a blind eye to anything they see us doing, if they possibly can. But listen—I can't put any of them at risk by revealing anything about Derek or his plans. Lizana . . . is different."

"Why?"

"If she wants to tell you, she will." He gave me an apologetic look. "It's her business to tell, not mine. You should know she's to be trusted. Also, she and Derek are old friends. She introduced us, in fact."

Peitar headed slowly down the path. I took a shortcut through the trees and scrambled up to my room, my skirts as usual doing their best to hinder me.

Once inside, I was impatient to write up what I'd heard. But, remembering Derek's and Peitar's warnings, I tiptoed to the door to make certain I was safe—and everything winkled out of my head when I saw Lizana's worried face as she bustled downstairs.

What was wrong? I peered over the carved railing. Two footmen, as well as Father's valet, crossed the foyer to Father's rooms. As soon as they were out of sight, Peitar appeared in the foyer, breathless from effort, and came upstairs as fast as he could.

More confused than ever, I trailed him to the rooms that he had had before the accident. He closed the door, sat down, and tied a stocking carefully around the bottom of his crutch. "Keeps me quiet in this passage. I don't use it often. Almost got caught a few years ago when Father threatened to have the walls torn out in order to search for rats."

Then he opened the wardrobe, pushed past the old clothes hung neatly at either side, and pressed a knothole. The entire back of the closet slid into the wall, revealing— *another* passage!

He wormed his fingers under a pile of folded blankets, pulled out a palm-sized glass sphere, and whispered a word. The sphere glowed with blue-white light. An extra glowglobe! Holding it high with his free hand, he led the way.

Even with the glowglobe, it was difficult to see. There was a very narrow stairway to negotiate and then two sharp turns. We must have been at the back of the house under the guest chambers, just outside my father's library.

One more corner, then Peitar said something under his breath, and we were in darkness. My eyes adjusted to a faint line of golden light.

It turned out to be a gap in the back of one of the bookshelves, just above my own eye level, though Peitar could see.

". . . I do not know, Your Highness. He says he's on a secret mission for you." It was the head steward.

"I never sent anyone on a secret mission. What do I have to be secret about? Are you certain he named me as his master?"

"Well, Your Highness, he did in a, ah, metaphorical sense."

"Stop talking twaddle and bring this fool in to me. Now! Get moving!"

Footsteps, and then, "You!" Father exclaimed. "I should have had you hanged years ago! Well, you'll hang tonight."

"Hail to you too, Prince Gobble," came a familiar, laughing voice—Derek!

"Why do you keep spying around my home? My valet swears he's seen you here before. Do you know someone in the household?"

Derek laughed again. "If I did, do you think I'd be lurking around? I wanted to see for myself just how well off you are, in contrast to the families starving in Riveredge."

"Who are you spying for?"

"No one. I wish to become a voice of conscience, and that means I have to look where the power lies, don't I? The Selennas are the oldest family in the entire country. Older even than the ruling Irads. You wanted to marry an Irad princess, so you permitted the king to tax your guilds on top of your own taxes. Not that it affects *you*. It's the people of Selenna who pay."

"You're as ignorant as you are arrogant," Father snapped.

"Why, Your Highness! You care what a *commoner* thinks? Your face is as red as the strawberries I stole on my last visit to your overstocked garden. Why isn't some of that food going to Riveredge?"

Father said nastily, "I won't hang you tonight. I think the king might like some sport first. You there! Ride to Miraleste and find out if His Majesty wants this spy. Tell him it's the Diamagan rat. Be back by morning." There were the sounds of someone departing. "And you. Take this fool to the old treasure room and lock him up. Post two at the door, fully armed."

The narrow ray of light illuminated Peitar's sudden, surprising smile. He nudged me, and we left. As soon as we were back in his old rooms, I checked outside. No one was there.

Peitar sank into his armchair, forehead beaded with sweat. "Don't fret. Father has just ensured Derek's escape."

"*Another* passage?"

"Yes. This house, as well as the palace, is full of 'em. One can tell how trusting our ancestors were of one another."

"The palace, too? How did you *find* secret passages?"

"Mother told me about this one," he said, surprising me again. "It was our secret together, after my accident. She discovered it. She used to scout the ones at the palace when she was small, too."

"But this house is where Father grew up. Why doesn't he know about them?"

"When Mother asked, he said he'd only heard of one, and his grandfather had had it walled up a long time ago. Father's never been interested in creeping down dusty corridors or knocking on walls."

"So *Mother* loved secret passages," I exclaimed in delight.

Peitar went on. "After Mother died, I discovered I had a knack for finding them—it has to do with seeing how spaces fit together. The toughest part is finding the release mechanisms. Some are obvious. Others, you really have to search for. I'm about to give you your first dangerous job, Lilah. You'll have to be the one to let Derek out. The passage is too steep and twists too much for me."

I couldn't wait. "Where is it?"

"The library." Peitar removed the stocking from the bottom of his crutch. "Wear dark colors so no one sees you. The release is the lower right-hand brick in the fireplace."

He went on to describe the passage very carefully so I would know just what to expect. "Avoid treading on the last step until you are both in the passage, or one of you will be left inside the treasure room, and there is no way to open it from the inside. Then hide him in your room. Lizana will take him from there—she says she has a plan."

"When should I go?"

"Soon as night falls. He can get away then, especially if it rains as threatened." He leaned over to tuck the stocking in a drawer.

At last I was getting answers! I hurried to another question. What is 'black wool and ambition'?"

"I knew you'd ask that. An adventure that befell Derek and Bernal—his brother—when someone captured boys and girls with the idea of training them up to do evil things. It changed his mind about including kids in his plans."

"So, what about—"

"Shh." Peitar raised a hand.

We heard our father on the landing. Peitar motioned, and I dove under the bed.

The door opened, and Father said, "Peitar? There you are. What are you doing up here?"

"Sorting my boyhood books, looking for—"

"Will you join me for the midday meal?"

"I'm happy to oblige, Father. But I'm not really hungry. Can we not meet for dinner in our customary manner?"

"Very well."

Father left, and I crawled out from under the bed and made for my room.

Lizana was there, straightening the bed things. Peitar had told me to trust her. I took a deep breath and said, "Peitar says that you're in on our plan to rescue Derek. Peitar told me about the secret passage to the old treasure room. It goes through Father's study."

"Ah. That was the first one your mother found, not long after we came here," Lizana said. She looked grim. "He was caught on my account. I will not sleep easy until he's on his way."

As soon as she was gone, I opened my window. Big drops of rain spattered my face, warm and wet. It would be a big help if the storm made a lot of noise.

I sat down to write up the day's adventures. By the time I was done, the sky had turned a threatening purple-gray, and the thunder was much nearer. Lightning flashed off to the west.

Once again time crawled. When the dinner bell rang at last, I changed into my dark blue nightgown and opened my door. From Father's formal dining room came his and Peitar's voices and the ring of crystal.

My father's mealtime ritual was old-fashioned. First, he and Peitar would sit in the library, over wine. Then they'd go to the dining room.

On the way downstairs, I rehearsed a reason to be in the library in case I was caught—I'd say I wanted to read a family history. Father was proud of the Selennas and our past. No one was posted by the double doors to my father's wing. He clearly wasn't worried Derek might escape.

I slipped inside the library and quietly closed the door. Just in case, I selected a book and laid it down near the fireplace. Then, after double-checking, I pressed the lower right-hand brick.

Thunder covered the faint *graunch* of heavy stone and metal. I snatched a candle from one of the candelabra, lit it with the sparker, and ducked into the space behind the grating. When I trod on the first step of the hidden staircase, the stone gave, and I almost lost my balance. The fireplace slid closed behind me.

I carefully made my way down the steps, which were narrow and uneven, made scarier by the flickering of the candle. When I stepped on the bottom step, it sank, and with a low rumble the wall before me slid open.

Derek's eyes widened in surprise. Experienced spy that he was, he said nothing.

He was seated on the stone floor, his hands and feet tightly bound by curtain cords. I knelt and set the candle down, nervous giggles bubbling inside me. Curtain cords!

I wrestled with the knots until Derek wrenched free on his own, rubbing at his wrists and wincing. He untied his feet, then picked up the cords. I took the candle, whispering, "Use the second step," as I motioned him inside the passage. When I put my weight on the first stone, the wall slid closed.

Then we started upward. "Thank you," he murmured, close to my ear.

"It's Peitar and Lizana's plan," I whispered back, delighted it was working. If this was the worst danger I ever faced—well, I could do it forever!

At the top, I peered through the opening. The library was empty.

We were soon inside. I closed the passage, snuffed and replaced the candle, picked up my book, and sprang to the doors. The way to the grand staircase seemed impossibly open and exposed. From the dining room came the sound of my brother's voice, blabbing away gamely. Father laughed once. A rare sound.

"Servants' stairs," I muttered. And, to Derek, "Stay close." Down the hall. Open the narrow door just under the stairs—and we were in!

We raced up to my floor, and I opened the door a crack. No one in sight. I grabbed Derek's sleeve, pulling him toward my room. Then came the clack of Father's shoes right below us! I opened the door and shoved Derek inside.

"Lilah?"

Shock panged through me. I peered over the landing. My father stood below, holding his whiskey glass. "I thought I heard someone in the library. Was that you, child?"

"I wanted a book." I held it up. "Don't come near, Father, I'm still sick!"

My father frowned. "There's a dangerous criminal in the

house. Though he's under lock and key, I want you to keep to your room. Who is that with you?"

I turned my head, wildly, reaching for excuses.

Lizana stood in the doorway, holding a tray. "Lizana," I said gratefully.

"Good. She can stay with you until morning, when we'll be rid of this villain."

He went back to his meal, and Lizana and I closed ourselves in my room, where Derek stood, his clothing rumpled and torn, bruises over one eye and on his jaw. He handed Lizana the curtain cords. "Maybe they will think I escaped by magic if they don't find these."

"Good thinking," Lizana whispered. "Now, children—"

"Children?" I gawked at her

"To me, Derek's just a child. Put this on, young man." She held out the cloth she'd carried under my dinner tray.

Derek shook out the gray fabric, and grinned. "A dress!"

"You are going to be Merilda, the downstairs maid. She's going to be very, very ill, and must go home. You can't make it over the wall tonight," Lizana explained. "It's too well patrolled. You need to leave while the storm is at its worst. No one will want to get a thorough drenching just to examine a sick maid."

Derek pulled the gown over his clothes. Lizana handed him two balled-up rags to stuff down the front, and then wrapped a shawl around his head, hiding his hair.

"Stoop a little," she said. "Small steps. And straighten

that bosom! You have one side up and the other escaping into your armpit!"

I smothered my giggles as Derek struggled to reshape his front. Then, under Lizana's eye, he practiced walking. Once, he looked at me and minced across the room, sashaying like any noble girl at a ball, his wrists arched as if he held a fan—shoved his drooping bosom back into place—waggled his hips around.

I had to bite my pillow to keep from howling.

"That's enough. Children!" Lizana whispered, but she was smiling.

"I make a handsome lady, don't I?" Derek fluttered his eyelashes.

"Terrible!" I wheezed. "T—t—"

"You'll do. Come along," Lizana said crisply as she checked outside my door.

Derek hunched his shoulders, flipped an end of his shawl at me, and followed Lizana, his steps slow and small. I admired the way he managed to seem shorter and older.

When they were out of sight I gulped down my food, then recorded Derek's rescue.

seven

Nothing happened for the next few days, other than a series of storms that kept me inside. Just as well, for as far as Father knew, my cold was lingering on, and I wanted to visit Bren and the kids and brag about rescuing Derek.

On the first nice morning, Peitar appeared at my door. "We're leaving tomorrow for Miraleste."

"Tomorrow!" I sat up in bed. "Then I've *got* to go to the village!"

"Are you sure that's wise?"

"I've got to say good-bye." *And tell them what happened to Derek.*

"All right," he said at last. "I'll ask Lizana to use my old dodge with Father. It used to buy me a day of freedom when I needed it."

"What's that?"

"A supposed 'special medicine' that will make you sleep all day, but you'll waken on the morrow completely recovered." He spoke with that funny tone that was half mockery and half something harder to define. A little like sadness, maybe regret. Then it was gone. "Be careful. Father was exceptionally angry about Derek's escape."

Soon I was in my Larei clothes, in the garden. Extra guards had been posted, pacing slowly in the hot sun as they looked for anyone who might sneak in. But I was patient. When they were out of sight, I got over the wall and ran until I reached the old bridge. As I crossed, I noticed a group of people farther up the banks scrubbing at clothes and laying them on rocks or the sparse grass to dry. It was horrible that no one had cleaning frames.

Bren must be at the guardhouse. The idea of going there was scary, but I had to trust my disguise. I loitered slowly toward the stable. Several of the guards stood about in the shade—and there he was, on the other end of the porch, busy cleaning horse tack.

I kicked some pebbles, and he looked up. I walked on by, and heard him say, "Gotta go get some grub. Be back later!"

"Just see that you do," came a lazy reply. "You've got more work awaiting you, brat."

I kept walking. Bren caught up, his face red. "Larei," he gasped. "Looking for Derek? Because he's—"

"Gone, I think to Miraleste," I finished. "He got caught, but then he got rescued."

"He did?" Bren's eyes widened. "How?"

My moment had come. "I did it," I said, striving to sound casual instead of proud. "Secret passage in Selenna House." *Now* let him think I wasn't any good, or trustworthy!

Bren whistled. "Nice work. How did you manage that?"

"He was talking to someone and got caught. They locked him in the cellar, and there's a secret passage out. Derek *did* assign me to spy at Selenna House," I finished defensively, because Bren was eyeing me with far more question than admiration.

His face cleared. "That he did. So did Prince Greedy get steamed?"

"Oh, yes. He was boiling! Now he's taking u—uh, them to Miraleste." I could have kicked myself. What was wrong with me?

"Them?" Bren asked, and he made that crook-leg sign. "Lord Cripple and Lady Fluffbrain?"

I bit my lip. "Yes. So what have *you* learned?"

"Nothing. They think kids are as smart as rocks, so they talk a lot, right in front of me. But it's all just stupid blabber about gambling, drinking, and what they do when they have free time. Not a hint about secret plans or anything interesting."

"They might not know any."

"My aunt sent Deon to the capital—remember, Derek asked her? So once Prince Greedy and his brats are gone, will you be coming here to help?"

"Can't." I fumed at myself for not thinking everything through.

"Can't? Why not?"

"I'm . . . going along. I have my job, after all!" There was a silence. *So much for bragging,* I thought. *It's never as good as*

you think it's going to be. Not if it causes questions you can't answer.
"Maybe I'd better go back."

"Don't. Let's find the others and have a game. I'm sick of doing all the guards' worst chores, and it's too muggy for spying anyway."

"You can just go?"

"Sure." Bren shrugged. "It's not like they actually hired me. All I get is dinner scraps."

He knew where all his particular friends were to be found, at the other end of the village. We played a complicated game whose rules kept evolving. Running, hiding, capture and rescue, silly dares—the day sped by. As darkness fell, the smaller kids headed home. I left reluctantly.

How awful that I had found friends at last, just in time to leave them. And for Miraleste, which I hated. I had no friends among the children of the courtiers. How could I? We never acted normal, not with all the grown-ups worried about position, and tattling servants, and, above all, the cold, watchful gaze of my uncle, the king. Peitar told me that we kids were pieces to be moved about on the game boards of the adults, though we hadn't a notion of what the game was, nor its rules.

One New Year's Week they'd forced us to prove our courtly manners by talking exclusively in Sartoran. Though the court fashion for speaking exclusively in Sartoran had ended three generations before, when Sartor was taken by

Norsunder, it was still considered important to know the language, so Sartoran lessons were part of my training to become a lady.

A lady! And ladies got betrothed. I kicked at some rocks. To have to wear some horrible dress, all stiff with ribbons and gems and whatnot, and stand there for everyone to stare at, next to some arrogant bore I'd probably loathe on sight! Ugh!

Everything seemed so *unfair*. As I trudged home, my spirits sank. I couldn't even enjoy the triumph of rescuing Derek. I hopped the wall as usual, the clouds and the darkness so thick that the sentries couldn't see far. When I reached my room, Peitar stuck his head in, his anxious face relaxing when he saw me. "I'm glad you're back," he said.

I sighed. "Oh, Peitar, I shouldn't have gone. I did so many stupid things—"

He looked worried, and I hastened to say, "Nothing life-threatening. But I'm going to miss them all, so much! Oh! Deon got sent to the palace. New job. Do you think I can be Larei and find her?"

Peitar shook his head. "No, Lilah. It was risky enough here, and the palace is far better watched. If Uncle Darian catches you . . ."

"Ugh." I shuddered. "I forgot for a moment about *him*."

"Don't. Don't *ever* forget him. And we don't want to do anything that can jeopardize Derek or any of his people."

The door opened, and Lizana came in with my dinner. "Good," she said when she saw me, then nodded at Peitar and left.

"That reminds me," I said once we were alone. "If Derek overthrows our uncle, and I hope he does, is he going to be the king?"

"I don't know. There's a lot to happen between now and then."

"I think I'll take my Larei clothes along. So when the gang yells things at our carriage tomorrow, I can pretend to be Larei and it won't feel so horrible."

"Only if you take care never to let anyone but Lizana see those clothes. Now eat and get some rest. Tomorrow will be a long day." And he was gone.

I frowned at all that steaming food on the tray, and decided I'd take a bath first. I was beginning to unlace my tunic when a voice squawked, "Ulp! *Lady Lilah!* No!"

I froze. The branches thrashed outside my open window, and Bren landed on the sill. "You followed me! And you were listening at my window!"

Bren's expression was a peculiar combination of triumph and embarrassment and fear and curiosity. "I had to!" He sounded strangled. "You're a girl," he added.

"I never would have guessed," I snarled.

"You're really a Selenna. A noble, and you dressed like . . . You didn't tell us." He sounded more perplexed than angry.

"You said you'd never make friends with us 'scummy nobles.'"

"But this is different!"

"How was I to know? That's what you said."

"You let us call you all those names. . . ."

"Look. Just take back what you said about Peitar. Including doing that awful thing with the fingers."

Bren mumbled, "I know it's stupid. Derek told us it was."

"Then why do they do it?"

"Because your brother will never be a leader. He couldn't fight a duel or lead an army in—well, uh, that's what the grown-ups say." He stopped, his face the reddest I'd ever seen.

"Well, duels are stupid, and Lasva the Wanderer said that all wars do is make messes that other people have to clean up. And, by the way, some of the servants here are Derek's friends."

Bren stared down at my carpet. "Never again." He looked up. "If you'll—"

"If *you'll*—" Forgive me. He didn't want to say the word any more than I did. I nodded.

And we shook on it. We were still friends, then.

Bren took a long breath as he looked around. "This is quite a room."

"Oh, you should see my father's suite. Mine's plain compared to his."

He shook his head, but I could tell he wasn't really thinking about my father's fashionable furnishings. "Will you take me along? I want to help spy in the capital. I think the guardhouse is a waste of time."

I motioned him inside, and he stepped on my carpet as if eggs were squishing between his toes. I tried to hide my grin. "We'll have to ask Lizana." I pulled the summons bell.

Bren noticed the alcove, where Lizana had left a cool bath waiting.

I said, feeling very awkward, "My cleaning frame is in there, too. Want to use it?"

He shook his head quickly, obviously as uncomfortable as I. "No. Nobody at home has one, and they'd notice." Then he glanced at my untouched supper, and away.

"Help yourself. I'm not hungry. And no one will know."

Bren's cheeks were soon bulging.

Lizana appeared, her brows lifting when she saw him. "He wants to come with us," I said. "To Miraleste. I was hoping he could. It would be good to have a friend."

"What about the guardhouse in the village?" she asked.

Bren looked surprised that she knew. "Tim can take over."

"Your mother—"

"My mother would be happy if I went to Miraleste." Bren grimaced. "She's a real—"

"Snob," I finished, remembering what she'd named him.

"She'd love it if I got a job there. And I'd be one less mouth to feed."

Lizana pointed at me. "You. Get to sleep." She turned to Bren. "You go back down that tree, get out, and make it right with your family. Tell them you'll draw footman pay, though you'll start as a page. That ought to help. At dawn, be at the kitchen entrance. Go in the gate, all nice and legal. I'll have the proper clothes waiting for you."

Bren finished my dinner and licked his fingers clean before he climbed out the window.

eight

A trip to Miraleste meant my hair had to be washed, perfumed, and wrapped in curling rags. I endured it without my usual whining, happy at the prospect of allies in the scary rectitude of the royal castle.

The next morning I made sure that my Larei clothes were secretly packed, along with my fashion book, before I sailed out in my heavy linen-silk traveling gown. As I approached the stairs, someone came from the other direction.

I stopped. Bren and I stared at one another.

He was respectably outfitted in a Selenna servant's gray-and-blue long tunic, knee breeches, and hose, though they hung on him—there had been no time for alterations. In contrast, the shoes must have been too small, because he winced at each step. His mop of brown hair had been skinned back and tied into a tiny puff at his nape.

He was usually all bony angles, but now he stood stiff and straight as wood slats, his expression uneasy. "You sure look different."

"So do you," I said.

He wrinkled his upper lip. "If I think of it as a disguise, it's not so bad. Except for these shoes. *And* there's pay, which will help at home. Anyway, since I'm now Lord

Peitar's official page, I was sent to tell you the carriage is waiting."

"Father?" I asked, in a whisper.

"In his own carriage," Bren muttered with a hasty look around the open entry hall. "In case the medicine didn't work and you still have that cold."

Relief! Now the journey would be enjoyable instead of boring.

Wearing a formal gown meant I had to reduce my normal walk to tiny court steps. I minced down the stairs to the front entry, Bren following in the correct place, stiff and self-conscious. When my father emerged from his wing, resplendent in his velvet traveling suit and his very best formal red wig, he didn't give Bren a second glance.

Soon we were off. Bren, as Peitar's page, rode with us. He ran his hands over the satin cushions. "This is nacky," he exclaimed, launching back and forth between the windows so he could see the view from both sides.

"You'll get tired of the scenery soon enough," I warned. "Especially since Father won't let us out, even at the posting houses when they change horses."

"Why not?"

"He always says they don't cook well, but I think it's because we don't pay well."

"But you—he—everyone knows the Selennas are rich!"

"It looks it, but we really aren't." I looked at my brother. "Ugh, Peitar, you explain."

"There are levels to being rich, Bren." Peitar sat back. "It's true we have a fine house, but we inherited it. The furnishings . . . everything is old and carefully repaired. We have plenty to eat, but that's because it's from our home farms. The tax money really does all go to the Blue Guard—and most of them are training with the army. We pay for them, but they aren't here."

"But all that velvet, the lace, and that wig!"

"It's true our father dresses well, but those suits are strictly for court. And he hasn't ordered a new one in years."

I laughed. "As for the wig, that's left over from the queen, our great-great-grandmother, who was a Selenna. Her red hair was famous, and when she got old, she wore red wigs. So everyone at court wore red wigs. Uncle Darian hates wigs, and curls, so all the men his age, especially the army-mad ones, just tie their hair back. But Father sticks to his wig because it's a Selenna privilege."

Peitar pulled his travel desk from the shelf below his seat. "I have to finish some letters," he said.

I wished that I'd thought to carry my fashion book, but I didn't have anything new to report—getting my hair tormented into proper curls didn't count. The book and my Larei clothes were somewhere in the baggage coach. When we got to Miraleste, Lizana would make sure that none of my uncle's servants unpacked my things.

We rolled through the village. As usual, some kids shied rocks. This time I recognized the boys and girl who made the crook-leg sign, yelling insults. I had played games with them the day before, but if I stepped outside the carriage they would hate me.

Bren sent a worried glance at Peitar, who didn't seem to notice. Instead, he was looking at the chalk drawings on one of the village fences. This seemed to worry Bren even more. Peitar glanced at Bren, then back at the fence. He gazed so intently that he turned his head, studying the drawings until they were out of sight.

"There's an artist in Riveredge, I see," he finally said.

When Bren's face turned tomato red, I exclaimed, "*You* did those drawings?"

Bren stared down at his hands. "Derek told you? I wish he hadn't."

I was even more amazed when Peitar smiled. "It's all right, Bren. My mirror has already told me what I look like."

"No, Lord Peitar," Bren said to his lap. "It's mean. Like Lilah said."

Peitar made a placating gesture. "I'll live. The most important thing is your talent. After we get things resolved, you ought to be sent to one of the art guilds for training. As for my title, you can drop that in private. I agree wholeheartedly with Derek that titles, used to divide people from one another, are pernicious."

"Derek says art is for nobles," Bren mumbled, and when Peitar went back to his letter, he stared out the window as if his life depended on watching the countryside.

As the morning wore on, the flat fields and meadows gave way gradually to hills, farms, and dark green stretches of woodland. We changed horses twice and kept going at a fast pace. There were a few old castles, most dating back to the days when Sarendan was a lot of tiny duchies and princedoms all squabbling with one another.

"Do you know who lives in that one?" Bren asked almost every time.

"That castle has an exciting history, but boring people live there now," I'd say, or, "They're all a bunch of snobs, but their ancestors had great adventures." Finally Bren turned on me. "Why is it you think everybody in history is interesting, but everyone now is boring?"

"That's because they are."

"That's because we wear our masks yet," Peitar murmured. "And only when time passes will the masks come off, in memoirs."

Peitar did not mean real masks, of course. Lasva the Wanderer had talked about the masks of falsity, the way we hid what we were really thinking as we displayed our good manners. Well, we had to, didn't we? If we told our uncle what we really thought, there'd be trouble. I wasn't sure what kind, but I could feel the tension in the adults if he was in a bad mood, and I saw the way they watched him for reactions.

That was why the histories were interesting, because

people *did* things. I'd just begun doing interesting things, but that was because of Derek. Now I'd be stuck at court.

I kept brooding until Peitar set his letter down and said, "Shall we eat? It's past midday."

"I'm supposed to serve you." Bren knelt on the floor of the coach and reached into the shelf below our seat.

"We can all help ourselves. And you eat, too," Peitar said. "But if you're ever with Father, remember to stand in the background, ready for orders."

Bren pulled out the hamper. The bread was still warm. I helped unpack fishcakes, four kinds of fruit tarts, cheese, bread and butter, and two jugs, one of water and one of Cook's fruit punch that was tart, not sweet. Bren attacked the food with such enthusiasm it was fun to watch. Peitar toyed with his, as usual.

Afterward, my brother said slowly, "Lilah. Bren, you too. In case the trouble that faces the kingdom gets too much to bear, you should know a secret. You may tell your cousin, Bren, but that's all."

Bren looked up, surprised.

Peitar turned his attention to me. "Have you heard of the Valley of Delfina? Mother used to go there after she'd been ill. When I was small she took me."

"It's in a bunch of our histories," I said. But that was all I knew.

"It lies to the south, in the highest mountains. Only one way in, and that's by magic."

"Magic!" Bren and I said it together.

"Mother taught me the spell before she died. She said to use it as a retreat if I needed it, once I got old enough to travel on my own, and I was to choose the time to tell you. I think . . . that time might be now. See this?" He made a different complicated gesture with each hand, at the same time.

"Yergh," I said. "It looks like you're making your fingers into knots."

"Practice. It's not meant to be easy."

We practiced. Bren's clever fingers got it much sooner than my clumsy ones. Peitar made us practice more, until we could do it without thinking. Then he taught us the words to say while we were doing the signs. They sounded like Old Sartoran.

When he was sure we had it, he said, "This will only work if you reach a certain point in the mountains, though exactly where I don't remember." He smiled. "Once you're high enough, you make the sign." His smile flashed briefly into a grin. "You'll figure out what to do. I'm going to leave it as a surprise, partly because you'll enjoy it, and partly because it has to stay a secret. If ever you need to get away, that's where you can go to be safe." He looked at us intently, and we both nodded.

"South?" I asked. "But—wait. Those mountains are behind Diannah Forest, and we all know it's infested with criminals."

"You'll be all right," Peitar said.

I glared at him. "How? I've heard Father talking about them, and even Uncle was complaining once that he sends warriors but the thieves always seem to know when they're coming, and vanish—but reappear as soon as there's a trade caravan. Or nobles. Like *us*."

Bren said, "Even *I've* heard bad things about Diannah Forest."

Peitar shook his head. "Just promise you'll do as I say, will you?"

"Yes. But I *hate* secrets that you won't share for some stupid reason."

"And *I* hate the possession of secrets that are not mine to share."

My mind filled with questions, but Peitar's brow was tense again, the faint pain-lines beside his mouth deeper. He returned to writing his letter—something he clearly was not enjoying—and said nothing more.

Bren glanced my way and made a face. I suspected he wanted to discuss this as much as I did—but later, when we could be alone. He was intimidated by Peitar, though I couldn't imagine why. Peitar was just Peitar, my gentle brother, and no threat to anyone.

As THE DAY waned, the road took us through a close-growing pine wood, and then wound down toward the long, snaky lake called Tseos.

"That's beautiful," Bren exclaimed.

We let the window down, and then he almost fell out of the carriage looking at Miraleste, built along the hills over the lake. I'd read in several histories how beautiful everyone thought the city, but to me, it had always meant boredom—or worse, *him*. My uncle.

"That side of the lake's all built up," Bren said, pointing. "Why not the other?"

"It's crown land," Peitar said. "All private preserve. There are a few summer residences, but they are all hidden away."

"Supposedly everyone wants to stay at the lake palaces in the summer," I added. "I don't know why, since my uncle hates parties and boat races."

"The attraction of power overcomes a lot of social defects," Peitar said, sitting back on his cushions. "They have the parties same as always, and Uncle Darian is the first one invited. Even if he never goes." His sardonic expression brought our uncle to mind, and I shuddered.

Bren poked me. "What's wrong?"

"He looked just like Uncle when he said that."

"That's probably the worst thing you've ever said to me, Lilah."

"Well, it's true," I began defensively, and then I realized Peitar was only teasing.

Bren gazed round-eyed from Peitar to me. "You really *don't* like the king, do you?"

"Is that so hard to believe? You don't, either!" I exclaimed.

"Well, that's different. I mean, he's your uncle, and you're nobles, and I guess I always believed all the nobles liked the king."

Peitar observed, "I'm afraid of him, and sometimes I'm afraid *for* him." Bren's eyebrows rose, but Peitar's gaze had gone distant, and so Bren turned to me.

I couldn't resist. "He almost had me *executed* when I was little!"

Bren's mouth dropped open.

I sneaked a peek at Peitar, whose thoughts weren't so distant anymore. He gave me a funny look, and I amended, "Well, Father thought so, anyway."

"What happened?" Bren asked.

"I don't remember a lot of it," I admitted. "It wasn't long after Mother died. They made me dress up fancier than ever, so I couldn't move. And Great-Aunt Tislah would tweak me and pinch me and mutter about how *good* and *sweet* my mother always was as a little girl, and how *she* never, ever mussed her gowns. Anyway, I guess Uncle missed Mother. . . ."

"I think Mother was the only real friend he ever had," Peitar said. "The only person he loved."

"I don't think he loves anyone," I cut in. "That's why I hate him! See, Bren, the older relatives kept pushing me at him, telling me to smile, to be sweet."

"They were hoping you'd become a court favorite," Peitar said, again with the smile I hated so much.

"Well, I sure ended that! When Aunt Tislah put me on his lap, I shoved him away and said in as loud a voice as I could that he felt like a snail."

Bren nearly collapsed. "A s-snail! The king! A snail!" He hiccupped, and then said, "Why, is he all clammy and moist?"

"No, not at all. But he's so . . . so, oh, so cold. It was all I could think of. I was really little," I added.

"Snail. Hoola-loo! So you were gonna be executed for that?"

"Father swept me away, that's all I remember, and shoved me in the coach, and yelled at me the entire time. Then Uncle's men came and made the coach turn around, and Father was screaming about how they'd kill us." The memory sent chilly prickles along my arms.

"And what happened when you got back to the palace?"

"I was crying and apologized as best as I could, but Uncle Darian just laughed. It's the only time I've ever seen him laugh, but it wasn't a nice laugh. Then he said, 'Get her out of my sight,' in that winter voice of his. Lizana is always telling me I have no tact, and I sure hadn't then. Before we got out the door, I said, 'You aren't gonna . . . hexacute me?' and he said, 'No, you're too small.' He was joking."

Bren whistled. "That's a joke?"

"My uncle's kind of joke. He's pretty much ignored me ever since."

"So that ended Lilah's political career," Peitar said. "That is, until this visit."

Now Bren looked confused. "We're going so I can get betrothed," I moaned.

"Well, that's pretty disgusting," he said, making a hideous face. "Marriage! And that's another reason I'm glad I'm not a noble."

Peitar gave him a wry look. "I'm reliably told that most people, whatever their degree in life, eventually grow up, pair off, and have families."

"Maybe. But no one makes you when you're a kid, just because of politics."

"There's the city gate ahead." Peitar gestured for us to get ready for our arrival.

"Yes," Bren said. "And a betrothal for Lilah!" He snickered all the way down the rest of the road, until we got there.

nine

~≈~

The gates stood open. All along the walls paced armed guards. One saluted our drivers with a gauntleted fist; the blade of his spear gleamed red in the light of the sinking sun.

The buildings on the south side were crowded together, and warriors patrolled in great numbers. Everything appeared orderly, but as we headed uphill to the west side, where the nobles lived, people stared, their faces closed. Twice someone threw things at our carriages. I jumped at a loud *thok!* against the door. The second time, there was a yell, "Soul-sucking noble! You're all thieves! Go to Norsunder where you belong!"

I stayed put, not wanting to see the angry face behind that voice—or what the warriors would do if they found the shouter.

Many of the fine mansions along the west side were empty. Nobles preferred to stay on their country estates during the summer, where it was cooler, if they weren't invited to the lake palaces.

At long last we neared the royal palace, on the highest hill overlooking the lake. Bren peered intently at the slate roofs and ironwork rails until we were waved through the palace gates. Our carriages rolled past the great flagstone parade court, through the carefully tended gardens, and came to a stop in the secluded, tiled entrance to the family wing.

"Once I'm out, take my desk," Peitar said to Bren. "Keep it with you. It's important. Don't let any of the king's or my father's servants near it."

Bren nodded, then opened the door and went to let down the stairs.

Father was just getting out of his coach, and his valet fluttered around him, making sure that the folds of the traveling coat draped properly over the jewel-chased sheath of the dress sword and twitching the side curls of Father's wig into place. I could hear Father complaining as another handed him his ensorcelled handkerchief of pure lace.

I followed my brother down the steps as a damp wind gusted off the lake, pulling at my hair and skirts. Bren, clutching Peitar's lap desk tightly, sent me a last, nervous look.

A steward bowed to Father. "You are requested to wait upon His Majesty at once, Your Highness, if that pleases you."

My father turned up his nose as he undid his baldric and handed his sword to his valet. "Well, then, I needn't keep that." No one went armed to private interviews with the king. He beckoned impatiently, and we took the wide, curving stair, our steps muffled by the thick violet and blue carpet until we reached Uncle Darian's informal parlor. Old, gray-haired Steward Halbrek opened the door, his face blank as he bowed us in.

Father swept a low courtly bow, for there was the king, standing by the window with its view of bleak sky and wind-ruffled lake. Everyone was supposed to dress formally, according to rank, but Uncle Darian wore a plain tunic and sash of dark violet with hints of gold—the Irad colors—long trousers, and riding boots.

The light on the king's face made him look very much like a grown version of Peitar, which was unsettling because I never really could think of him as an uncle, as family. At least Father did care for us in his way, despite his frowns and fusses. Uncle Darian was too remote, too cold, too dangerous in his moods—too much *the king* and never *our uncle.*

He gave a careless wave toward the fine chairs.

Father was, as usual, clearly disturbed by the king's impatience with what he considered proper courtly manners. Or maybe it was because Uncle Darian was in a bad mood. Still, he sank into the chair with a grateful sigh and mopped his brow.

The light then shifted on my uncle's stern face; it was our turn. I dropped my best curtsey. "Good evening, Uncle Darian." And I retreated to the farthest chair.

Peitar bowed, also murmuring his greeting.

Uncle Darian's mouth tightened. "Put that thing in the

fire," he said, gesturing at Peitar's crutch. "Leaning on it will never make you straight. You are not yet too old to learn strength of will."

Peitar's expression did not change. He did as ordered. Then, as the crutch began to burn, he made his painful way to the chair next to mine.

The king turned his attention back to Father. "Tasenja and his boy are here. You've explained?" I sat up straight as Father bowed his head in agreement. "Do you understand what's expected of you, Lilah?"

"Yes, Uncle," I bleated.

His brows contracted in a slight frown. "The betrothal ceremony will take place next month, but you and the boy will meet now."

I knew what he meant: he wanted us to meet in private now, in case I made a fuss. Though my last mistake had been made when I was barely old enough to talk, he'd clearly never forgotten it. I couldn't help but grimace.

He almost laughed as he said, "Prospect of a betrothal turns your stomach?"

"She'll do what she's told, Your Majesty," Father said.

"Yes, she will." Uncle Darian pulled the cord for the steward. "Bid Lord Tasenja and his son join us."

Peitar caught my eye and lifted his chin: *Courage*, he was saying, plain as anything.

Meeting this boy didn't mean I was marrying him—now or ever. If Derek had his way, the choice would be never.

Until then, I could play along. Wear a mask, as Peitar had said.

Lord Tasenja was vaguely familiar—short and plump, with blond hair carefully curled at the sides and back.

The son was also short, blond, and stocky. He strutted forward and tossed back his wrist-lace before bowing expertly before Uncle Darian, and then—in just the right degree—to my father. Two half-bows for Peitar and me, and then he stood, courtly nose in the air.

At a look from my father, I rose and made my curtseys. Lord Tasenja surveyed me, from the hair bows trying to hold back curls that were already unraveling to my embroidered slippers, which had grown tight since our last visit here. He did not appear impressed.

"Lilah Selenna," Uncle Darian said, stripping all the etiquette out of the introduction—which was actually rather a relief. "Innon Tasenja."

Their name, like ours, was the same as their holding. That meant a very old family.

"Come along," my uncle said to the two fathers. "We have much to discuss. Let them get acquainted." Peitar trailed behind, one hand surreptitiously resting against the wall every time he had to put weight on the bad leg.

I sat down on the fine sofa and busied my hands with smoothing out my skirts. What my uncle had done to Peitar filled me with rage. But I had to hide that! Here was my future, standing three paces away.

Then Innon spoke. "You aren't one, either."

That was an ordinary voice, not a snobbish drawl.

I stared. Despite the embroidered silk coat and the ruby shoe-fastenings, he looked just like an ordinary boy—as I must have looked like an ordinary girl, instead of a simpering courtier, while I was watching my brother struggle behind Uncle Darian and Father.

"A what?" I asked.

"A Court doll."

"Fheg!"

"How do you feel about romance?" he asked, his pale brows rising.

"Phoogh!" I exclaimed even more heartily.

Innon put his hands to his forehead as though about to faint. "And here my father's spent the entire ride south trying to force a lot of love poetry into my head so I could spout it at you. Hoo, what stuff!" He held his nose. "'Your lips, my love, are sweeter than blossoms in the spring. . . .'"

I made gagging noises, and Innon's light brown eyes were crescent moons of mirth. "Does anybody really like that muck?" I demanded.

Innon made a *who knows?* face. "My father said Mother was right fond of that one when they were courting. And I'm very sure that Thiannah Ferrad would lap it up as well. Until the king told my father that you and I were supposed to get hobbled, our parents had been forcing us on each other, hoping, I guess, to round out the estates someday." He looked skeptical. "And here I thought girls hadn't a thought in their heads beside gabbling about romance, and who's in fashion and who's out, all the day long."

I retorted promptly, "And I thought *boys* hadn't a thought in *their* heads beside gabbling about their stupid sword-fighting lessons and who's stronger, and hoola loola loo."

"Well, the only girls I've ever met are like that. I spend all my time in our wood when they come visiting." Then he brightened. "That's why I was so glad when you made that face after the king shut the door."

I laughed. "Whew! Well, I roamed our garden, until I met . . ." I stopped.

"Met?" Innon asked.

"Well, some village boys and girls," I said hastily. "They have great games."

"No one plays games in Tasenja." Innon sighed. "Everyone works. It's this drought, and the king won't let us have mages."

"We had a mage just a couple of years ago, to renew the cleaning frames and the heating spells for the baths and the fire sticks for the stoves and hearths. But that was only at Selenna House. I don't understand why we don't have them fix the village near us."

Innon flung himself down on the other end of the couch and tapped one of his fancy blackweave shoes. "It's the king," he said. "Doesn't like mages because one of 'em spoke out against his taxes."

"Everybody complains about taxes."

"Not to the king's face." Innon leaned forward. "My mother said this mage is real powerful. That is, he's old and as rickety as a bad fence, but he's been around since Sartor was free, and he knows enough magic that the king kicked him out, saying if he crossed the border without invitation, it would be his last move. And there's been no welcome for any mage since."

"I didn't think you could do anything with magic besides fix glowglobes and fire sticks and cast spells on water barrels and buckets to keep the water pure."

"Well, with the bad kind of magic, the kind they use in Norsunder, you can do anything. My father says the king is convinced this mage is just as dangerous."

"So *that's* why our mage had guards. Father said it was to protect her, but I thought mages were good at protecting themselves."

Innon shook his head. "She was an exception. The people at court complained, so the king permitted one to visit just the palace and the homes of nobles. I don't know what'll happen when the last fire stick won't light or the last cleaning frame won't take the dirt out of clothes. We'll be all right, because we have servants. But what will the common folk do?"

"Well, maybe they won't have to worry about that," I said. My heart thumped.

Innon's eyes rounded. "How?"

I hesitated. So far, Innon was the opposite of what I'd expected—just as I'd turned out to be the opposite of what Bren had expected. Maybe I'd been unfair about court kids myself.

I leaned toward him and whispered, "Revolution."

"What?" Innon stared in surprise.

"If I tell you more, you have to promise not to tell anyone."

He shook his head. "No one I'd want to tell! My father would either not believe me, or he'd feel it his duty to go to the king."

"The other boys here?"

"Army-mad." Innon grimaced. His face was so round and good-humored that his expression made me want to laugh. "Just like you said. They don't care about anyone else—more'n half of 'em come from holdings where the people are starving, or nearly. They just want to be good enough in the competitions to catch the king's eye and get promoted to the officers' training up at Obrin. That's why they're here."

"You don't want any of that?" I asked, testing.

Innon said, "Don't want to kill anybody. Oh, if the Norsundrians really do come, sure. Except I won't be any good at it. I'm slow, and judging from my father, I'll always be slow. Slow and short doesn't make much of an officer." From his expression he didn't seem to care. "'Sides, I prefer figuring."

"Figuring? What's that?"

"Numbers." Innon twiddled his fingers. "Less messy than people. You always know where you *are*, with numbers. And you can find out where things will be. I love numbers!"

"Well, maybe you can help," I said. I was doubtful, but I tried to be encouraging. "I mean about the numbers. Derek must need some of that."

"Derek?"

Here was the moment.

Should I trust him? From what he said, most of the court kids were exactly the way I thought they were. And I knew that some of the Riveredge kids would have hated me if they'd found out about my disguise. But Innon was different, that much was clear.

I wondered if this was what Bren had felt like when he recruited me.

"Be quiet and listen." I began to tell him more, leaving out Bren and Deon's names, when we were interrupted by a whirring sound from the wall beside the fireplace.

Innon blanched. I fell silent as a panel slid smoothly behind the panel next to it, leaving an open gap in the wall.

ten

I held my breath—and Peitar stepped out.

"I could have been one of Uncle Darian's people." Though his voice was soft, it was very serious. "The fathers are discussing settlements with the king, and sent me off. I thought I would test this passage and check on you two. I'm glad I did."

"But Peitar, Innon is one of us!"

"I don't know that I'm any revolutionary," Innon said, looking uncomfortable. "But I do know there are problems. A lot of problems, is what my parents say, when we're at home."

"I wouldn't call myself a revolutionary, either," Peitar said. "But that's for later." He turned to me. "Lilah, we'll have to talk about how to recruit people. You need to be more careful."

"I was," I protested, trying to keep my voice low. "I can't imagine Uncle Darian in that secret passage, spying on us. I bet he doesn't even know about it!" In answer, Peitar pointed to the door.

Innon lightfooted over and crouched down. He peered under the bottom of the door, then straightened up and shook his head.

Peitar smiled his approval and leaned against the hidden doorway. "Who do you think taught Mother to be so good at detecting passages? He and Mother didn't use them for spying, though—they used them to escape our grandfather. Uncle Darian thinks the palace is safe with his guards everywhere, the servants silent and obedient, and the nobles loyal. Let's not give him reason to be suspicious, all right?" He didn't wait for an answer, but continued. "This used to be Mother's favorite sitting room in summer. It was once the heralds' secret chamber, which is why there's a passage. Entrance is through the old archive room—which has always been an archive room—beside the fireplace, like here. You can see and hear through holes in the carving." He indicated the panels. "Heard you talking about Derek."

I groaned. Softly. "Sorry."

"Don't be sorry. Be careful." Peitar turned to Innon. "Glad you're sympathetic."

Innon grinned. "If the kingdom is going to get better, I'm all for it, but I think I have some questions."

"Naturally you do." Peitar pushed himself upright. "We'll take a walk in the garden after dinner." He looked over at me. "A few quick things. We are in new rooms this time, a sign of royal favor. Or royal importance. We might not have any private moments after I leave, so I'll tell you now that there's a passage in your room, in the back of the wardrobe— but beware, it goes to the small study in the king's rooms. Innon, you're down at the end of the guest suites?"

"Oh, please, is there a secret passage in *our* rooms?"

"If you're in the suite with the green wall hangings, walnut furnishings, carvings like leaves, yes. Goes to the library."

Innon was delighted. "Secret passages! There are only two at Tasenja. Easy to figure where they are, if you know how houses are made, but the catches stump me."

"That's the part I like best." Peitar smiled. "I'd better take my own advice and be gone. By now they ought to be finishing up the legalities, and I'm supposed to be in my room, changing for dinner." He stepped back, and the panel whirred softly shut.

"Interesting fellow, your brother," Innon said.

There was just enough discovery in his tone to make me suspicious. "I suppose the other boys say rotten stuff about him behind his back? He can't help that leg of his."

Innon said, "Never really heard much about his leg, just that he's got a sharp tongue. Surprised me, because Father said he's a dreamer. Others don't think him worth interest because he's never been at Obrin, or even in the training salle here." He canted a glance toward me, then said, "Mind if I ask what happened?"

I told him. "And Uncle Darian throws Peitar's crutch in the fire, and makes a lot of noise about how anyone can have the strength of will to overcome a minor annoyance like a broken bone if he just sets his mind to it. I'm sure it's easy for *him*. He's good at everything he does, or so everyone at court says. But of *course* they let him win at horseracing and mock duels and the rest of that footle, or else he'll execute 'em."

"No, it's true. He really *is* one of the best. You haven't seen. I have."

"I still don't see why he has to treat my brother that way."

"Well, if the gossip my grandfather told me is true, when King Darian was our age, the old king used to have him beaten every single time he lost. Grandpa says he even had broken bones once or twice. Of course, they set 'em. But still. He used to do the same thing to King Darian's father—your grandfather—when he was young."

"Nobody ever told me that."

Innon made a face. "Grandpa told me these old stories. I can stop now, if you want."

Though I felt sick inside, I said, "Better tell me everything. All I know is that my grandfather died when my uncle and mother were young, and that something was wrong with him."

"Nobody ever talked about it in the old days. Everyone was afraid of the old king except the prince, and the two of them argued all the time about gambling and drinking parties, until he was thrown during a horse race. Afterward, he wasn't quite right—he did whatever the king told him to, including having kids so there'd be a new heir. He got worse and worse, and then he died. King Darian became the heir when he was not quite nine—"

"When Mother was seven," I whispered.

"—and the old king started in on *him*. That's what Grandpa says, and he was at court." Innon leaned forward. "One of my cousins—he's a lot older—said that when they were boys, after sword practice, they all used the garrison baths. Your uncle—he was the prince then—was all covered with scars." I shuddered. "If Grandpa had been like that, I would've run away and joined a caravan as a horse-tender, crown or no crown."

We had a moment's warning—the sound of footsteps beyond the door—and Uncle Darian came in alone.

My heart clattered against my ribs as Innon lifted his nose in the air and bowed.

"Well?" Uncle Darian said.

Innon drawled, "We find one another's company most agreeable."

"Yes, Uncle," I managed. My voice squeaked.

"Then we'll make the announcement now, and we'll give you a fine party next month. The entire court will be there, and you'll have plenty of new gowns, Lilah."

I curtseyed, proud of the way I did *not* show my utter disgust. My uncle looked faintly pleased, faintly relieved, and mostly bored. "Now, come along. You two will accompany me to dinner."

And so we followed my uncle to the formal dining room—the big one, not the little one where we sometimes went with Father and the king and one or two important adults, or our usual place, the royal schoolroom dining area.

It was a pretty room, the ceiling carved rosewood, with embroidered silk hangings from Colend between the gold-framed portraits. The three crystal chandeliers sparkled with reflections from their lit candles, as did the goblets held high by the grown-ups as they wished us long life and happiness.

At underage betrothals, mushy poetry and speeches weren't considered appropriate, which was a relief. Innon and I, who were seated side by side at the far end of the long table from Uncle Darian, tried to outdo each other in snobbish manners. I don't even know how it started. I was conscientiously lifting my punch glass, curling my pinky, and I caught his eye. Then he did it, too, but his pinky was much more curled—and the game was on.

Father was so pleased he smiled at us. What a disgusting pair Innon and I made! Peitar's eyes narrowed with skeptical humor, but the adults paid no attention, just kept talking and laughing in well-bred voices, as the painted eyes of past kings and queens looked down on us. Most of them had sat in this same room going through the same sort of ritual.

After a very fine cake made up of alternating layers of pastry and custard, my uncle said that an impromptu dance had been arranged. This meant that nobody had to change into formal clothes. As it wasn't the actual betrothal, Innon and I didn't have to go; the fathers and my uncle did the honors for us.

Peitar was six months shy of his official coming of age, so he didn't have to go either. He waited until all the adults had filed out in order of rank to join us out on the terrace overlooking the moonlit lake.

The wind had stopped, and the air was balmy. "We'll have to dance next month, you know," I said morosely to Innon. "Maybe we can make a game of it, like we just did in there."

"The food will be even better than tonight. They'll make a point of having all our favorites," he answered.

We heard Peitar's uneven steps as he caught up, but Innon didn't turn to stare, for which I was grateful. "Now we can talk," Peitar whispered, as he leaned against the stone railing. "But keep your voices low."

I looked around, for the first time really aware of the guards patrolling the top walls at various levels, picked out against the sky by torchlight, the occasional glint on drawn weapons. We'd be easily identifiable, but what was more natural than the two Selenna toffs blabbing with the Tasenja heir who was to ally with their family?

"This castle must look splendid from the water," I said.

"It does." Peitar's smile could be heard in his voice. "It's also an effective reminder of who truly holds power."

"My father doesn't," Innon observed. "Not outside Tasenja."

"Your father is one of the most popular courtiers in the

kingdom," Peitar said, to our surprise. "If he backs the king's new policies, they'll have even more support."

"Your father didn't look like he approved much of me," I said.

Innon snickered. "That's just his court face. Truth is, there isn't much he disapproves of, except maybe bad stewardship at home. And maybe the latest taxes."

"Your father's life," Peitar observed, "has been a long, pleasant series of mild gratifications, removing the need to see farther, to exert. Our father's, on the other hand, has been a long series of thwarted ambitions, though to the outside eye it would seem they enjoy much the same sorts of advantages. It's a difference in character."

I sighed. When Peitar talked like that, I had trouble understanding him, and I was afraid if I asked him to explain, he'd start in about politics. "Why don't you tell him what he needs to know?" I suggested. "I think I'll go in. It's been a long day."

Peitar inclined his head. Innon made me a flourishing court bow. I curtseyed as if to a king and heard his laughter as I retreated inside the dining room. Servants were clearing the vast table, and they paused to bow. I waved awkwardly, wondering for the first time if some of those impassive faces hid revolutionaries.

Our chambers were royal, all right. My room was enormous, lit by many glowglobes. The walls were decorated in elaborate plasterwork—climbing golden-leafed vines and tiny roses of every shade of pink, with buds made from coral. The curtains and upholstery were embroidered with gold leaves and pink roses.

I looked more closely at the flowers on the walls. Whose hands had set them there, and when? What unknown artist had painted each one so carefully that the plaster petals showed gradations of color? What princess had looked at them in the past, and what had been her feelings?

My thoughts were broken when an almost invisible door opened beside the wardrobe. Out stepped Deon, all clean and neat and dressed in servant gray! She grinned at my surprise. "Hi, Lilah."

I gaped. "Who told you?" Because there was no chance she would have been so friendly if she hadn't known about my Larei disguise.

"Bren. And Lizana put me in charge of hiding your secret things, and here they are." She pulled out the bottom drawer of the wardrobe. There were my underclothes, neatly folded, dried rose petals scattered among them. She lifted everything up to reveal my Larei disguise and the fashion book. I exhaled in relief. "I'm supposed to ask if you want anything before I go down to the guest suite and wait on those snobs."

"Well, the father might be a snob, but the boy—Innon—is on our side."

Deon put her hands on her hips. "Really?" I nodded. "I'll be sure to tell Lizana. And Bren . . . and Derek," she ended, in a testing sort of voice.

"Good," I said. "As for what I want . . . just for something to happen! Something besides the boredom here, I mean."

"Derek says soon. What a prime place for some *real* slam justice!" I'd heard that phrase from Bren, too. Before I could ask what it meant, Deon gave me a challenging look. "Do you want me to brush out your hair or something?"

"No, I do all that myself. I don't want a lady's maid."

"And everyone talks about how you don't yet have one, as if that's a bad thing. Hoo, do they gossip! You'll have to have one when you turn sixteen, Lizana said."

"All the more reason for a revolution," I retorted with careless cheer. "I don't want somebody lurking around whose entire job is to make me fashionable and tattle when I go barefoot."

"Who'd actually *want* to be a maid?" Deon looked around in disgust. "*I'm* doing it for Derek. Though I have to admit, it's nice to have baths each morning—as long as we're out before sunrise, so you nobles can use them the rest of the day." She was still challenging me. I shrugged—it wasn't as if *I* could change things. She scowled at the rose-colored carpet. "And it's good to get plenty of food, but it's turned everyone here into tamed pets."

"You mean the servants? They don't want a revolution?"

"None that I've met. Oh, they all complain about the

nobles—you ought to hear them!" She hooted. "But *change*? Not a chance! They like living in a palace right fine. As for a fight for freedom, they act like it's a horrible idea."

"No freedom?" I picked up my hairbrush and set to. No use in being careful; the curl had already fallen out. I'd be forced to put rags in before I slept.

"Oleus is the steward in charge of pages. The second day I got here, he said, 'What's the use in everyone being forced to scrabble for bread—those who are still alive? That's all a civil war will do for us.' Me, I'd just love to see that nasty Lady Arnathan scrabble for *her* bread!"

I thought of Lady Arnathan, who was always on the watch for proper etiquette and deference. If anyone she considered lower in rank tried to enter a room first, she used her bony elbows to painful effect.

We laughed, then Deon left, and I ran down to the baths for a soak before I put up my hair and climbed into the enormous canopied bed.

eleven

One of my biggest problems is that I don't always think ahead.

The next morning I woke early and went out onto the balcony. Dawn was just a bluish smear in the eastern sky. The soft, still air carried scents from the wildflowers on the hills below. The lake was almost invisible, except as a vast black shadow.

There were lights here and there throughout the city, where people were preparing for market. The servants' windows were lit—those and the enormous ones in the grand pavilion, which housed the ballrooms. The last dancers had probably left just a short time ago.

I went inside to take the rags out of my hair. Then I put on a morning gown and sat down to record yesterday's events. I wrote fast, my handwriting getting tinier as I tried to fit as much as I could on the page. About halfway along I stopped— I'd forgotten to use my codes! So I started abbreviating, which was easier to remember. It felt good when I was done, but after I hid away the book, I wondered what to do next.

I eyed the back of the closet, where Peitar had said the secret passage was.

I'd never been to Uncle Darian's rooms, but I'd heard

about the formal study where he met diplomats and other important visitors, the parlors for courtiers, the grand bed-chamber almost as big as the ballroom, the enormous royal bath. The passage didn't lead to any of these, but to a small room where I was sure he held secret talks. What else would you do with a small side room? I envisioned myself eaves-dropping on some crucially important conference and being the one to tell Derek. I just *had* to take a quick, careful peek.

The closet was carved with twining roses. I pressed each in turn, and sure enough, one at the bottom corner sank into the wood. With a familiar whirring sound, the door slid back, revealing an opening that smelled of old wood and dust, with a faint whiff of damp stone. As the door closed, a tiny glowglobe blinked on, lighting the way.

The passage twisted and twisted again, braiding around the royal suites. If my uncle, who must have been dancing until late, was snoring away in the royal bedroom, there wouldn't be a secret conference, but maybe I'd find some papers. When I reached the end I searched for a peephole. Nothing. I pressed my ear to the wooden panel. No sound at all. I ran my fingers along it, and found a carved handle. It twisted slightly—and the door slid out of my hand and into the wall.

Leaving me and my uncle staring at one another.

He was seated on the edge of an ordinary narrow bed—nothing like a king was supposed to have. At that moment he looked like a normal person, in trousers and an unlaced shirt, holding a stocking, his boots on the floor beside him. His uncombed hair hung down over his shoulders.

My uncle's blue eyes were no longer surprised but annoyed. "What are you doing?"

I closed my mouth, swallowed—or tried to, my throat had gone dry as paper—and managed, "Testing a passage I found." I added, improvising, "Mother used to make it a game for Peitar, finding passages. Selenna House's full of 'em. And he taught me."

Uncle Darian resumed pulling on his stocking. "That passage was put in by one of our distinguished ancestresses, for receiving favorites," he said wryly, studying me. Not with irritation, I discovered uneasily, but with interest.

I looked from him to the room, confused. "But this isn't one of the royal chambers!"

My uncle laughed. An actual laugh, the second I'd ever heard from him. "When you're a king—or a queen," he said, "you can use your rooms however you want. But until you are, I'd advise you not to go poking about uninvited."

"All right," I bleated.

He smiled frostily and picked up his other stocking. "May I finish dressing?"

"Oh! Uh, sorry, Uncle."

I stepped back into the passage, fumbled for the door handle, and it slid closed. Then I hurried away, fighting the sense that I was still being watched by those cold blue eyes. I scolded myself: *He can't be bothered with me—to him, I'm just a stupid brat.*

Only when the wardrobe door shut behind me did I breathe easily. Then I hurried to write what had happened.

I had just stashed the book and was about to go find Bren when there was a quick tap at the servants' door. Surely that couldn't be Deon. Servants didn't tap; they entered and left noiselessly.

When I pulled the latch, Derek stepped into the room. I stared in amazement. He was almost unrecognizable, dressed in ill-fitting servants' gray, his ragged hair smoothed back.

"Where's Peitar?" he demanded.

The room, large as it was, suddenly felt too small. Derek prowled the perimeter, examining everything; I stared witlessly at him until he snapped, "Lilah! Did you hear me?"

"Oh! Um, I don't know. Haven't seen him since last night. His is the next room down."

"Gone. I need him. Fast."

"Maybe he's at breakfast. Or outside. He goes outside to talk so he can't be overheard."

Derek frowned. "All the more reason to burn down this damned blight." He kicked one of the delicate chairs, which skidded toward the window. I jumped up, fearful it would crash into the glass, but it reached the edge of the rug and tipped over. I righted the chair with trembling fingers.

"You want to stay here, and I'll go find him? No one will come in except Deon or Lizana, and—and it's a pretty view, and a pretty room," I added lamely, trying to calm him, I suppose.

That was a mistake.

Derek whirled around, his eyes angry. *"Pretty!"* He practically spat the word as he sneered at the coral rosebuds on the wall. "What was paid for one of those pieces of offal would feed an entire family for a year."

I sucked in a breath. "B-but it was done a long time ago. It's art. Isn't there a place for art?" Bren and his drawing flickered in my mind.

"And who gets to see this *art?*" Derek retorted. "Some thieving noble who bleeds the common folk until they drop. I'd like to burn it all." He glared out the window, his entire body tight with rage. "I could speak one word and torch this entire city," he said in a soft voice. "The kingdom! Everyone is in place. The main part of the army is on maneuvers at Obrin, and the best of the city guard training in the west. All that's here are the young trainees and the guards near retirement. The time has come, but it all waits on a single person. Your brother." He began to pace the length of the room. "And now, I can no longer wait even on him," he said, his voice hard. "Not unless he can perform miracles."

The day had scarcely begun, and this was the second powerful person mad at me.

"I-I-I'll go find Peitar," I stuttered, crammed my feet into my slippers, and fled.

The great dining hall, the small dining room, and the library were all empty, except for servants. Peitar couldn't walk far. He had to be nearby.

The gardens, I thought, and raced outside.

Starting with the closest, I worked my way around in a circle, every so often calling his name. On the third try, I found him. He was with Innon, who carried a chalk and slate.

"Derek," I said in a croaking whisper. "He's here . . . he wants you. . . ."

"Lilah." Peitar's voice was soft. "Have you been running all over calling my name?"

I turned cold. "Only three times."

He turned to Innon. "Make yourself scarce. *Now.*" Innon looked at me, his round face serious, then vanished in the other direction. "All right, Lilah." Peitar looked even more tense than Derek had. "Here, lend me your arm. Let's go, and tell me everything. Quiet voice, now. And smile if we meet anyone we know. Let's not draw attention."

"Derek's in my room," I whispered, adjusting myself as Peitar leaned on me. "Something is really, really wrong. He was saying things—"

"Hold. Let's wait until we get inside." We were now within earshot of strolling courtiers, and a few servants bearing trays.

We walked up a flower-bordered path and inside the big building. Peitar smiled at two friends of Father's on their way to breakfast. We bowed, and they bowed. The woman glanced at my still-unbrushed hair, and her upper lip lengthened.

When we reached my room, Derek was there, alone.

He whirled around, his hand going to his side, but eased when he saw us. "Peitar. King Dirty Hands has Bernal. So far they don't seem to know who he is. As near as I can find out, he was arrested for loitering, but if some soul-sucking captain decides the men need some entertainment and puts him to the question—"

Peitar winced and rubbed his forehead.

"What do you suggest, O clairvoyant one?" Derek asked, but his expression was not at all humorous. It was desperate.

"I'm not clairvoyant. If I were, we wouldn't be sitting here wondering about the future."

I noticed the wary, guarded way that they looked at one another and remembered Derek saying that everything depended on Peitar's word. A strange silence stretched out, almost like a contest. Or a duel.

Finally Peitar said, "Have you read my letter?"

"The time for sitting about in comfortable armchairs and theorizing is over. It's over."

The servants' door flew open. Derek moved fast, pulling a knife from somewhere in his clothes as Deon ran in, looking at me. She said, "Dirty Hands wants you."

At the discreet tap on my bedroom door she vanished back into the servants' corridor, Derek right behind her.

"Coming," I called.

There stood one of the stewards. She said politely, "His Majesty requests an interview."

"Me? Right now? But I haven't really finished dressing." I indicated my hair, glad of its messiness for once.

"Now, Lady Lilah," she said in a respectful but firm voice. "You must come as you are."

I tried to sound unconcerned. "Well, all right, lead the way." Before we turned the corner, I noticed four of the guards approaching my room from the other direction.

I tried to calm myself. I *knew* no one had heard me say anything to Peitar. Then I spotted Innon in the hall, mincing along behind another steward, his nose in the air. Of course—this was about the betrothal! The steward opened the door. My uncle was alone. "Sit down, children."

He looked at me coldly, then turned away. I wondered if he'd decided to be angry about my mistake with the secret passage. But it wasn't as if I'd ever do it again!

Innon and I exchanged puzzled glances.

My uncle seemed to be waiting for something. Finally he turned around and said conversationally, "What can you tell me about Bernal Diamagan?"

The question was so unexpected that I jumped. Innon only looked confused.

Darian's eyes narrowed. "I thought so." His tone made my head ring with warning. "You may go, boy."

Innon shot me a worried look before the door closed silently behind him.

My uncle said, "I'd assumed you were just stupid, but it appears that you are a stupid, conniving little traitor." As he spoke, he moved straight to the panel beside the fireplace.

The door slid open, and there was Peitar.

"Step out," Darian said.

Peitar did. All the walking he'd done so far had told considerably. The two looked at one another, so alike in unexpected ways. Their expressions strengthened the resemblance.

"So," Darian said, "you do have an interest in high politics after all." Silence from Peitar. "You'll regret it."

"No." Peitar's voice was just as devoid of tone as our uncle's, but the atmosphere in the room was so terrible my heart hammered and my hands trembled.   .

"Yes, you will, my noble young heroes. I can promise you that much." Now our uncle's glance included me.

The door opened, and armed guards came in.

Any one of the four tall, strong men could easily have defeated us both. The biggest, I noticed with a strange, detached part of my mind, had thick red hair like my own.

He reached for Peitar, and I tried to protect my brother. The guard gave me what he probably thought was a mild swat. I fell back on the couch, my skirts billowing.

Then a calloused hand pulled me to my feet, and we were marched not to the main halls but to the hidden byways of the palace, ones used only by Darian's silent guards.

twelve

I knew when we had descended to the garrison prison because the air abruptly became cold and still. We were escorted into a room, and the door slammed and locked behind us.

"You can look around now, Lilah." Peitar was breathless, but his voice was kindly. "There's nothing to see."

And there wasn't. Instead of a dungeon full of torture instruments, we were in a room that might have been anywhere, except that it had no windows. A glowglobe was set high on one whitewashed wall. There was a cot, a table with two chairs, and a bench.

The door opened again, and a tall, grizzled warrior in a violet battle tunic came in, incongruously carrying a tray. He set it down on the table and bowed, a quick motion not quite toward either of us.

"Thank you, Captain Avnos," Peitar said as he sank onto the cot.

"You know him?" I asked after the door closed.

"He used to carry me around on his shoulder when I was eight or nine, when Uncle Darian had gotten rid of my crutch," Peitar murmured. "Before he was made a captain."

Mind scouting that breakfast? I don't think I can get up again so easily. It's been a difficult morning."

"Difficult!" I repeated, springing to my feet. "It's a *nightmare*! Why are we even *in* here? We didn't *do* anything!"

Peitar just shook his head, so I turned to the tray. The scent of steeped gingerroot drifted up from a clay teapot. There was a plate of toasted bread, a hunk of cheese, and a bowl of boiled oats with honey, as well as cups and utensils.

I set the food down near Peitar. "Do you think Captain Avnos brought this in secret? Is he one of us?"

"No, he's loyal to Uncle Darian." Peitar poured out the steeped gingerroot. "This is on our uncle's orders, I'm certain. I'm also certain that nothing will happen to us until I have an interview with him. It's the interim that worries me."

"You mean, after we eat, he's going to have us tortured?"

"Not that." Peitar's smile was rueful, but his eyes looked terrible. It wasn't anger, it was grief—real grief. The sheen of tears brightened his lower lids. "Oh, Lilah." He sat back, holding his cup. One of the tears slid down his cheek, but he didn't seem to notice. "Something betrayed us, if not someone. Tell me what happened with Derek?"

I gave a shuddering sigh. "I don't know if it means anything, but before Derek came, I went exploring in that passage. . . ."

"Lilah. You didn't." He winced and shook his head. "My fault, my fault. I never should have told you. Go on. I take it you ran straight into our uncle."

"Yes. He was right in the middle of getting dressed! How was I supposed to know that he'd turned the study into a bedroom?"

"I should have guessed he would avoid the old king's rooms. Tell me everything, just as it happened, please?" When I had finished, he said, his voice very soft, "Lilah. You didn't think to check the passage?"

"I—no! I, I forgot when I saw Derek." I groaned. "It's *my* fault. Our uncle must have sent a spy after I left, and they heard everything Derek said!"

"And when you ran all over the gardens looking for me, Uncle Darian was busy closing the trap around us. Carefully, quietly, so no one would know. Including us." Peitar sighed. "That's why there were guards in the hall when you were summoned—they were sent to find Derek."

"Do you think they sent some up the passage from Uncle's rooms, too?"

"Probably. But they couldn't know that Derek was dressed in servant gray, and we saw him go out that way. I hope it means he escaped." Peitar shook his head. "We'd better eat. Yes, we are in trouble, but it could get worse. Very quickly. We need to be able to think."

"*You* have to think. I've already ruined everything." My throat closed up, and tears of self-pity burned in my eyes.

"*We* have to think." Peitar drank off his steeped ginger-root. "Things are fairly desperate, I'll admit, but that doesn't mean they can't be made worse. We have to prevent that, if we can."

I fought back the tears. "All right. Here, you take some oats first." We ate in silence.

"Is Derek mad at you for something?" I finally asked.

"Not with me, but with my ideas. We disagree not on fundamental needs but on how to accomplish them."

"He almost sounded like he didn't trust you."

"Oh, he does. That is, he did." Peitar set down the bowl. Despite his words, he hadn't eaten much.

Instead, he poured more steeped gingerroot and held the cup as he stared through the opposite wall to distant places and times and people, and said, "You probably don't know this, but Derek's father was a groom in the royal stable. Our mother fell in love with him—and our great-grandfather was furious."

Another surprise. "Because he wasn't a noble?" I asked, and when Peitar nodded, I said, "I just don't understand why our great-grandfather, or anyone, should care."

Peitar said, "Adamas Dei says that you cannot exploit people you respect. The things Derek is angry about aren't Uncle Darian's fault, or even our great-grandfather's. They're the result of a series of increasingly damaging attitudes going back several hundred years."

"Oh," I said.

"When our parents were betrothed, Derek's father was banished to the eastern half of the kingdom, where he started a family. He raised Derek and Bernal to love two things: justice and the shadow of our mother. The day he got the news of her death, he walked into a snow bank, hoping to be reunited with her beyond this world—it inspired a lot of tragic love ballads. Anyway, after that— after hearing about us all his life—Derek made his way to Selenna, risking his life when he was hardly older than you are now. He found out that we agreed on a lot of the same principles, and included me in his plans. Lizana protected him as much as she could, but it was still dangerous."

"Love! Every time I hear about it, I'm glad I'm too young."

Peitar shook his head. "Love is love, it's ineffable. But when it's mixed with politics, it becomes a stain on the spirit."

"Will that ever make sense?" I asked, pulling the oatmeal bowl toward me. "It sure doesn't now."

"Is that your kindly way of saying that I'm talking a lot of hot air?"

The ring of boot heels outside silenced us. The door opened, and a battered young man was shoved in. He crumpled to the floor, moaning.

"Lilah. Help him." My hands shook as I moved the tray to the table. By then, Peitar had reached the stranger, whose bruised, puffy face resembled Derek's. His hands had been tied behind him. Together we managed to shift him to the cot. He was unconscious.

We attempted to undo the knots around his wrists, but

they were too tight, and blood-soaked besides. Finally Peitar straightened up, his face drained of color.

"Is—is this Bernal?" I asked, my voice too high.

"A reminder, sent by Uncle Darian, of the price of high politics," Peitar said. "He will be summoning me very soon. I'll try to get some bandages and things brought here, if I can. If I can't, I want you to help Bernal. Try to make him comfortable."

"Is this going to happen to us next?" I asked, my voice quavering.

"I don't know. What I do know is that we have effectively vanished. Our uncle had just enough time to plan it while you sought me in the garden. No one knows where we are—not servants nor courtiers, much less spies in the city. He must have tried to do the same with Derek. It means he no longer trusts anyone—anyone at all." He looked up at me soberly. "Derek's words in your room had to have been a strike to his heart."

"Uncle Dirty Hands doesn't have a heart," I snapped.

"Yes, he does. But it's banded by thick scars."

For a time we sat in silence, me beside the cot, my insides knotted with fear, and Peitar on the chair, looking down at Bernal.

Presently, just as he had predicted, the guards came for him.

There was nothing I could do for Bernal until he woke up, so I just sat there, waiting. I have no idea how much time passed, for there was no candle to burn down or light to change. Time was measured in Bernal's painful breaths, in and out. Tears ran down my face, hot, then cold.

When they stopped I remained crouching, watching a spider spin a web on one of the legs of the cot. The little creature lived its life unheeding. I wished I was back at Selenna House, playing in the garden and dreaming about what was over the wall.

Bernal's breathing changed just before I heard noise again. I wiped my face on my silken sleeve and waited.

The door was unlocked, and Peitar came in, his forehead tight with pain. I looked at him questioningly. He sat and gave that sardonic smile that jolted me with its resemblance to our uncle's. "We had a discourse on duty."

Then Bernal moved. He was awake. "Peitar," he whispered.

"This is my sister, Lilah," Peitar said. "Shall we help you bind those wounds we can reach?" He smiled slightly. "Lilah is carrying a bit of superfluous cloth."

I looked down at all my petticoats but didn't feel like laughing.

"No matter," Bernal managed. "I—why are you here?"

"I'm afraid my uncle found out about our participation."

"Does Derek know I got caught?" Bernal's brown eyes were anxious.

"Yes," Peitar and I said together.

He made an unhappy sound. "Then he'll do something.

Tonight." At Peitar's questioning look, he went on. "Because tomorrow I'm to be put to death. Public. City square."

I crouched in a ball, almost biting through my lip, but I felt no pain.

The two of them just talked, their voices low murmurs. Not about Derek or plans or anything like that. Bernal didn't rail against courtiers or even against Uncle Darian. Instead, they spoke of Arnathan, the province where the Diamagans had spent their childhoods, and horses. I got a feeling that if Bernal hadn't devoted himself to Derek's cause, he would be raising them.

Time passed, and I helped Bernal drink the rest of the gingerroot, and then he slept.

Peitar laid his head on his crossed arms, and after a time, I heard his breathing slow down.

I tried thinking, *I am Lasva Dei the Wanderer, and this is my adventure,* but I was too scared to believe it. So I sat there and studied the little spider in her web.

PART II

Enemies

one

Finally I fell asleep, curled up on the stone, head pillowed on a swath of my skirts.

Approaching noise woke us. The door slammed open, smashing into the wall, and a crowd of armed people roared in, led by . . . Derek!

"Castle's ours!" he cried, waving a blood-streaked sword. A long knife was stuck through his ragged sash. "City will be soon." His companions cheered. Their weapons and spattered clothing made me shudder.

"My uncle?" Peitar asked.

"Ours! It took more than ten of us to capture him. Who would have known all those swords he's got on the walls weren't bolted down?"

"His own guards died, I take it?"

Derek's smile faded. I suspect he'd forgotten that those "guards" were men Peitar had known all his life. "Only four." Then, in a sharper voice, "And the king either killed or wounded as many of my people before they disarmed him. He's a prisoner, bound and guarded." Derek said to the others, "There's my brother, Bernal—and my friend Peitar, and his sister, Lilah. See to it they are safe."

And he was gone, along with most of the crowd.

Someone bent to cut Bernal free. "I've got to join my brother," he whispered to me as he got shakily to his feet and began to work his cramped arms and legs.

He was helped out, leaving Peitar and me alone.

"Lilah, get yourself to one of the passages and hide. . . ."

"No chance." I helped him up. "Here's my shoulder. We'll stay together."

"All right," he said reluctantly, because we both knew he couldn't walk. "But we should get out of these clothes before some of Derek's rioters attack us."

Out in the hall, I saw everything I dreaded. The floor and walls were splashed with blood. People were sprawled everywhere, some unmoving, others in obvious pain. We stopped by the first few wounded, though there was nothing we could do. Peitar told them we would try and get help, but I was afraid Derek's followers wouldn't show the mercy that Captain Avnos had.

The door between the garrison and the palace was ajar, smoke drifting through, bringing the sounds of distant cries and the crash and tinkle of windows breaking.

Twice we ducked into archways to avoid shouting, singing rioters, their arms full of loot. It was horrible, seeing Selenna servant blue and gray among the fallen. Terror made me shaky, but Peitar seemed to have acquired some kind of strength, because he kept us moving. Though he looked at everything, long and grim, as if memorizing it.

Finally, we reached the residence gardens and found our

first dead courtiers. I knew them for courtiers only because of the blood-soaked silk and velvet and brocade. All their jewels were gone.

The rioters had not yet reached our floor. Father's suite was empty. "It looks like there was some warning after all," Peitar said, looking around the vast chamber. He shook his head once, as though it hurt. "I have to find Derek. Get his people to see to the wounded."

My room streamed with morning light. It finally caught up with me—a complete day and night had passed while we were in the garrison. I hurriedly changed into my Larei clothes, braided up my hair, and crammed on my cap. Then I stuffed the fashion book into the waist of my knee pants.

Peitar met me in the hall. Gone were the jeweled hair tie and the fine shoe clasps. He wore a plain shirt and leaned on his extra cane.

No one would recognize us as nobles now.

So this was revolution. I remembered how impatient I'd been for it to happen—just so I wouldn't have to curl my hair. But in my idea of revolution, people gathered to make stirring speeches about how we could better our lives, followed by cheers and exciting trumpet blasts as . . . things somehow changed. Not this horror.

We made our slow way downstairs and came upon people emerging from one of the suites. A teenage girl had pulled a costly ball gown over her clothing. Her companion waved a sword. "Damnation to the nobles!" he shouted, jabbing a tapestry on the wall.

"Long live King Derek!" the girl shrilled. Giving us a wave, they vanished into another room.

I looked at my brother. "King Derek?"

"Not his idea. The problem is, he hasn't replaced it with anything else."

Outside, on the grand terrace, more rioters swarmed back and forth, some laughing like it was a picnic. We joined the crowd entering the royal pavilion, where government had taken place for so many generations.

The floor was littered with shards of glass and broken statuary. The tapestries depicting famous historical scenes hung in tatters. The air was hot and gritty.

Derek and several others stood on the dais in the throne room, making speeches. The musicians' gallery and the wall alcoves were filled, but not everyone was listening. Knots of adults talked furtively, while kids pulled at the banners on the walls.

A middle-aged woman in a cook's apron was speaking. As the crowd shoved us forward we began to catch words. "Death . . . blood . . . clean! . . . a new beginning!" she cried. Swords, axes, spears, hoes, and scythes were thrust into the air. "Today will live in history, as the blood of the nobles waters the seeds of freedom!" She threw her arms wide. A cheer echoed through the hall, the crowd shifted— and we came face to face with Bren and Deon.

"Peitar! Lilah!" They too had changed from palace clothes. Deon bounced with excitement, but Bren's grin seemed forced.

"There are the Selennas," I heard Derek call. The crowd parted around us, and we joined him. "My best friend and guide, Peitar Selenna," he proclaimed, throwing an arm around my brother's shoulders. There were a few mutterings—some in question, others in anger.

Derek cleared his throat, then whispered, "Gah, I'm thirsty." He lifted his voice. "Unknown to you all, Peitar was my earliest recruit, my right hand, second only to my brother. I wish you all to protect him and his sister, Lilah, who is also one of us. Peitar, share some of your thoughts."

My brother tried, but his quiet voice didn't carry. Behind me, a burly man grumbled. Several people laughed, and as the talking got louder, my stomach clenched.

Peitar shook his head and turned to Derek. "There are wounded people who need tending. On both sides."

"The nobles can look to themselves for a change. As for the others . . ." Derek raised his voice to a powerful shout. "Hear me! Can someone help the wounded? Our fallen brothers and sisters rely on our help!" The people cheered again, but if anyone moved to do his bidding, I couldn't see it. He turned back to Peitar. "Come! Celebrate with us. Your uncle was going to hang my brother today, and probably you tomorrow. Instead, *he'll* be on the execution stand, but he won't get an easy hanging. We'll make it last a couple of days, if we can."

Peitar gave him a long look, then shook his head. "Derek. When you want to talk again, you'll know where to find me."

We retreated—Deon, with many backward glances. I thought I saw Innon, looking dirty and disheveled, but he was swallowed by the crowd before I could be sure.

Finally we were on the grand terrace. Peitar leaned against a half-smashed marble bench. "Those people are so stupid," I muttered, sitting down. And when he gave me a distracted glance, "I heard one say your mind is as twisted as your leg, and all nobles should die. And *he's* going to make a new government?"

Peitar shrugged. "My leg is crooked, anyone can see that. And he knows nothing of my mind."

"I'd like to smack him over the head with a cook pot."

"Passing the hurt back, eh? Let it go."

"Foo!" I exclaimed. "It's all very well to be high-minded like your legendary Adamas Dei—if he even lived—but the fact is, even if that man's words can't hurt us, his sword can."

"Yes. Which is why there's nothing more for us here. It's too dangerous to stay, and I don't know how to fix it. Let's go home."

"I'll go with you." Bren scowled. "C'mon, Deon. . . ."

Deon scowled right back. "No. I don't want to see my family again—noble-loving fools! Well, not Gran. But I'm staying to help. Derek says this is where freedom is being born and history made!"

"Deon . . ."

She shook her head. "I'm off!" And she ran.

I turned to my brother. "Peitar, we have to find Lizana . . . and make sure Father—"

"He's gone," Bren said, interrupting, as he watched his cousin vanish inside. "Lizana warned people to leave. I thought she was betraying the cause . . . but I think now she was right. That was last night, after the king sent your father home. I helped put food in his carriage."

"Lizana knows how to take care of herself," Peitar said. "Let's find mounts, if we can."

"Are you angry that Deon stayed, Bren?" I asked as we walked. "She just wants to help." When he didn't answer, I whispered, "I didn't think it would be like this—all the killing."

He let his breath out in a rush. "Oh, I did. Sort of. After all, you can't go to the worst nobles and say, 'Hand over your estates,' and expect them to do it. And a lot of them fought. One duke, he must have slashed up a dozen people before they got him. But some were kids our age! They tied one girl up and gagged her and threw her in the lake, and laughed as she struggled." He shook his head. "And when she drowned."

Sickened, I asked, "What was her name?"

"All I know is, her own maid was the ringleader. Kept saying horrible things, like how she'd been beaten for dropping a hairbrush. Had her fingers smashed for wrinkling a gown. But I thought, 'Make the noble brats earn their bread. That'll cure 'em. Don't *kill* 'em.'"

Peitar said, "The murders of children were not on Derek's orders, Bren."

"I know. But that's the other thing! They aren't *listening* to his orders! They're just doing whatever they want." Bren took a deep breath. "You're right, Lilah. Deon just wants to help Derek. And she will. Even if no one else does," he finished in an undertone.

We picked our way past evidence of fighting, into the deserted stable. The horses were uneasy, ears flicking and flattening. Bren bridled and saddled three as I worried about Peitar, who had not ridden since his accident. We had to help him mount.

Then it was my turn. I'd never been on horseback, and it was frightening to be seated so high on a shifting animal. But Bren said, "Hold on with your knees, and follow me. Don't kick, or yank the reins, and you'll be all right. We won't gallop—we have to make the horses last."

Knees? Forget that! I clutched the horse's mane in a death grip. We began riding slowly into the city, Peitar also clutching the reins so hard his knuckles were white. After a while, when we realized that the animals never went faster than a walk, he relaxed a little, and so did I.

Finally Peitar said, "We were in prison all day yesterday. Can you tell us what happened?"

Bren said, "Derek gave the command at midnight. They set fire to noble houses in four separate places. We could see the fires from the servants' quarters."

"And while the guard was assisting with the fire lines

down to the lake, the rest attacked guard posts, and converged on the palace?" Peitar clearly knew what Derek had planned.

"Yes. Deon took me to a drill my first night. I didn't want to kill sleeping people, not even nobles. I wanted to do something else, like put out the fires, but there were never any plans for *that*."

We continued in silence. Smoke billowed from the center of the city, drifting in a frightening brown haze over the lake. I wondered if some courtiers had hidden on their boats or gone out the day before and had no idea anything was wrong until they saw the flames. I did not know which would be worse.

When we reached the market section near the south gate, bigger crowds surged down the streets. Some of the stores had hastily painted signs to forestall looters—FREEDOM! and HAIL THE REVOLUTION!—but others had armed people stationed outside. The streets were covered with glass and smashed furniture and even food, which amazed me. How could people who had complained about hunger destroy food?

No one paid attention to us as we rode out through the open and unguarded gates. People streamed past, some carrying goods in baskets and knapsacks. Others had carts, and there were coaches, pulled by horses, by goats and oxen, and even by people, many roaring drunk.

At last the crowds thinned out, and we started toward the east, and Selenna.

I finally burst out, "I've always hated Uncle Dirty Hands,

but that—what Derek said, about making his execution last for days. He never did *that* to anybody, not that I ever heard of."

"No. He hates torture. He has had people roughly handled, like Bernal. And killed. But never as entertainment." Peitar drew in a long, shaky breath. "I won't be a part of that, even passively."

Neither Bren nor I knew how to respond. But I could tell that Bren wanted to say something more.

"I saw your letter," he finally told Peitar, in a rush. "Yesterday morning, late. I'd just talked to Derek, in the garden where the servants go. After, I thought of a question, and turned back, but he was reading. Then he crumpled up the papers and threw them down. After he left— well, I was curious."

"What did you think?" Peitar asked gently.

"You're right. You're right, and Derek can't see it." Bren's voice cracked—he was crying. "I thought every man being king for himself would work—would mean peace!"

"Maybe it can work if each person governs only him- or herself. I read somewhere that the problem comes when people seek to command one another. I believe Derek will see that this way, with violence, doesn't work."

I hoped so.

two

At nightfall, we camped. That is, we stopped on a hillside just above a stream, the horses tethered nearby, since we had nothing to make camp with. It was the first time I had ever slept outside. We had no blankets, and I hadn't eaten since we'd been in the garrison. I was stiff and hungry when I woke.

Bren readied the horses, then showed us how to stretch out our aching legs. Peitar's face blanched with effort. We mounted up and began the first of two long days on the road.

The weather stayed clear and hot. Bren knew which wild berries were safe to eat; otherwise, we went hungry. Whenever we saw a stream, we drank, and turned the horses loose. We did not talk much, except about horses, berries, where to sleep. We were all lost in our separate thoughts.

When we finally reached the Selenna House gates, the guards stared at us in surprise—especially when they saw me in my Larei clothes, with my braid hanging down.

"There's been violence in Miraleste," Peitar called up at the sentries. "Against the homes of nobles. We had to evacuate, but it's spreading. They may well come here."

The guard in charge looked back grimly. "We're short-handed, my lord."

"Do your best," Peitar said as we passed inside.

Two stable hands took our horses, as if everything was normal. Yet here I was in my disguise, still smelling of torched city. Peitar gave me a troubled glance. "Lilah, watch your tongue. Bren, you too."

"Why?" I asked, feeling unsettled and crabby. "What can Father do to us now?"

"Lilah, Uncle Darian must have told him we were traitors before ordering him home, or Father wouldn't have left without us. Don't force him into a position of having to choose between two loyalties."

Loyalties? I was still working that out when we reached the front doors. The hall was dark, and though shadows gathered, no one had lit the great chandelier. It sparkled with dim, ghostly shards of light, reminding me of the rooms in the palace that had not yet been looted.

"Where are the servants?" I whispered.

"Most of them are probably still gone," Peitar said. "Remember, we were supposed to be in Miraleste all week. As for the rest . . . I don't know. We'll have to shift for ourselves. I'll go talk to Father."

"Well, I'm hungry. Come on, Bren, let's find something to eat."

"Sure," he said with some of his old enthusiasm.

The kitchens were empty but clean. Neither of us could

find the fire stick, so Bren used the sparker to light the lamps and the wood laid ready in the grate. The smell reminded me horribly of Miraleste. Bren and I managed to cobble together a meal—reheated barley soup, as well as bread, cheese, and fruit. Peitar joined us, and said, "Lilah, take Father's share on a tray to him, please."

Father sat in his study, staring into the fire. When I appeared, he glanced up but said nothing. I left as fast as I could.

When I got back to the kitchen, I asked Peitar, "What did you tell him?"

"That Uncle Darian had been mistaken, which was why we were free. He didn't ask me anything more."

He paused when Father's valet appeared, casting us a narrow-eyed glance as he went straight to the wine closet, selected a bottle and a goblet, and vanished again.

"Better leave him some food, too," Peitar said.

I was tired and filthy, but I didn't want to sleep in my room. "I think I'll get some blankets from the linen closet," I said, "and stay right here."

Bren curled up on the other side of the fireplace. It was warm, and I felt the fears of the days before slip away. *Maybe things will get better,* I thought as my eyelids closed.

LAST NIGHT'S MESS looked worse in daylight. I felt grimy and reeked of smoke.

"Peitar, Bren. I'm going upstairs to use my cleaning frame."

"I'm coming with you," Bren said, throwing off his blanket.

It had never felt better to step through the frame and feel magic take the dirt and smoky grit from my skin and hair and clothes. I wished we could do the same for the dirty dishes, but I had no idea where the cleaning spells were.

Father's valet came in soon after and showed us the small barrel of water and the drying cloth. We dipped the dishes once, and they came out sparkling. Magic buzzed through my fingers as I worked.

Afterward, we poked around the larder and found potatoes, onions, and cabbage. I, of course, had never cooked. Bren tried to remember how his mother made potato pancakes, and we worked together. We served them with new grapes from the vine out back, and Peitar took some to Father and his valet. The meal was delicious.

When the kitchen was clean again, it was already noon. "What do we do now?" I asked Peitar.

"Maybe I should go home," Bren said. He didn't sound all that eager, and I wondered if he was afraid that if he went home, he wouldn't get paid. I knew his family was counting on that money.

"Can you wait?" Peitar asked. "I think we're better off staying quietly here, at least for a day. Maybe you can go scout things tomorrow." He walked toward the stairs.

Bren scowled. "I'm not going to go into the village and yell about you being here, and tell them to attack," he muttered.

I'd forgotten that to Riveredge, we were still Lady Fluffbrain and Lord Cripple, brats of Prince Greedy. But Peitar hadn't forgotten. "Maybe Selenna Leader would tell them to attack anyway," I said, and Bren scowled even harder. But he didn't disagree.

We counted up the various foods stocked in the larder, tried to figure out how to cook things, then finally decided to make potato pancakes again. By then the shadows had grown long.

Sudden, loud pounding on the front door startled us. We ran out to the foyer. Peitar was on the stairs, carrying a pile of books and papers. Father and his valet appeared in the doorway to their suite. The pounding came again, even louder.

One look at the valet's face made it clear that he had never answered a door and was not about to begin. So I did.

"Gate sentry," the man said. "Villagers are rioting. Tell His Highness—"

"What?" My father came up behind me, interrupting the sentry.

"Your orders, Highness?"

"Turn them away!"

"But there are only a dozen of us, Highness."

"You have the gates, and the weapons."

"But there are too many to count. . . ."

"Hold them off! Kill anyone you have to!" And, as the man ran back into the night, "Shut the doors," Father ordered. He glanced somewhere between Bren and me and said, "Please bring me my dinner."

We finished cooking, eating our share as we did. As Bren began the cleaning, I picked up Father's tray—

And almost dropped it when I saw the windows flickering with the wicked flare of many torches. I ran to Father's study.

My father's valet had fled, and he was alone. "Lock the door."

Then we faced one another. Without his wig, my father seemed older than he was. Pity, fear—a snake pit of conflicting feelings squirmed inside me.

"Are you afraid?" he asked.

It seemed a strange question, but I whispered, "Yes."

"Then I take it these are not here on your invitation."

"Oh, no." My voice quavered. "I . . . when I saw what happened in Miraleste, it was—"

He raised a hand, and his rings sparkled. "I hope," he said in a quick, low voice, "that the two of you will amount to something someday. But your time is now, and mine is past." Then he was again the father I knew. "Go to the library. I'll hold them here as long as I can." He took up his fine sword. *"Go!"*

Someone battered against the door. "Come out, you bloodsucking noble soul-eater!"

I fled to the library, and the secret passage in the fireplace—but how would I get out the other end? Trembling, I hid behind a chair as people stampeded in.

"No one here!" I yelled, just as the first man saw me.

I got a perplexed stare, but the villagers had no interest in a scruffy urchin. One started pulling books off the shelves and flinging them into the fireplace, as another lit the sparker. A few hacked at the furniture, one with a sword, another with a scythe. A woman grabbed my mother's porcelain figurines and stuffed them into her bodice.

I dodged past, into the parlor, where Father lay in a heap on the floor, his sword gone. I ran, sobs tearing at my throat for him, for the careless violence destroying the only home I'd known.

The hall was filled with smoke. I lurched blindly toward the kitchen, and bumped into someone who dropped his booty and cursed me. I was sobbing too hard to care. The kitchen was empty, but I spotted the fashion book tossed aside on the floor, and stuffed it inside my tunic.

If Bren and Peitar were hiding, I knew where.

I didn't feel safe until I was in the passage. As the fountain slid closed over my head, I felt my way along the damp walls until I heard Peitar call my name. They were in the room where he had met with Derek. Candlelight wavered on the walls.

"I helped Peitar escape." Bren's voice was tight. "They meant to kill everybody."

"Did you bring Father?" Peitar demanded anxiously.

I stood there, my breathing ragged.

"They got him, didn't they," Bren said.

"He—he—s-said we'd better amount to something, and he told me to go, and I wouldn't, and he ordered me, and they s-smashed everything, and—and I went after my book, because . . ."

I couldn't talk anymore. I was crying too hard.

Peitar caressed my cheek, but I felt the tremble in his fingers, because he was crying, too.

Bren crouched on the ground, all bony arms and legs. "I saw them. I *know* them. My own brother Tam. Just a year ago he wanted to be in the army, training horses. And today, he was as bad as those people in Miraleste."

"I've learned something about crowds." Peitar's voice was unsteady. "People are no longer themselves when they join crowds. There's a group mood. It's like a magic coercion." Bren was listening, even if his face was pinched and miserable in the light of the candle. "They seem to take on the ugliness or goodness of the leader. Today it was ugly. Tam might not remember what he did when he wakes up tomorrow."

"But *I'll* remember," Bren whispered.

three

We hid for two days, while above us the villagers destroyed everything they couldn't take. It was a good thing Bren was with us. Before he helped Peitar to safety, he had made sure to grab as much food as he could.

We slept a lot. When I woke and remembered what had happened, I felt so sick I wanted to go back to sleep again. Bren poked around, examining the golden candlesticks and carved boxes and old clothes of stiff brocade and gemmed velvet, while Peitar, as usual, took solace in reading the books he'd managed to save. I forced myself to write down everything that had happened, using the pen and ink Peitar had brought.

The second day, he read to us from the memoirs of Adamas Dei of the Black Sword, a legendary warrior who had left Sartor in search of peace. Although Bren didn't say much, he seemed to be interested, so Peitar lent it to him.

Our food was gone by the third day. Bren and I listened through the fountain, and when we heard nothing, dared to venture out. The vegetable garden was stripped, the closest fields empty, but we managed to dig up some roots and drank from the kitchen well.

Later, we found Peitar sitting on the front steps in the

ash and rubble, looking distraught. "I said the Words of Disappearance over Father. And over the others who had fallen."

I'd been afraid to go back into the parlor. "I'm glad," I said, thinking of Father's remains, now a part of the soil where our ancestors lay, and though I hadn't been there when Peitar did the Disappearance magic, I silently recited the poem wishing peace to Father's fled spirit.

Then it was underground to sleep again, amid the gleaming treasures of ancient Selennas.

IN THE MORNING, Peitar said, "Just before the raid I burned all my letters." He paused. "Now I believe I must return to Miraleste."

"Miraleste! Isn't that going right into worse danger?" I exclaimed, and even Bren looked startled. "You said there was nothing more for us there. Why go back?"

"There's even less for us here," he said. His smile was bleak. "And the danger is probably about equal. Also, Lizana hasn't returned. I think that means . . . Derek might need my help."

"He didn't listen when we were there before," I argued.

"Maybe he will now. I did promise. I have to try."

Bren and I traded glances. "We'll go with you," he said.

Peitar sighed, and I knew what he was thinking: *No place is safe anymore.* "We'll have to have mounts."

"I believe I know where to get some." Bren turned away, scowling.

I joined him—but first, the two of us went deep into the garden to see if any fruit remained. We devoured what we found, saving some for Peitar, then hurried to Riveredge. The gatehouse was wrecked, but there were no bodies; someone had, at least, said the words of Disappearance over them. I wondered who had fought, who had joined the looters, and who had fled, like Father's valet. And I wondered if anyone had yet Disappeared the dead of Miraleste.

After everything that had happened, I was stunned to find the village almost the same. Things from Selenna House were proudly displayed on porches and in windows—here a silver candlestick, there part of a tapestry. I spotted a bedraggled girl with one of my old dolls.

Bren found his brothers at the village stable. Sure enough, the looters had gotten most of our horses. He wheedled them out of three older mounts, plus a basket of stale biscuits, cheese, and grapes. It was Derek's name that did the trick. Bren lied and said that Derek expected us to report back.

"You'll tell him what we did, won't you, Bren?" Tim asked, his face earnest and proud. "You'll tell him that the horses are from us, and we won't sell 'em to nobles."

"Sure I will." Bren gave a convincing grin. "Very first thing I say."

⌣ ⌣ ⌣

WE RODE FOR Miraleste. I could see from Peitar's profile that he felt as terrible as I did about Father's death. Bren was restless and broody, constantly fingering the reins.

Eventually he burst out, "So you're the Prince of Selenna now?"

"No," said Peitar. "Nothing changes until one swears the oath of allegiance before the throne. Titles are granted by the crown."

"Then you can't fix anything here."

"No one would listen to me. We saw that already, didn't we?"

"Maybe things will be better in Miraleste now." Bren looked hopeful. "Derek's sure to have them organized, like he did before."

"Maybe. I hope so." Peitar turned my way, smiling. "Lilah, I expect that book you've been writing is going to be the most notorious memoir since the Esalan brothers' *Our Provident Careers.*"

I could see he was trying to cheer me up. And yes, it was true that I'd witnessed most of the important events so far—but that was because they were my fault. If only I hadn't stuck my nose into that stupid passage!

"Esalan brothers?" Bren asked. "Who are they?"

"Old thieves," I said morosely. "Peitar used to tell me their stories."

"They were sons of a baron, impoverished through unfair circumstances," my brother explained. "Long ago, in a time like this—with a great divide between those of rank and everyone else. The brothers lived double lives, robbing the wealthy of Miraleste and, once they were truly successful, doing good for the needy. They used daring and imagination and never killed anyone."

"Then the crown prince joined their gang," I put in, trying to shake off my dark mood. "Only they didn't know it."

"The old queen died, and the prince was to be crowned, and the celebration was to be the brothers' biggest caper." Peitar's voice quickened. "The day arrived, and so did the brothers. But when they saw the new king, they were amazed and swore off stealing."

"The royal pardon helped," I added.

Peitar smiled. "And the crown prince had learned most of their secrets. But he did promise that whoever overtaxed their people might just get a visit from the brothers—on the king's command. And so they retired honorably and wrote up their memoir. Our mother read it to me when I was small."

"How come I've never heard of them?" Bren asked.

"Because the nobles have chosen to rewrite the part of history when 'Esalan justice' was slang for justice outside the law."

"'Esalan justice' . . ." Bren snapped his fingers. "Slam justice! Is *that* where it came from?"

Peitar nodded. "Soon after we first met, I told Derek about the Esalans, and he asked for more about them on every visit."

"But he never told us."

"Probably because they were nobles themselves."

"How about another story?" Bren asked.

So Peitar whiled away the long ride with their adventures, finishing when we camped alongside a stream that night. As I listened, I realized that Derek had woven that sense of humor and camaraderie through his own tales— and hearing about the brothers in Peitar's voice made me feel a bit better.

THE FIRST THING we noticed when we rode through the unguarded city gates was the stench.

"Ugh," Bren exclaimed. "Did they burn all the wands, too?" The Wand Guild was definitely not using their magic to get rid of horse and animal droppings.

"Maybe the guilds have disbanded," Peitar said.

Most of the houses that remained bore signs related to Derek's cause. The first inn we saw, the Three Princes, was now Freedom Alehouse. Everywhere we looked, people had scrawled their opinions on walls and fences.

Nearly all were against my uncle. We passed one that said:

DIAMAGAN ↑
DIRTY HANDS ↓

Next to it, in larger letters:

EAT AT THE RED RAVEN—
NO NOBLES ALLOWED!

Merchants worked on repairing their shops. The streets were filled with people with nothing to do. Many of the noble houses had been burned to the ground, and others were in ruins.

At the royal stables, we were confronted by a man dressed in the red smock of the bricklayers' guild. "Where you goin' with them nags?"

"We have business with Derek," I replied.

He spat on the ground. "Everyone has business with Derek. If you leave them nags, they're mine. If you want 'em back, it's six golders apiece." Six! Before, you could *buy* a horse for two.

"What if we haven't any money?" Peitar said.

"That's your lookout. I got a business to run, and fodder isn't cheap."

"We'll keep the horses by us."

"Hah!" was the derisive answer. "Some free advice—don't let go o' them bridles, and don't turn your back on anyone."

"Thank you."

The man gave him an odd look, and I gulped. Peitar's

manners—noble manners—were not acceptable anymore, that was for certain. But nothing happened as we rode toward the damaged but still standing royal pavilion.

We helped Peitar dismount, then Bren said, "I'll stay with the horses. Don't worry," he added in a hard voice. "They'll be here when you return. And so will I." To me, he whispered, "Find out where Deon is, will you?"

I nodded and followed my brother inside, where bodies lay all over—not dead, but drunk, judging from the stink. Someone had found the royal wine cellar.

The throne room had been stripped of its furnishings and ancient flags. Voices came from the old treaty library, where we discovered Derek with a few people his age, and . . .

"Innon!" I exclaimed thankfully. "I *did* see you! You're safe!"

Derek's expression changed from tense to surprised to relieved. "Peitar." He said it like he hadn't expected to see us alive again. His next words shocked my wits right out of me: "Peitar, Darian Irad escaped."

I think my brother wasn't sorry, but he didn't show it. "That's not surprising."

"You don't think he'll leave the kingdom?" Peitar shook his head. "It's been a nightmare. The treasury is completely empty. I don't know if Irad arranged it, or if looters got it all—but I have nothing. I can't *do* anything. Innon and I have been sitting here trying to figure out some ways to manage. . . ." He sighed. "Truth is, we don't even know where to begin."

Derek and *Innon*? Where were all the experienced adults? Dead, if they were nobles—or in hiding. There were only three others in the room, and they were all Derek's age.

Innon gave me a weary smile. It was clear he had been working a long time. The slate in his hand was scribbled over, his grubby clothes covered in chalk dust. The room was stuffy and smelled of sweat.

Derek flicked us a quick smile, then turned back to Peitar. "I hope you aren't hungry."

"We have three biscuits left. Glad to share." He didn't mention that they were hard as rocks.

Derek waved away the offer. "Our main threat is going to be Dirty Hands."

"Yes. His own sense of duty will bring him back," Peitar warned. "Unless you were able to deal with his army at Obrin. . . ."

"That was a mirage, thinking that I could send untrained farmers and laborers against the army. My leaders were successful against nobles who knew nothing of defense, or who were caught by surprise, but when it was time to march to Obrin, they started deserting in larger numbers. My captains came to me two days ago, saying that the volunteers I had left were making all kinds of excuses—so I had to send *them* home, too. Irad must be on his way to Obrin now. And we can't do anything to stop him from coming back." Derek looked away, then back at Peitar. "Your father?"

"Dead." My brother's mouth tightened, making him look unsettlingly like our uncle. I wondered if he felt the same horrible jolt of memory.

If anything, Derek seemed almost as upset. Then he straightened and clapped his hands on his knees. "Sideos. Farian. Linnah. I need to speak with Peitar. You know where we have to begin. Can you get started, each to recruit one person for a specific job? Just like the old days."

Linnah sent a glance Peitar's way, more perplexed than angry. Then they were gone, and Peitar sat down, giving a grateful sigh.

Innon sighed, too, as I joined him on the floor. "What happened after my uncle sent you out of the parlor?"

"People were acting odd—servants carrying bundles of stuff, guards running, weapons out. Then Derek spotted me. He said that Deon had told him about me, but just as we began talking, everything started happening. He said to wait, and sent Lizana. She'd told my father to escape, and I hope he did—I hope he didn't come back to search for me. I got rid of my toff clothes and mussed myself up. By then the mob was looking for courtiers to chase and kill."

I shuddered. "Bren said she was warning people. Do you know why? Did she go against the revolution?"

"No. She acted on Derek's orders. She told me one of the last arguments he and Peitar had was over the fact that all nobles weren't evil—that some were good for their lands, and if they were all killed, everyone would suffer. I guess he changed his mind at the very end, because he made her a list of people to tip off."

"Did she get to them all?"

"No." Innon's face was bleak. "And some refused. Said loyalty meant staying to help the king. So a lot of those died," he finished in a flat, tired voice.

I stopped asking questions, as they were only upsetting us both, and we turned our attention to Derek and Peitar.

". . . I should have remembered that his warriors were dedicated. They struck fast. There were a lot of volunteer guards around Irad—they enjoyed shouting things at him, throwing garbage. . . ."

I said, "Did you let them torture him?"

Derek didn't meet my eyes. "No," he admitted, as though he'd been weak. "I know I promised a good show, but first I wanted there to be a trial. I suspect only that kept their hands off him. They practiced their speeches while he sat there bound and gagged—"

Peitar cut in. "You needn't elaborate. Go on. So some of the royal guard rescued him."

"Yes. They were outnumbered, but my volunteers weren't experienced. Irad's raiders killed the ones who didn't run, which is probably what's going to happen to us when he returns. He got away in the one coach I'd managed to save. I'd saved it for you, actually, but you left too soon." Derek smiled grimly. "You expected something like this, didn't you?"

"His guards are disciplined and loyal. And as you say, your people had passionate hatred but no unity. No one in authority that they will recognize, and no training."

"Yes, well, here's something you didn't foresee. Irad seems to have Bren's cousin Deon." When I gasped in surprise, Derek turned to me. "She was my best message runner and volunteered at the kitchen in trade for meals. She was sent by one of the cooks to clean the carriage, and I don't think Irad's guard knew she was in it when they seized it."

"Have you searched?" Peitar asked.

"Yes. No sign of her."

"That means she'll be borne off to wherever their camp lies and put to work fetching water and cooking. They'll be low on servants." He sighed. "His mood must be vile."

Derek cursed under his breath. "And he'll return. That's what I keep telling everyone, but they all think if they could beat him once, a second time will be easy. They don't listen, Peitar, except if it's something *they* want to do! *Authority*, you said. Everywhere I'm hailed as a hero, the author of freedom, but when I ask them to band together to fix a bridge or rebuild a house, everyone is busy looking for more nobles or bartering what they took. When all that is used up, where are we to get new goods?"

Peitar rubbed his forehead. "I don't know."

"And when Irad returns, it's going to be me—and you—he comes after first."

"Yes. That's the main reason I'm here."

"You'll stay, then?"

"I'll stay." He did not sound particularly happy, but he did sound decisive. "And we can test the truth of what I said in my letter. We should speak of making law that protects everyone, low and high."

Derek shook his head. "I hope you're right."

"But you must not stay, Lilah," my brother said. "I'm afraid it's going to get worse before it gets better. There is one worry that would haunt me, and that is your safety. Promise me you'll leave, now, for Mother's refuge?" Mother's refuge—he meant Delfina Valley, far away in the mountains down south!

"But I want to help!" I protested.

Derek gave me a serious look. "You can help best," he said, "by going there." By the way he spoke, I knew that Peitar had told him about Delfina Valley.

"I appreciate your desire to help, Lilah," my brother added. "But the situation here is beyond your experience." When I was about to say that it was beyond *Peitar's* experience as well, he added in a low voice, "And I don't want you hurt by any more well-intentioned mistakes."

Or, put less nicely, I'd already landed us in prison once. He was afraid I might do it again. I knew he was right. And

I had no stomach for fighting and killing. My throat hurt too much to speak, so I just nodded.

Peitar looked relieved. "Good. And you, Innon, I wish you'd go with her."

Innon sat up, looking surprised.

Derek gave him a pat on the shoulder. "I do, too. You've been a great help, but Peitar can take your place. If we settle Miraleste, we'll send word to you both. And take Bren, would you? I don't want any more of you kids disappearing."

I dreaded having to tell Bren about Deon.

Innon turned to Peitar. "Where are you sending us?"

"Lilah will show you. Down south."

"I hope you don't mean anywhere near Diannah Wood!"

"Through it, actually."

Innon grimaced. "You want to get rid of us permanently? People *disappear* there!"

Peitar turned to me. "I won't ask Innon to trust me. He doesn't know me. But will *you* trust me, Lilah, when I tell you that you will be safe?"

"All right," I said, surprised and very curious. "Then let's go. I don't know how long Bren can protect our horses."

Peitar smiled and touched my brow. "Go in safety, Lilah."

I did not look back as we walked away, but Innon did, and then he looked at me. "What's wrong?" I asked.

"You didn't hug him. Are you mad at him?"

I thought about that—how I used to climb on Peitar's

lap, until I learned that it hurt him. But nobody hugged at Selenna House. Lizana wasn't allowed, Father didn't think it was appropriate . . . the last hug I remembered getting was from my mother.

And I wasn't going to say that. "I'm not mad," I said, as we reached the stable, where Bren was waiting. I gathered my courage and blurted out the bad news about Deon.

To my surprise, he said, "Deon? *She'll* be all right. She'll think it's an adventure . . . except if she gets put to work! Then she'll be making up insult songs to sing for us when she does manage to escape." He paused, then said doubtfully, "So are we really going to just . . . run away?"

Innon pushed back his filthy hair and listened.

"I still want to help," I said. "I think the revolution's made a mess of things. Peitar seems to want to fix it. I want to help him, but I don't know how."

"It would worry him to find you anywhere in the city," Innon said. "It's been terrible, and reports are, it's worse in the countryside. That's why I didn't try to go home."

"I know. It was . . . horrible at my house. But it seems cowardly to just leave Peitar to deal with it."

"And Derek. So let's figure something out," Bren said.

"I tried," Innon put in. "But there was too much to do, and everybody wanted to be in charge and not listen to anyone else."

"All right," I said. "How about this. We keep our promise and go south. But we stay there just long enough to figure out a way—a *good* way—to help. One that won't make Peitar worry."

"And Derek," Bren put in.

I didn't say, *This is his fault,* but I thought it. "And Derek. Then we will return and do what we can. Agreed?"

Bren smiled for the first time in days. "I'll try the kitchens. Maybe I can talk us into some food."

Innon and I waited with the horses until he returned with a small bag of provisions, then the three of us were off to Delfina—and Diannah Wood.

four

～※～

"That book by Adamas Dei of the Black Sword was so old-fashioned I didn't get very far. Who was he, exactly?" asked Bren, later that day.

"He wrote a lot of wise stuff that Peitar likes to quote," I replied. "He was an ancestor of Lasva Dei the Wanderer, that's all I know. I'd rather read about *her*."

Innon said, "He's one of the very first of the Dei family, who go back at least a thousand years. They were really important in Sartor, almost as important as the ruling family, the Landises."

"But isn't Sartor controlled by Norsunder?" Bren asked.

"For the past century. Nobody can get in or out. Anyway, Adamas supposedly had a sword whose blade was black steel and could cut a rose petal without making a bruise, but he gave up being a warrior and became . . . what did Peitar say, the first day I met him? A visionary." Innon grinned at me. "Like your brother is. Minus the sword."

"Ha!" I exclaimed. "So that's why nothing he quotes from Adamas makes sense—half the time Peitar doesn't either. Two buds on a branch."

Bren snorted. "No wonder I had trouble reading it.

Sounds like a noble poetical spouter—that's what Derek calls 'em."

There was a pause, and Innon squinted upward. "It's good to get out of Miraleste, but ugh! It's hot."

"Nasty weather for anything," I said, looking around the parched but untouched land. Maybe the revolutionaries had only been in towns, estates, and cities. "I vote for a swim as soon as we reach the Miseos River."

Our horses plodded steadily southward into a wide valley. Patches of tangled hickory and red cedar dappled us with shade. Wild blueberries grew everywhere. We stopped a few times to pick and eat them.

I think our horses were as glad to see the river as we were. We watered and tethered them loosely so they could crop grass and watercress, then splashed in fully clothed. The boys had a water fight. I just floated, my eyes closed against the blazing sun as a couple of lazy fish nibbled at my toes. Songbirds warbled in the brush.

My mind kept going back through the horrors of the past week—like when you can't help touching a bruise just to see if it hurts as much as you think it does. I couldn't quite believe that Father was really dead. I wondered what Peitar was doing.

Finally we dragged ourselves out, our clothes wet and heavy, but cool, and shared out a small loaf that had been stuffed with greens, chicken, and cheese. It was so small that afterward I was still hungry—but Bren was used to hunger, and Innon and I had begun getting used to it.

We resumed our ride. The road turned from the river to the mountains, which grew larger through the day, fading at last into shadows a shade darker than the sky. By then we were dry, but thirsty and ravenous. The horses were drooping. Finally, the road crossed one of the Orleos River's branches.

"How about camping near that bridge?" Bren suggested. "My dad taught me how to catch fish with my hands, and I got a sparker from the palace."

After we saw to the animals, Innon and I went to gather sticks. Bren had caught two small fish by the time we returned, and they were soon cooking over a merry fire. Along with a stale bun and an end of cheese, it was a delicious meal. But those were the last of our provisions. Tomorrow we'd have to forage.

We lay on sweet-smelling grass under a clear, starlit sky, listening to the rush and chuckle of water, and in the distance the rustlings of small animals, the cries of night birds. The air was too warm for us to need blankets, and everything was peaceful, but my heart seemed to lie inside my chest like a stone.

Bren said, "Lilah? Peitar will be all right. Derek'll make sure that no one harms him."

"I wish that was true." Memory arrowed back to Derek's words in that hot, stuffy little room. "He might want to. He might try. But if anyone wants to hurt Peitar, can Derek really protect him? And I don't mean just rioters—my uncle's out there, too. I know he blames Peitar because Peitar is friends with Derek. I think Uncle Dirty Hands is the biggest threat of all."

Innon sat up, silhouetted against the stars. "D'you wish Derek had killed the king, then?"

"Not like that," I said quickly. "And . . . oh, I don't know *what* I feel, except I don't want to see him again—ever, *ever.*" My throat tightened. "I just know I need to find a way to help Peitar make things right again. Somehow. And I don't want to talk about it anymore."

Silence from the boys.

I managed to sleep, but the murmur of voices filtered in, twisting my dreams into nightmares. I woke with a start to hear two soft, fierce almost-whispers.

". . . I don't care what Derek says he is. I mean, I like Peitar, too, but he's not a leader. He's not." Innon's anger didn't match up with the easygoing boy I'd first met.

"So the revolution's all in our heads?" Bren, on the other hand, had not lost a jot of his sarcasm. "Derek told me that Peitar was Number One—and Derek *is* a leader."

"No, he isn't. He *started* that revolution—anyone can start a fight. You didn't spend a week in Miraleste, watching bullies beat people up and take what they wanted. Derek makes all kinds of speeches, but he can't stop it."

"He says people have to decide for themselves. That's what freedom *is.* No one is a lord, or everyone is a lord for himself."

"My father says most people are content to follow—"

"Your dad's a noble! Of *course* he'll say that! Derek's strong. He's fought off a lot of the *king's* bullies."

"Strong doesn't mean smart. Stupid, mean, and evil can be strong—and that's who's going to be ruling under Derek's 'freedom.'"

"He isn't going to just sit around and watch that happen," Bren retorted.

"He *can't* stop it. I tell you, I was *there*. I walked around yesterday, trying to find something to eat, and heard people wishing that the king would come back. And they weren't nobles—there aren't any nobles around the city anymore."

"I don't believe anyone said they want Dirty Hands back." Bren sounded fierce.

Innon didn't answer, and I drifted off, not waking until morning.

WE CONTINUED SOUTH. Most of the time we were alone on the road, as there are no great cities or market towns just south of Miraleste. To the west stretched the plains on which flax and wheat had grown in better times. To the east lay the broadening river valley, where rice beds stretched between river branches.

And to the south lay the long, dark line of Diannah Forest.

"I really don't like having to go there," Innon said finally.

"Peitar told us that we'd be safe," I reminded him.

"How? *No one's* safe in Diannah Wood! The king mounted a couple of surprise attacks to clean it out—both times, the outlaws found out and vanished. And I guess there wasn't enough money in the treasury to put a garrison in the forest just for a few caravans."

"Peitar seemed to think we'd be all right," I repeated. "Derek, too. Maybe the outlaws only come out for nobles and rich traders. I'm not going to worry."

THE NEXT TWO days brought us ever nearer to Diannah. Bren was the best at catching and cooking fish for our meals, but Innon was handy, too. He'd roamed for entire days up in Tasenja, his parents' province, and had learned what was good to eat and what to avoid.

Finally, great trees closed around us, blocking even the mountains from view as we rode into the cool, shady maple forest that bounded the deep heart of the wood. Our horses picked their way over mossy logs and spongy under-growth. The occasional broad-wing hawk drifted silently through the dark canopy above, making us feel we were being watched.

It was a strange feeling, especially after so many days in which we'd seen almost no one. I thought it was my imagination until I saw Innon looking around uneasily—Bren, too, as the light began to fade. He pulled out the small paring knife he'd taken from Selenna House.

Dark came faster than it had out in the open. Bren said, "Maybe we'd better dismount and scout out a campsite. Lilah, you see best in the dark—"

"Halt," a voice ordered.

"Uh-oh," Innon muttered. "Let's get out of here!"

"Which way?" I asked—just as someone grabbed the bridle of my horse. Then I was pulled from the saddle and landed with a thump on the mossy ground. Innon stood silently near his horse, a slim woman beside him, her drawn sword resting point down. Bren tried to defend himself, but a man knocked the knife out of his hand.

We were led through dense forest to a sheltered, campfire-lit grotto and an older, bearded man, standing with a group of adults. Bren glowered, Innon looked terrified, and I kept thinking over and over, *Peitar said we'd be safe, Peitar said we'd be safe.*

"We haven't done anything to anybody," Bren said.

I was about to add that we had nothing of value, when fingers twitched the book out of my sash, and I yelled, "Hey! That's mine!"

"Who are you, little fire-eater?" the bearded man asked.

"Lilah Selenna," I blurted before I could think, and Bren moaned.

The man accepted the book from the forester behind me. "And these others?"

"Innon Tasenja," Innon said, coming to stand beside me.

"Bren Breneoson." He sighed.

"Well. Let's just see what we have. Fashion sketches?" the bearded man said in a voice of amazement, and the other adults laughed. I fumed. By the light of the fire, he read out some of the descriptions of the gowns, to more laughter. Then he paused. "Now, *here's* something different." He continued reading in silence, then looked up and frowned. "I see Selenna's name—not surprising. But here's Derek Diamagan, and King Darian Irad. Would that be the same as 'Uncle Darian'? I can't make out many of the words. Come here, girl. You read it to us."

"I refuse!"

"Then I'll throw it in the fire," the man said.

I remembered what Peitar had done with his letters. "So burn it."

"All that work, so quickly consigned to ash? What can you be concealing, I wonder?"

I looked at the waiting adults. They looked back, and though they knew two of us were nobles, and one wasn't, they hadn't separated us or made any threats. *Peitar said we'd be safe.*

So I started reading aloud, faltering when my abbreviations confused me. There were some chuckles at first. Otherwise, they listened in silence.

When I paused for breath, the man said, "Skip to the mention of the king."

I paged to the day of the revolution, and read to where Peitar, Bren, and I left Miraleste. Then I shut the book, for I wasn't going to talk about what had happened to Father.

It seemed to be enough. The man stared down into the fire, then looked up. "So. You were there for this revolt. What have you to say for either cause?"

He wasn't looking at the boys but at me.

I shrugged, feeling awkward. "I don't know. I want—I want justice, and freedom, and all the things Derek talked about, but I don't want it the way it's been. I don't want any more people getting killed."

"Do you think your brother knows what to do?"

"If anyone does, it's Peitar," I said stoutly. "Or if he doesn't now, he will. That much I'm sure of. It's just that I don't know if anyone will listen to him, because he can't fight with a sword, and he has that crooked leg, and he doesn't always make sense."

"Your account of his words makes plenty of sense," the man retorted, but not unkindly. Then his tone changed. "When you see Lord Peitar Selenna again, you tell him if he has need, he can send a message here to Diannah Wood, to Deveral, and there will be what help we can muster." I gaped at him. "Deveral. Can you remember that?"

"Deveral. Diannah Wood." I added in a tentative voice, "Um, how should he send a message? How will you know to believe it?"

Deveral gave a sudden smile. "If he speaks to Lizana, the message will get to us. When she's not by, he's to send someone and use her name." *Lizana?* More secrets! He addressed the others by the fire. "Feed them, and in the morning put them on the road to the valley."

five

A girl not much older than us brought our horses and led us down a path. Shafts of gold-green morning light filtered down overhead, birds called to each other, and there were more wildflowers than I'd ever seen in the tangled garden at Selenna House. The sight and scent squeezed my heart with unexpected sadness for all we had lost.

Our guide talked readily enough. "This is one of the oldest forests in the world, though I'm told that the woodland up in Everon and Wnelder Vee is older—there, and even farther north."

"Are there any morvende here? Or any of the other magic races?" I asked.

She shook her head. "There's been no sign of the morvende since Norsunder took Sartor." She jerked her thumb westward. "Those mountains make the border, you know. We're close—damn close."

The bad word seemed uncomfortably apt. None of us had ever seen Norsundrians, but everyone knew that their country existed outside of time. Its rulers were more powerful than mages and did evil things. You could go there to avoid death and live as long as you liked—except the

Norsundrians owned your soul and could consume it, and you, to make them stronger.

"So what do you do?" Bren asked. "Are you thieves?"

"Sometimes." She was not in the least apologetic. "Though not many worth robbing come through Diannah. You can call us 'guardians,' for that's nearer the truth." She patted the nose of Bren's mare. "We're still going to exact a price from you. We want your mounts when you reach the transfer. Just send them back down the trail."

"But the mountains go on and on," I protested. "And some of them have snow all year!"

She grinned at me, her dark eyes friendly. "You won't need the horses, once you do the spell. I promise you."

At noon, she gave Innon a parcel of food and said, "Follow this trail all the way up, until you come out of the wood. You'll know when. Fare well." She clucked, and her longhaired pony trotted down the trail until the shadows swallowed them.

By late afternoon, the forest had thinned, and we stopped by a stream. The parcel contained nutbread, which served as dinner.

"When do we get to the magic?" I wondered.

"I tried it. Nothing happened," Bren replied cheerily, rubbing down his horse.

Peitar said we'd be safe, I thought.

⌄ ⌄ ⌄

NEXT DAY'S RIDE took us steadily uphill, past rocky cliffs and soughing stands of pine. By midday the path had narrowed, skirting the edges of increasingly steep escarpments.

"I think it's time to let the animals go," Bren said.

Innon grimaced. "I don't much look forward to walking up this cliff."

But it was too dangerous for horses, so we sent them back down the trail to the foresters.

"Shall we try the magic?" I asked.

Innon looked dubious. "If it doesn't work, it won't do something terrible, will it?"

"Like make your ears fall off, or turn you into a tree stump?" Bren snickered.

"I don't know anything about magic, remember?"

"I don't either, really," I said, "but Lasva Dei said there are two kinds—light and dark. Light magic either works or it doesn't. Dark magic can destroy you if you do it wrong—it's more powerful, but it's dangerous. And there aren't any safeguards."

Now Innon sounded even more anxious. "What kind is ours, light or dark?"

"It has to be light. After all, we aren't harming anything."

"Well, let's try, then," Bren suggested.

I tucked the book more securely into my sash. We taught Innon as Peitar had taught us, in the carriage to Miraleste—gestures first, then the words. After we were sure he knew it as well as we did, we tried for real.

And nothing happened. We tried again, slower. Nothing.

"I guess we need to keep going." I sighed.

So we climbed until all three of us were panting. My feet began to slip.

We tried the magic again. And, again, nothing. Bren sat down, pressing the heels of his hands to his eyes. "What now? Did we learn it wrong?"

I took a deep breath to answer and felt strange. Tingly, the way I felt stepping through a cleaning frame. And then curiously light, as if I could run uphill. I tried a leap over a rock—and came down softly, as if I were in water.

"How'd you do that?" Innon asked behind me.

I tried another leap, this time higher, and my body stayed suspended for a long breath before it began drifting down. I flung up my arms—and I rose into the air!

Bren gave a wild yell of joy. "Deon will *love* this!" He shot past me, soaring upward with frightening speed. Then Innon launched himself into the air, his arms windmilling. He turned in a slow circle, making noises of surprise and delight.

We were flying!

"Arms up for speed, out for steady," Bren called. "Point your head toward where you want to go." He skimmed across the sky, silhouetted against the sun, his body straight, his arms wide, fingers curved like the wingtips of a raptor.

I imitated him and found myself going faster. Innon soon appeared beside me.

At first we stayed close to the rocky cliffside, but gradually gained height until we sailed just above the treetops. It was then that I felt the power of the magic drawing us in a specific direction. It didn't control us—it was more like guidance. Up ahead, Bren was experimenting, swooping and diving and climbing again.

"Oh," Innon said, his eyes wide, with the biggest grin I'd ever seen. "Oh. This is what I've wanted all my life."

"Me too," I cried. "Me too!"

We circled spectacular cliffs of varicolored rock, and old, twisted trees, sometimes diving down into shadow, then emerging into sunlight again. Up and up, until we reached the mighty summits we'd seen from far below. Sometimes my shadow appeared below me, rippling over patches of blue ice in crevasses that never saw sunlight, and ground that might never have been touched by human feet.

I flew in a great arc in order to look at Sarendan stretching into the hazy distance, its silvery-white rivers like glowing ribbons. Then I raised my arms, arched my back, and the world turned upside down. Vertigo clawed at my insides, and I stuck out my arms and legs to steady myself. The boys were far ahead.

I raced faster and faster until air whistled past my ears, and I caught up with the others. Together we soared upward, until we rounded one ice-laced crest and saw land stretching out to the south.

Magic drew us slightly to the east and finally down,

toward a lake surrounded by six or eight mountains over-shadowed by a great sky-touching peak.

The valley was framed with ledges cut into the sides of the cliffs, one much larger than the others, all of them green with trees and grass. On the largest lay a village, built around a meadow dotted with blossoms the pale gold of a harvest moon. Sheep milled about, and here and there goats trotted up trails too narrow for human feet.

As we were pulled slowly down into the village, I scanned the well-kept houses. Each had a small patch of vegetables as well as flowers, orderly and pretty—so different from Riveredge.

Bren was the first to land. He put his hands out to slow himself, touched down, and ran a few steps to a stop.

Several kids came out of a nearby house, and a moment later a woman joined them. They wore bright, embroidered clothes, and I was instantly aware of our filthy, tattered selves.

"Who are you?" the woman asked, without alarm or even any surprise.

"There was a revolution back in Sarendan. We were told to come—" Bren began.

"My mother had a house here," I interrupted. "Sharannah Irad?"

The woman beamed. "Oh, Rana was my friend when we were young! You are her daughter?" I nodded, and she eyed me in a friendly manner. "Definitely a resemblance." I must have looked dubious, because she added, "In you I see her smile again. I am Seriah Evris. Be welcome!" She turned to a girl our age. "Dawn, please show them to Irad House."

Dawn was short and much lighter in build than I, with neat brown braids and a round face. Like the others, she wore a long, colorful tunic over loose trousers gathered at the ankle.

"There's someone already at Irad House," she said.

"A man?" I thought uneasily of my uncle.

She shook her head. "Woman." Dawn did the magic with blurring speed, lightly leaped straight up, and hovered in the air, waiting for us to follow.

We found it easier to take off this time, and flew after her. The meadow fell away behind us, and we headed toward a ledge with a tangle of forest around a steep stone roof.

One by one we landed on a path through this wild garden.

"Come back to visit when you have time," Dawn said to me before she departed. "Everyone else who visits is an adult—I've never met a girl from outside before."

The garden was shaded with alder and several kinds of hemlock and poplar, with juniper bushes everywhere. I counted five different shades of roses, wild grapes, and blueberry bushes.

A sudden turn in the path brought us to the house. It was wood and stone, built into a hill, with corners and dormers and interesting angles everywhere. Here was my mother's retreat, her true home.

My eyes burned. I blinked fast. Bren and Innon didn't notice, for which I was grateful. They bounded up the steps ahead of me but stopped at the wooden door carved with vines and leaves. It was I who pushed it firmly open.

And we found ourselves face-to-face with Lizana.

"Ah, you made it safely," Lizana said, as if we'd just parted that morning. "Are you hungry? Thirsty?"

"Later," I cried impatiently, before the boys could speak. "Where—how—?"

"Did Peitar come with you?" she asked, looking past us.

"He's with Derek. In Miraleste," I said, all the old worries rushing back. "Father . . . Father is dead."

"I am so sorry, child." Lizana patted my cheek, and that small gesture made me feel better. "As for your brother, I know you couldn't have stopped him. Come in, boys. I'll show all three of you the house and explain the rules over a good meal." She guided us first to a cozy sitting room with cream-colored walls, black walnut furnishings, and a slate fireplace.

"Who's that?" Bren asked.

Over the mantelpiece hung a painting of a dark-haired girl in an old-fashioned gown of maroon satin. She had a heart-shaped face, slanted blue eyes, and a gentle smile.

"Mother," I whispered.

"This was her favorite room," Lizana said to me. "Come."

As I followed her familiar, stout figure in Selenna blue and gray, my mind bloomed with questions. But I knew there was no use in asking until she was ready to answer.

We passed through a sunny kitchen and a book-lined library, ending up at the front door again. She indicated a staircase next to the library. "That leads to your bedrooms. Lilah, you'll have your mother's old room. You boys will share the one with the bunk beds. I'm down here, near the kitchen."

"Where will Deon stay?" Bren asked warily. "I know she'll come. Derek will tell her where. When she escapes wherever Dirty Hands has her."

"She will stay with Lilah, of course," Lizana said, and when she turned my way, I asked, "What happened to you?"

"I helped as many people as I could, after Derek promised me he'd find you and free you. I thought you'd be all right at Selenna House, so I stayed to try to get things back to order. But it turned out to be more than one person could do." She led us back into the kitchen, where we sat around the table. "So I left, thinking that either you'd stay with your father or else Peitar would find a way to bring you here."

Bren began, "But Derek said Dirty Hands—"

"I wish," she said sternly, "you would refrain from using that name in my presence. He is Lilah's uncle. And he's not, as so many would conveniently assume, an evil man. Though he has done evil things."

"So doing evil things makes him a good man?" Bren crossed his arms.

Lizana considered him, lips pursed. "Peitar could probably answer you more quickly, for he has been reading a great deal about the nature of evil. My own answer would take a long time, as long as experience, so only ask if you really want to hear it."

He shook his head. "No. I think Dir—Darian Irad is an evil king. I hope he's dead. But . . . I won't call him Dirty Hands in this house, if that's your rule."

"Fair enough," she said. And then, to Innon, "Your question?"

"Why did Deveral in Diannah Wood use your name?"

One side of Lizana's mouth quirked. "He's my brother."

"Hah!" Bren said. "I *knew* there was something, I just knew it." And, when she raised her eyebrows, "Lilah's name mattered to him. And he looked familiar." He touched his cheeks. "It's the resemblance."

"You do have the eye of an artist," Lizana said, and he colored.

Innon pressed on, "One of the foresters claimed they were guardians. But what do they guard?"

"They guard the wood against enemies that—as yet—do not turn their eyes this way. The caravans they rob are few, and Deveral makes certain the owners can well afford to lose what's taken. It keeps attention away from Diannah—and, incidentally, from this village up here and what it, in its turn, guards." I could tell the boys were as curious as I was. "Enough of that," Lizana said, disappointingly. "While I prepare a meal, you three go upstairs and change. We've cleaning frames. There's also a bath. You will like the bath," she added, smiling at me. "And there are clothes in the wardrobes." She looked at Innon and shook her head. "Peitar's old clothes should fit Bren, but I'm afraid you'll have to make do."

I ran upstairs. On the left were three bedrooms, and windows on the right overlooked the garden and a glimpse of winking blue lake. The first room had bunk beds. The next was very plain—austere, almost. The last had warm rosewood furniture, a thick rug, a quilt, and chair cushions of indigo and white with faint silver tracings. I loved it at once.

The first thing I did, after putting down my book, was open the wardrobe. There were old-fashioned gowns and clothes like Dawn and her friends had worn. Tears threatened again as I looked at my mother's things. I backed up a step, impatient with myself. I was not a crier, so why was I acting like one?

Well, stop it, I told myself. I picked a rose-colored gown and went off in search of the bath.

Lizana was right—I did like it. The window looked out on a fern-dotted cliffside, and the bath itself was more like a pool, fed by a spout near the ceiling. The water gently steamed and never spilled over. Magic—had to be!

I shucked my grimy Larei clothes and slid in. The zing of magic made me feel as clean as if I'd scrubbed with a brush.

Soon I was back in Mother's room, looking at myself
in her mirror. The gown laced, so it fit pretty much anyone my size, but it was a little short, and the sleeves were
tight. It was strange, wearing something my mother had
once worn. How I wished things were different—that I
could see her again, that I had some real memories, not
just blurry ones of her smile, her soft hands, the smell of
roses in her hair. . . .

I grabbed her brush. When at last my hair had been
tamed, my arm ached, my scalp smarted, and my eyes
stung, but I was clean and neatly dressed, and I knew that
Lizana would approve. I put my Larei clothes through the
cleaning frame, folded them, and laid them in the bureau.
Then I went down to the kitchen.

Bren was already there, looking completely unlike himself in Peitar's clothes—especially the shirt with full sleeves
and old-fashioned point lace at the wrists. "There wasn't
much of a choice." He tried to frown, but the corners of
his mouth betrayed him. "I don't know what Derek would
think of this toff rig."

"You look fine," I said. His ears turned bright red.

Lizana was just putting out the dishes. The smell of fishcakes with onions made my stomach rumble.

Innon spoke uncertainly from behind us. "I think I'd as
soon wear what I came in."

We turned around—and I tried hard not to laugh. The
ruffled, robin's-egg-blue shirt he'd found was enormous.

The sleeves hid his hands, and there was so much extra shirt tucked into the striped, pleated satin trousers that he looked like he had a potbelly all the way around.

"Well, *this* is worse," he said, and yanked the shirt out. It hung down past his knees. Then the trousers began to slip. He clutched them and hobbled away as fast as he could.

Bren howled. I gave up and joined him. Lizana just shook her head.

When Innon returned, he wore his old clothes, which were now clean. "I guess these'll have to last," he said cheerily. "Whew! At home I must have had ten suits, and my mother was always nagging that that was scarcely enough."

"You are all going to learn to sew," Lizana said.

"That means I can cut some of those old ones up?" Innon asked.

"Yes. But that's later. Right now, supper."

We sat down to the meal, to which she had added a vegetable stew. "Now, all of you, listen," she said, as we served ourselves. "You're free to explore the valley and swim in the lake—but not the far end, where the purple-blue flowers grow right down to the water. They're called Lure, and for a reason. If you get close, you'll begin feeling you're invincible, and if you get nearer, you'll slide into sleep—and it's a dangerous, magical sleep—unless someone pulls you away at great risk to themselves. The valley youngsters are not permitted to fly alone until they can be trusted to avoid the Lure. Do you understand?" We nodded. "Next. Here, we all work. No one is the servant, no one the master. You will each keep your rooms clean, and all help in the kitchen. It isn't hard. Tsauderei, the mage here, has given us many magical aids."

More nods—Bren suspiciously, but when he saw Innon and me agree, the slight frown above his eyes eased.

"Those are all the rules," she concluded. "Now, do you want to talk about what happened after you went back to Selenna?"

I gave the shortest explanation I could. Bren glowered, and Innon ate stolidly, not looking at any of us, until I got to the part where we found Derek and Innon working things out on the chalkboard.

"Trying to figure out how people can trade," he broke in. "You know, a sack of onions gets you half a wheelbarrow of bricks. Or one day of carpentry work gets you half a sack, but if you're a glassmaker who puts in a window, you get a whole sack."

I was about to say that you could just pay for what you needed, but then I remembered that nobody had any money. For the first time, I wondered how people had figured out the worth of all these things as Bren said, "*You* were doing that?"

Innon flushed. "I've got a head for numbers."

"And all the rest of 'em were arguing, right?"

"No. Yes. Linnah wanted to get the guild chiefs together to negotiate new taxes for rebuilding the city, but Sideos thought guild chiefs as bad as nobles and wanted to let the members of each guild start over with their own rules. That's where we were when you arrived."

"Well, *I* am glad you're here," Lizana said, neatly laying her fork and knife on her plate. "I trust you enjoyed flying?"

Our enthusiasm was so loud she covered her ears. I tried to imagine her flying. Of course she would do it with dignity.

She rose, plate in hand. "Vegetable peelings go through this frame here, which transfers them to the garden compost. There's the bucket for dishes. You dip them, dry them with this cloth, and put them here." The shelves held more of the old-fashioned clay dishes, edged with blue and painted with twining vines and crimson flowers.

"The water comes from the fall around that corner. When you're done with the dishes, you snap the towel— like this—twice, and it's dry and clean. Hang it on its hook. Over in that corner is the mop. Anything on the floor will stick to it. When you finish, shake it out the door."

We hopped to it, and the kitchen was soon cleaned to her satisfaction.

Then Innon tore upstairs and reappeared in ancient knee-pants. "Going swimming!" he called, and was gone.

I sat down at Mother's desk. My battered fashion book seemed out of place on the polished wood. I opened a drawer to find a pen and ink and discovered a diary bound in blue, with a gilt rose on the outside.

It had to be my mother's. I felt the way I had when I first began to fly.

Across the first page, in a large, slanting script, were the words

THIS IS RANA'S BOOK

And below that:

> *So I will remember every visit*
> *to my real, true home.*

The diary started when she was very small, with long, scrawled descriptions of the house and garden.

I skipped ahead to where her handwriting improved. She seemed to be around my age, writing about how much she missed "Ian" and how she wished he'd visit, and how he would surely like "f." F? *Flying*, I finally realized. It must have been a secret back then, too.

The entries were filled with *Ian said this, Ian said that*—and her worries about Ian. It took a while before I realized that Ian was Uncle Darian.

I closed the book and put it away, feeling sick and strange and upset. Oh, I knew he had to have been a boy, but to find him there in my mother's diary, his spoken words transcribed with such care, her concern for him—so like my concern for Peitar—*that*, I couldn't understand.

Going downstairs to explore didn't banish the feeling. I prowled around until Lizana emerged from her own room and took a look at my face.

"Problem, child?"

"My mother's diary. I, um, looked at it. I know I shouldn't have," I added hastily.

"Why not? Who better to read it than her own daughter? I think it's appropriate."

"Appropriate?" I repeated. "I don't know . . . there are things I think I'm too young to read about."

Lizana put her hands on her hips. "Why is it that when faced with something you don't want to do, you children claim to be too young, but when it comes to poking your nose in matters that interest you, or running around in disguise talking of revolution, you protest that we shouldn't stop you, that we treat you like you're babies?"

I flushed, wanting to argue, but I knew she was right.

"That's a reprehensible excuse, 'I'm too young,'" she continued. No smile, no anger either, but very serious. "How young was your uncle when your great-grandfather finally figured out the one way to control him, even worse than beatings: to threaten to flog your mother while he watched?"

I gasped. "But she never said—"

"He never told her. She had enough burdens, living with her grandfather's harsh words. From a very *young* age."

"I only meant that I'm too young to read about marriage and being in love and all that."

I was lying, and she knew it. "If there was anything inappropriate, I would not have left it for you," she said.

I stared at her, thinking that she'd been young once too. When had she gone to work for my horrible great-grandfather? There was no use in asking. I was surprised she had even revealed that Deveral was her brother.

She shut the door behind her, leaving me alone.

I stepped back, and back, as though I could leave the horrible subject of my uncle on the spotless kitchen tiles. Then I whirled and ran out the front door, did the flying spell, and launched myself into the air. I flew upward as hard and as fast as I could, until my hair whipped my face and my eyes stung.

When I returned, Bren was waiting. "There you are! Let's go to the lake!"

I ran upstairs and changed into my mother's swimming things, but no matter how hard I yelled and played and splashed, I was always aware of the diary in the desk.

seven

Days slid by, balmy and clear—Sarendan and its problems receded into the distance, except for Bren wondering when Deon would show up.

I hadn't yet worked out a way to help Peitar. Until I did, I wanted to have fun. Innon and Bren were my first real friends, and what had happened in Miraleste bound us together. I was in my mother's "true home," and I felt close to her. There was flying and swimming, and exploring her garden.

And there was the library. Most of the books were very old, beautifully copied out in the difficult handwriting of centuries past, but oh, they were dull—histories of law-making, kings, and battles. Thankfully, there was also a set of plays, which I took for nighttime reading.

Innon went to the lake every day, swimming with the local kids once they finished chores. Some days Bren joined us, but others, he plain disappeared—he'd come to meals, but when we talked about what we'd done, he stayed quiet. I kept myself too busy to read Mother's diary, but I couldn't stop myself from thinking about it.

As the days turned into a week I became restless, and one morning decided that instead of swimming I wanted to talk—and I thought of Dawn. A girl my age! And our mothers had been friends.

Before I left, I visited Mother's portrait in the sitting room. If I stood just the right way, it was as if she looked at me. I thought she would approve of where I was going—and why.

As I flew over the garden, I thought I saw movement below me, but the trees were so thick I couldn't be sure.

Dawn's house, I remembered, had light blue shutters. Through the big diamond-paned window, I saw her and a boy at looms, their fingers darting fast, in and out in rhythm with the shuttle. A small girl was busy combing out wool. Seriah Evris oversaw everything as she worked at embroidery.

Dawn saw me and smiled a welcome. The door was open, and I found my way to the workroom. To my surprise, they did their tasks to the sound of a woman's voice—but not Seriah's. She made a quick gesture with three fingers, and the voice ceased.

More magic! It seemed to be a spell that had captured someone reading aloud and could be listened to over and over.

"We're almost done," she said. "Want to join us? There's elderberry cordial in the kitchen, if you'd like to pour yourself a glass."

When I came back, the voice was speaking again.

". . . and as I traveled northward, to kingdoms and countries that were unknown to us in the south, I discovered that there are familiar rituals to life all over Sartorias-deles. One is the Name Day Ritual. Though Name Day customs vary, nearly all people have them. And further, those that perform the ritual with music tend to have music as part of everyday life, whereas those who perform the ritual with speech do not. . . ."

Like us, I thought. Music was something you heard only at court, mostly for dancing. As the voice told of the old melodies people sang during the grape harvest, and games that involved music, I thought about how silent Selenna House had been. My father never had music played. He said it was just noise.

A bell tolled outside, and almost immediately some little kids scampered in to tug at Dawn.

"There." Seriah Evris stopped the voice, put down her sewing, and made shooing motions. "Noon! You are free." She smiled at me and picked up the empty glasses to take to the kitchen. *Next time,* I thought, *I'll ask her about my mother.*

Dawn hurriedly tidied her loom. Then she said, "What's for today? A swim? Or are we playing Riddle?"

"Riddle!" one of her brothers said, jumping up and down. "*We* already did swimming in the morning, and in Riddle we're ahead! We're ahead!"

Outside, other kids were coming out of their houses. The older ones took the hands of the littles, and all launched into the air, flying down to the western edge of the lake, opposite the end where the bright but deadly Lure flowers grew. High above the shoreline the kids played Riddle, which was a kind of chase-and-guess game. I found it more fun to watch than to play, for I couldn't fly as fast or as well as even the seven-year-olds. Presently a new boy arrived, and Dawn gave up her spot.

She sat down next to me. "It's fun," she said, "but I can do that any time. What I *don't* get to do is talk to others from over the mountain. Most have no interest in life outside the valley, but I do!"

"Well, I want to know more about things here," I said.

Dawn laughed. "Fair trade."

"I was also hoping you might tell me where Tsauderei lives, and how I might meet him."

Her eyes widened with delight. "You also have an interest in magic?"

"My favorite thing is history, but magic comes next."

"I really want to learn. Tsauderei said he'd start teaching me next year, and if I do well, he'll send me to the mage school in Bereth Ferian."

She flew us to a high ledge, just wide enough for the small house tucked into the side of the mountain. "He lives there. You ought to go visit him—my mother says he was a great friend of your family." Now I was the one who was surprised.

After we talked a bit about history—she, too, loved Lasva Dei the Wanderer—a kid showed up to call her back to the game, but not before she said, "There's someone I think you should meet. I have to get permission first."

As she left, I wondered why she didn't mention a name—and, anyway, who could be more mysterious than a mage?

I took a deep breath, and knocked on Tsauderei's plain wooden door.

"Come in!" he called. I entered a large room, with three walls of books. The fourth was a huge window overlooking the lake. Before it sat an old man in a rocker, a book on his lap.

He had a long, gray-streaked white beard. His braided hair was nearly as long as mine. Two gemstones, dangling on gold chains, winked from his left ear. He wore the clothes of my grandparents' generation—a paneled blue robe over another of dark red linen, both embroidered with the vine-and-flower pattern that I'd seen all over the valley. His voice was soft and old as history. "You've got the Selenna family eyes."

"I know," I said, surprised by his abruptness. "Lizana told me. Good for seeing at night."

He grunted. "So, what did you want?" I must have gaped, because he added, "You want something, I'll wager, or you would not have come up here."

"I do?" I asked. Then my face burned with embarrassment. "Does that mean you don't want visitors?"

Tsauderei waved a hand. "Never mind that. Forgive me. I

have no occasion to remember the niceties of manners, for people here understand me well enough, and I understand them. So. You are not here to beg me to fix your life with some magical spell?"

"I did have a question about magic," I admitted. "But not about you doing spells. Dawn said that you might teach her magic. Can I learn, too?"

"From what I know about your brother," he said, smiling, "you two are more alike than I had thought."

"Does that mean you'll teach me?"

"It means that you would have to catch up on your education first." He saw I was about to protest. "Lizana told me that your father forbade her to continue your lessons. I also know that you read on your own, but it's undisciplined reading. For entertainment. Nothing wrong with that," he said. "But first must come the basics. Learning magic is more than illusions to impress courtiers at parties."

"How?" I asked.

"Before you can begin to learn magic you must understand its cost. I do not mean an exchange of coins for services. I mean consequences, and that means understanding history enough to perceive new patterns—how things are changing. So tell me about your reading."

"It's all gone now," I said sadly.

His voice was gentle. "Selenna House was destroyed?"

"Yes. Most of it, anyway. The villagers set fire to the library."

"Your mother gave me a fairly detailed catalogue. Most of those books were copies."

"Really?" I asked. "Did she visit you here?"

"No," Tsauderei said dryly. "Strictly forbidden. Her grandfather hated me from the time we were boys, you see."

"You knew my *great-grandfather*?"

"We knew . . . *of* one another, you might say. My father was the pastry cook, so the prince would have nothing to do with me. It didn't help that I was the best at games." He laughed. "You wouldn't think it, but at one time I could vault onto the back of a cantering horse and throw a lance through a ring this small." He made a little circle with his hands. "They wanted me for the army, but I thought drilling and marching a stupid way to spend your life. So I went off to learn magic instead."

"And my great-grandfather hated you because of *that*?"

"Only in part. He hated me because I kept winning. In his mind, princes always won, and peasants gawked in awe and followed obediently. Don't know where he got that, either," Tsauderei shrugged. "The queen, your great-great-grandmother, was an easygoing woman. The point being, when I saw injustice, I spoke my mind . . . and ended up here." He laughed again. "Watching things from afar. As he well knew."

"But my uncle can't send warriors here, can he? He was never taught the magic spell."

"Exactly. He was only here once, when he was small.

Your mother was forbidden to come to my house, but the old king didn't know that everyone—including me—visited hers. Later, I met your brother, though he was very small. That's when she told me about Selenna House library."

"I've read a lot of histories, but nothing about the Selennas. I thought they'd be stuffy and boring, like my father's aunts."

"Wrong." Tsauderei shook his head, and the gemstones in his ear danced. "Your forebears were very interesting indeed. Anyway, their original records are safe. Your house just had copies. So. What do you read?"

I talked about Lasva and wanting adventure and the fashion book and court and what I knew about history and freedom and my mother's diary, and ended up surprising myself by telling him about the revolution.

"It's a pretty tangle," he said, but he made "pretty" sound like an insult, as Derek had.

"You mean in Sarendan?" He made a noise of agreement. "What's happening?" All the old memories and emotions had crowded back.

"You'll find out soon enough. Or will you?"

My throat hurt. "The boys and I made a vow to go back," I said quickly. "Though Peitar wants me here. All I did was cause problems before. And I don't ever want to see my uncle again. Maybe I shouldn't return."

"Leaving your brother to cope all alone?" Tsauderei asked, his white brows beetling.

That hit me hard. I cried, "What can I do, except make mistakes?"

"Well, now, that's for you to decide. But cease thinking you 'caused' anything. It sounds like your getting caught in that passage was just one spark among the many that caused this conflagration."

I thought again about my mother's diary, with Uncle Darian's name everywhere. I wiped my damp hands on my clothes. Going back, reading the diary, keeping my promise—it was all bound together somehow in my head.

Tsauderei said, "You are probably discovering that you can run, even to as remote and pleasant a site as this, but your problems do not remain behind, tidily packed away." I looked away. "Never mind. For now, if Dawn offers to introduce you to her friend, you might go. I think you'll be good for one another."

"Dawn and me?"

"No—that is, Dawn's a fine young person. Smart and focused. She'll make a good mage one day. No, the one I'm talking about is a secret." He hesitated.

"I can keep secrets," I said. "If I know it's a secret—and why."

"This one needs more than keeping—you can't even whisper her name to yourself while hiding in a closet, for Norsunder has tracer spells over half the world in case she survived the war a century ago. We can talk freely only here, because my protective wards are stronger still."

"How can someone survive a war a *century* ago?"

"The halting of time," he said dryly. "Think you're ready to hear more?"

I hesitated, then thought: *If Dawn can keep this secret, why can't I?* "Yes," I said.

"Very well. Dawn will introduce you, if you'd like to meet her. Living out at Hermit House is Princess Yustnesveas, the last living Landis, heir to ancient Sartor. I think you should meet her—you and your brother, if he ever shows up here."

eight

I couldn't figure out which of Tsauderei's revelations amazed me most. One thing I knew: I had to find Bren. If anyone could convince him that art training wasn't just for nobles, it was a mage whose father had been a pastry cook.

As I neared Irad House, I again saw movement in the garden. I touched down and walked along the winding paths, pausing only to breathe in the scents of my mother's favorite flowers. At the far end of the ledge, in a small clearing sheltered by enormous trees with an unimpeded view of the lake, stood Bren.

He was in front of an easel, so rapt in his work that he didn't hear me come up behind him. I watched him touch chalk to a corner of his picture, blending different shades of green to show how the sun filtered through the trees, edging each leaf with silver.

"Hoo," I exclaimed. "That's really *good!*"

Bren jumped, the chalk flying from his hand. He gave me such a strange look—midway between anger and embarrassment—that I laughed.

"Sorry, sorry!" I managed. "Oh, if you could see your face!"

"Why are you nosing around?" He sounded the way his face looked.

"I came to tell you about someone, but—why are you hiding? Your picture's wonderful!"

"Think so?" His expression was even more comical now, for mixed in with the embarrassment and anger was hope—but this time I managed not to laugh. "I can't get the light right. It's not showing . . ." He fought for the right word. "Depth? Distance? *Pheg!*"

"Peitar was right," I said. "You *do* need to train with artists."

"I told you, art is for nobles," he said quickly, picking up the chalk. "Derek says that artists who create things that only nobles see are just as bad as nobles."

"So you don't make art just for nobles. And that's why I was looking for you. I think you should talk to the mage— to Tsauderei. In fact, I think you should draw him. He's got the most *interesting* face I've ever seen." He was silent. "If you don't like it there, you can always fly away," I said.

"That makes me sound like a hatchling." He made a face. "I'll go."

THE MORNING AFTER I met Tsauderei I woke early, as I often did. I dressed quietly and warmly, because I could see frost making a silvery lace on the grass and leaves.

Then I took to the air. The lake was dark, the ledges

shrouded in blue shadow. The mountains made a frame, their eastern contours edged with peachy gold sunlight. I made a wide circle around the lake, the air ruffling over my skin and blowing through my hair. I watched lights glow in the windows of the houses as, above, the stars gradually winked out. To the west, clouds formed a dark line, blotting out the sky. Rain was on the way.

Reluctantly I headed back. Though I loved everything I did during the day, flying was my favorite of all.

After breakfast, the boys and I visited Tsauderei. With no preamble, he said to Bren, "Are you the artist?"

Bren gave me a betrayed glare. "How did you know?"

"Lizana's told me a little, but most of the evidence is there on your clothes. I take it you found the old paints in the attic, and the paper?"

"She said we could use whatever was in the house," he muttered.

Tsauderei waved a hand. "None of my business. But those paints are old and probably thick. If you need newer ones, you've only to ask. I can get some easily enough."

Bren dropped into a chair as if his legs wouldn't hold him up. "You can? You will?" He drew in a deep breath, then asked, "Can I draw you?"

"Why would you want to sketch a worn old stick like me? Of course you can. Just don't interrupt me when I'm working."

I could tell that Bren wanted to start right away—and

that he didn't want an audience. He gave us a grateful look when we made our excuses and left.

Innon raced to the lake, but I took my time, watching the slowly growing thunderheads, as I flew to Dawn's house. Through the great window with all its different-sized panes and bits of colored glass I could see her family at work, so I waved and made to leave, but she ran outside, calling me back.

"Mother said we can visit now. I'll do my share later, when the weather turns bad."

We flew to the very west end of the valley, where I'd never been. The ledge we landed on was green with old trees, mostly fir. The cottage called Hermit House was completely hidden. Only a thin column of pale smoke gave it away.

I followed Dawn up a narrow stone pathway. A waterfall plashed, and the air smelled like moss and pine and water. We rounded a huge tree and came upon a house as small and plain as Tsauderei's.

"Remember, she's called Atan," Dawn said. "Norsunder can't get into the valley, but that doesn't mean they don't have ways of spying."

The woman who opened the door was older than Lizana, tall and strong-looking, her hair silvery white. I liked her face at once. It was a strong, patient, thinking face.

"Come! It's a good time for a visit," she said, her voice husky and pleasant.

Like Tsauderei's, it was a one-room house, and it was warm and cozy with candlelight and lamps, smelling of cinnamon. There was a sleeping loft and, at the far end, a pool like our bath.

Next to it stood a tall, strongly built girl a few years older than I was. She was in the middle of combing out hair so long it hung in wet waves down to her ankles. When I looked at her face, I got a shock, for here was a real Landis—in the flesh, not painted or in a book.

Every drawing I'd ever seen of a Landis was a variation of her face: long mouth, straight brows over wide, heavy-lidded eyes, hers so deep a blue they looked violet. She was dressed in an old cotton shirt and baggy flying trousers, and her feet, like mine, were bare.

"Welcome," the princess said. She had a high, clear, musical voice that reminded me of Deon's. "Are you Lilah?" I nodded. "My mother's heart-name for me was Atan. It means 'sun' in my language. Tsauderei tells me you too are interested in history." Like the mage, she didn't ask the usual polite questions that people put to you when you meet.

I sat down on a hassock. "Well, I like adventure stories— the ones that really happened—and Lasva Dei the Wanderer."

"Do you feel the weight of their lives as well?" Atan asked.

"Weight?"

She looked up at the ceiling, but her gaze was so intense I had a feeling she didn't see it. It was uncannily like my brother's. Then she blinked and gave us a rueful smile. "Maybe it's just me being foolish. Gehlei thinks so." She indicated the older woman, who was taking something out of the oven.

"Not foolish. Different ways of seeing things." Gehlei set down a plate of cinnamon buns. "Look at this plate. What do you see? I see a weapon, if there was nothing else to hand."

"A thing to hold food," I said.

Dawn leaned forward. "I see the shape, and the color. And I try to guess when it was made."

Gehlei nodded at her, then turned to Atan. "So would your father have seen it, but he would have spared a thought to the hands that made it, and wondered if their owner was content with life."

"I'm like Dawn and my father. What would my mother have said?" Atan asked.

Gehlei's expression betrayed a quick sadness. "Ah, she would have agreed with me. She was always practical."

She looks sad because Atan is an orphan. That thought hurt. *As I am, now.*

"So I guessed." Atan smiled. "But only because she sounds so different from me."

Gehlei smiled back. "Remember, she chose to marry a man who would have been a poet if he could. You and your mother would not have seen the world the same way, but you would always have found one another interesting."

I was amazed by this princess who did not talk of fashions or court—and not just any princess, but the single living heir of the oldest royal family in the entire world.

On the roof outside came the gentle tapping of rain; the light in the windows was blue, subdued. "Every record I read adds another voice to my memory, and their passions become my passions," Atan said. "Sometimes they make me more afraid that I won't be equal to the task ahead."

"Here is where we begin to argue, for I have no patience with imaginary foes. Those real ones?" Gehlei looked westward and grimaced. "They will be bad enough one day."

The rain had increased to a steady downpour, and shadows made everything a deep, mysterious green. Gehlei excused herself and returned to her work.

Atan sat near the fire and spread her hair out to dry. She clasped her hands together—long, capable hands. "Gehlei hates to hear of our past, but even worse is my conviction that nothing will change until I act."

"Your past?" I repeated. "I don't understand. I thought that Norsunder conquered your kingdom generations ago."

"It's been a century here in Sarendan, and in the rest of the world. Both sides used magic enchantments that can alter time. Some of the spells have been broken, after years of magework. But there's one last enchantment binding Sartor outside of time, and it will end when I cross the border."

"There are magic spells on *you*?" I asked.

"There are spells on my family, and I'm the only survivor. Tsauderei and the Magic Council say that Norsunder doesn't think any Landises are still alive, but if I go to Sartor, they'd know instantly. Yet I have to do it, don't you agree?"

"But you're so—" I was going to say "young," then remembered Lizana's scorn.

"Alone? Untrained?" Atan said, giving me a rueful smile that reminded me, again, of Peitar. "Yes, but who else will do it? Sartor is forgotten by the rest of the world, just as Norsunder wanted. Who else *can* do it? As for training, Tsauderei says I know as much as a full mage, because the only thing I can do here is study. All I lack is experience, and that will be solved if I return home. As for youth . . . well, the longer I wait, the longer Sartor just lies under Norsunder's poison."

I thought of my own vow and shifted guiltily.

"What happened to her family is terrible," Dawn broke in. "Tsauderei told us the parts that Gehlei didn't know— like the king's last stand against the Norsundrian army."

Atan shook her head. "My father was a poet, not a war leader. It's a story of desperate courage, but it was a slaughter." She clasped her hands, looking down.

"After they killed the king and queen," Dawn continued, "they came after the children, who'd been hidden. But Gehlei, who was Atan's nurse, knew how to use a knife, though she took a terrible wound in the process."

Gehlei rubbed her shoulder.

"I was just a baby, so I don't remember," said Atan. "We

made it to the Sarendan border before we were caught in the time spell that closed Sartor off from the rest of the world. The edges of the spell have receded very gradually. Fifteen years ago, Tsauderei found us, frozen in time and place. He brought us here."

I thought about the destruction in Miraleste. This talk of time being altered, and children hunted down and killed, made my problems seem small.

Atan clearly sensed my mood, for she changed the subject, and we talked about Lasva the Wanderer until Dawn said, "The rain has let up. We should leave before the next band of clouds arrives."

"You'll come again?" Atan asked. "I enjoy company, but my life is quiet, as you see."

"I would like to very much," I said sincerely.

The rain started again on the way back, so my clothes were wet through when Dawn and I parted outside Irad House. I was delighted to find that Lizana had lit a fire. I took a hot bath, changed, and wrote up my day. It was very cozy, sitting at my mother's desk with the rain slanting down outside.

It was time to think about my vow, and that meant . . .

I drew a deep breath and took out the diary.

nine

Those first pages were about the garden, lessons, and pets. Sometimes she mentioned Lizana and "Father." He was a very shadowy figure. I couldn't even tell why he brought my mother to Delfina Valley, except when she wrote "we came on Grandfather's orders." By the time she turned eight, her father was dead.

She visited Delfina every summer. When she was about eleven, she started mentioning the names of friends, and how happy she was when Lizana taught her the flying spell.

Then I came to this:

It is prying, but I had to know who Lizana is. She always knows what to say and do, and never betrays herself. She is, in short, more polished in manner than any of the great court ladies, but she wears servant's gray. I must rethink everything I've been taught.

The bare facts are these: my grandfather exiled Lizana's family, and I cannot find out why. She has a sister and a brother. They were all rescued by a mage. The sister left Sarendan.

*The brother lives in secret. Lizana came here—
to the home of her enemy—to teach me.*

And then:

*I am here for my twelfth Name Day. I have
given up trying to get Ian to come. He gave
excuses, for he's always so mindful of my sen-
sibilities, but he confessed to Lizana that,
although flying was fun when he was small, he
prefers riding, and were he here, he would worry
about his duty at home, and how much time
he'd lose when he ought to be learning. He will
never please Grandfather—never. I can see it.
Kepreos sees it, all the way from the stable—*

I wondered if Kepreos was Derek's father.

*By reading in the archives, I found out why
Grandfather exiled Lizana's mother. She was a
mage! She sponsored Tsauderei's being sent to
study, and Grandfather was furious. I'm sure
Tsauderei arranged for Lizana to be hired for
me.*

Then there was a bit that made my neck prickle:

I am here, and I am thirteen. Thirteen! How strange it seems. Grandfather is already talking of betrothals, but Lizana and Ian insist it's another way of testing those at court. Kepreos gets angry if I mention it.

A year older than me, and I was betrothed to Innon already. Not that it felt quite real.

I am glad that I've been ill again, for I had to get away from Miraleste—it is so terrible, with Ian gone to the military school in Khanerenth for the next four years. I'm forbidden the stables, except to ride. Kepreos and I scarcely get a chance to talk. But it is a relief that Ian is at school. Now I can truly enjoy myself here and not feel guilt over leaving him to Grandfather's cruelty. He writes me such happy letters. How can he be so happy in a place where they study nothing but war? He says we are desperately behind, and that the only way to keep Norsunder at bay is . . .

I scanned rapidly down the page. Over the next years, the entries were all about Uncle Darian, and they were all worries. He'd returned for good, and their grandfather had

206 ∽ Sherwood Smith

put him to work reorganizing the training at the military academy at Obrin. Then came this:

> *The demonstration went well. It went too well. Ian hasn't seen it, but Grandfather has: the army is no longer loyal to Grandfather, or even to Sarendan—they are all following Ian.*

A page or two later:

> *I feel sick. Not sick physically—though that will probably come, for winter is nigh, but I had to get away from Miraleste, because Lizana and Ian were arguing again. I came in at the end, and heard him say, "You know nothing about it. You are a servant, and your responsibility is Rana's well-being, her clothes, and her curtseys at court. Don't interfere with me again." They pretended nothing happened, but I knew what the fight was about; I've heard people in the valley talk about how much better it would be for Sarendan if the army tax could be halved for just one year, to hire mages to go through the kingdom and fix weakening spells.*

That one made me feel sick as well—and angry at my uncle, despite Lizana's words about his not being evil.

And then . . . pages and pages about Kepreos. Descriptions of what he looked like, everything he said and thought, their secret picnics and rides, their talk of their future. Then, even though I knew what was coming, it was still a shock:

> *I have agreed to marry Oscarbidal Selenna, though my heart is forever destroyed. Many can blithely love one and marry another, but I cannot—that is, I will do it, for otherwise I am afraid for Ian's life. Grandfather is seeking the slightest excuse to kill him. He wants a tractable heir, and maybe he thinks he'll get one now. Oscar is a decent enough person—a rarity in Miraleste. We share little outside of a love for music, which makes conversation dull, but he is kind and very loyal to Ian. All he talks about is Ian's greatness, how his army will protect us from Norsunder. . . .*

I did not recognize this version of my father. I skipped the description of her wedding, about court and gowns and how sad she felt at Kepreos Diamagan's hurt.

Then her grandfather died—*Though Court mourned officially, not a person shed a tear*—and my uncle became king. She began worrying about the kingdom—bad growing seasons, poorhouses, taxes, the way people at court

never thought about the rest of the country. So much for
nobles never noticing! She longed to have her brother
talk to Tsauderei, but when it finally happened, it was a
disaster.

*Tsauderei is as blunt as Ian, and in his own
way as powerful. Though they agree that the
fundamental purpose of a king is to protect
the people, Ian sees that in military terms, and
Tsauderei is more concerned with protecting the
quality of life. When Ian said, "You tell us that
the enchantment over Sartor could break in our
lifetime. So what will you do if Norsunder comes
to take away our 'quality of life'—magically
clean their clothes for them?" Tsauderei retorted,
"You are very ignorant about the potential of
magic, for a king. Norsunder doesn't make that
mistake." Ian got angry and ordered Tsauderei
out of Sarendan, on pain of death if he ever
crossed the border again.*

*And when I tried to apologize—I should
have known better than to have them talk—
Ian said, "No, I am grateful, Rana. Until now I
never realized what mages in strategic locations
around the kingdom might do. We're best rid of
them all."*

The one good thing was my brother's birth.

She brought Peitar to the valley, and taught him to read early. He was eager to learn. She began to have hope again:

> *I really believe Peitar will be the answer to our ills. He is only four, but I find myself holding conversations with him as if he were older, his grasp of ideas is so quick, his thought so deep. And he is happy. I have begged Oscar to wait until he is seven to begin the everlasting war training, because I cannot bear to have my own boy made over as my brother was, into a young version of Grandfather. I can scarcely believe that the King Darian everyone has begun to fear was once my own dear brother Ian. Oscar has agreed to my request, mostly because Peitar is so small and fraily built. . . .*

Peitar "the answer to our ills"? I'd never thought about it before, but now I understood that Uncle Darian regarded my brother as a possible heir. He could be the next king. All that tension when the two of them disagreed—the stakes were not just the future of the kingdom, but Peitar's own future.

Ian once said he would never marry, for he could not bear to have anyone close whom he did not love, but he could not take the risk of loving. I thought it was the careless talk of the young military cadet, but I know now that he meant what he said. He always means what he says.

There were two more entries.

The first was about me, and it made my heart ache, because she wrote about how happy she was to have a daughter, and how much she looked forward to showing me all her favorite things. How much fun we'd have together.

I could barely read the last entry, but I forced myself.

. . . I stayed until I knew Peitar would recover. This time. I don't think I can bear to live anymore in so painful a world, for I cannot change what hurts me the deepest—that my beloved is gone forever to the other side of the kingdom, and that my own brother has turned against me. For the first time, I dared to speak my true thoughts. I told Ian everything I had been feeling, and we argued—Ian and I! Who have never before argued! He said it was not Oscar's fault, but mine, for "babying" Peitar, and that the accident would never have hap-

pened had he started training at the right age.
Between them, they're going to kill Peitar, just
as surely as our own father was killed—and
Ian can't see it, he can't—he's truly become our
grandfather.

That means, so far as I can see, that
Norsunder has won.

I gently closed the diary and wiped my eyes fiercely, full of grief and anger.

Now I had two vows to keep. First, if I ever fell in love, I was never going to let it destroy my life, even if it didn't work out. Some thought Kepreos's suicide romantic, but to me, it was *selfish*. Would Derek and Bernal have gotten into dangerous adventures if their father had put his sons first?

Second, the promise I made with the boys: I would *find* a way to help Peitar. I had been waiting for someone to tell me how, or at least give me my solution—and meanwhile he had had all the burdens and the worries.

If I couldn't find my answer around me, then it was time to do what my brother had done, and read. So I went back to the library, to learn about everybody who had a dream and made it happen.

DURING THE DAYS, when the weather was fine, I swam and visited Tsauderei, Dawn, and Atan. In the evenings, I read the Esalan brothers' *Our Provident Careers*, while Bren sketched and Innon studied histories full of treaties and tax laws.

Sometimes I read an especially funny caper to the boys. Innon loved the one where the brothers joined a troupe of minstrels. At a big noble party, two of them sang so loud and so badly that people clapped their hands over their ears—and the third sneaked around to pickpocket them all. If this was slam justice, I was all for it.

The night I reached the last page, I closed the book with regret and went downstairs. It was time to think about dinner. Before I could talk with Lizana, the boys flew in through the open windows.

"What's the fastest meal?" Bren asked.

"Bread and cheese," I replied.

"No." Lizana appeared in the doorway. "You'll eat properly. Now, if you chop potatoes small, and onions and turnips, you can cook them fast on this flat pan, once you've oiled it."

"Garlic, too." Innon tossed me a whole head of the stuff.

Lizana added, "And a dash of wine for flavor! Then—" She broke off.

I heard the front door open, then close.

Then a familiar uneven, scraping walk.

"Peitar!" I cried, and ran to meet him.

ten

"Fheg! You're dripping wet! Where's your cane?"

"And I'm happy to see you too, little sister." Peitar laughed, but his eyes were shadowed, his face more drawn than I'd ever seen it.

"Here, come into the kitchen so you can dry off."

"And some steeped listerblossom would be welcome." He leaned on my shoulder.

As soon as Lizana saw him, she handed him a towel. "You'll have that. And a good meal." She took over as we set the table, moving about the kitchen in a quick, sharp way I'd never seen before. Under her orders, we got dinner cooking much faster than usual.

Peitar dropped into one of the chairs with a long sigh. "The king holds Miraleste again." We all seemed to catch our breath at once. "One morning last week, we woke to find a detachment of the army lined up across the eastern horizon. The people who held the gate melted away, and no one opposed the king's force."

"Did anyone try to resist?" Lizana asked.

"A few groups. Enough for Uncle Darian to permit reprisals. It's called 'reestablishing order.'"

Bren gave him an anxious look. "Where's Derek?" Bren asked.

"He's as safe as can be expected. We argued once too often, so I came here. He knows where I am—and I'm sure Uncle Darian does, too, but as long as I'm not at the head of a rabble, I think he'll leave me be."

"And he doesn't know the magic spell," I said with relief.

"I hope Deveral fed you," said Lizana.

Peitar's expression brightened. "Splendidly. But it rained on the way. Even with the flying spell, it was a windy, difficult journey, and I don't think I've ever been more glad to see your lights below me."

"Derek Diamagan and the rest of the troubles can wait." She set down a steaming cup. "You need to eat and get yourself warm and dry, and sleep."

Peitar obeyed, too. Nothing more was said about Derek or Sarendan or Uncle Darian. Instead, he asked about our time in Delfina.

Innon gave an account of his new friends and their games on the lake. Then I prodded Bren to talk about drawing, and Peitar asked to see his sketches.

After cleanup, Bren went upstairs and got a sheaf of papers. He spread them out on the table, making one of those comical faces, part pride and part fear. There was the lake drawing, and others of the garden. They were very good, but his people were better: Seriah at her embroidery, her expression thoughtful; Innon flying with a delighted look on his face; a group of kids playing on the village green. And there were others: wary, angry people from the revolution; Deveral and Lizana, highlighting their resemblance; Derek in his storyteller mood.

"This," Peitar said, laying the last one down, "is very good. You have an exceptional talent, Bren—it ought to be cultivated."

"Derek thinks that art is only for nobles, and Bren should be a bricklayer," I put in.

"That's not true," Bren snapped, then said in a lower voice, "Well, not entirely."

"More true than not."

Peitar gave us a look, and we shut up. "You don't have to confine yourself to fine art, and even if you did, what's wrong with making art that anyone can have access to, rich or poor?"

First Tsauderei, now Peitar—I hoped it would be enough to make Bren change his mind.

THE NEXT MORNING my brother was still asleep, so I visited Atan. She knew much more history than I, but she was as eager to listen as to talk. Like me, she wanted to know *why* a person did what they did.

We got so involved in discussing whether JaJa the Pirate Queen was a real person or a story (and if she was real, which of her adventures were true), that I forgot the time—

forgot even that Peitar was in the valley—until I had to go back to Irad House.

That reminded me of something Tsauderei had said. After dinner, I caught Peitar alone. "Rested?" I asked.

"Much better, thank you." Peitar raised his eyebrows. "Why? You have some nefarious scheme afoot?"

"Come with me tomorrow, to meet someone."

"I visited Tsauderei today, if that's who you mean." I shook my head. "I want to spend some time at the lake. A swim without having to watch for danger will be a rare treat."

"Somebody new. Someone who reads a lot of the books you do, and talks about the same things."

He raised his hands in mock surrender. "You win. But afterward, the lake."

Peitar wasn't a fast flyer, but it was clear that it was easier for his entire body; like Bren, he was more graceful aloft. As we gained height, he lifted his head and the summer wind tangled his hair, and his face relaxed so much that, for once, he really did look nineteen.

"Is Uncle Darian really after you?" I asked as soon as we were high above Irad House.

"Probably. Yes. I wish I knew why."

"Ugh! What's to wonder about? He called us traitors!"

"That was said in anger. I don't believe he believes it. Remember when I talked to him the day of the revolution, when we were locked in the garrison? He was most angry that I was friends with Derek—and that I didn't tell him of Derek's plans. But he hadn't yet read my letter."

"How did he get the letter? Bren said he threw it away!"

"He threw it in the garden, and one of the king's men found it and gave it to Uncle Darian after he was freed. He probably didn't like seeing my opinion of his failings, but he'd also have seen that I'm against violence—that I refused to have any part in the uprising. He knows I can't lead a pony cart, much less an army. In short, I am no threat to anyone. Yet once he retook Miraleste, he sent people to hunt me down. I think it's because our interview was interrupted. Sometimes I think I ought to let them get me, just so we can talk again. But what if he decides to silence me forever?"

I said in my calmest but firmest voice, "You have to promise you won't let him get you. Promise!" And when he hesitated, I said, "Oh, Peitar, it'll be scary enough when we go back, without my thinking that you—"

"Not *we*," he said quickly. "You *can't* go back, Lilah. I couldn't do anything, knowing you were in danger."

"You can't make me stay here."

His voice was so soft I almost didn't hear it. "I can."

"A threat?" I cried. "Peitar—"

Then there was no time for speech, as we came in for a landing near Hermit House. He straightened up with an effort and faced me. "I could ask Tsauderei to amend the magic so that you cannot leave the valley. Lilah," he added quickly, almost desperately, "I believe in your courage and your good intentions. One of the best days of my life was when I caught sight of you sneaking past my window. It's a real gift that we can talk this freely. But Sarendan is in a state of war, and you don't have the training or the resources to survive it."

"You don't, either."

"I know," he said ruefully, "and I almost didn't survive."

"What? You didn't tell—"

"I see a house. Is someone inside? Let's go meet your friend, shall we? Ugly stories can wait." I had to give up—for now.

Atan answered the door, which meant either that Gehlei had seen us coming or Tsauderei was there, for they never relaxed their vigilance.

"This is my brother, Peitar," I said, and to him, as he looked at her with interest, "This is the person we call Atan. Her existence is a secret outside of the valley."

"I will tell him everything later," Tsauderei called from within. "Good thought, Lilah," he added.

The house smelled of herbs and honey and wax, as they were making candles. Atan clearly noted the way Peitar walked, but she didn't recoil, or stare—she just turned her attention to *him*.

"How nice to meet you," she exclaimed, and showed him to a chair. "Though truth to tell I've been apprehensive, for Lilah and Tsauderei describe you as a real scholar."

Peitar smiled. "Not even remotely, I'm afraid."

Tsauderei snorted.

"Steeped leaf? It's real Sartoran leaf," she added. "One of the few benefits of the time-freeze is that we still have some that's a century old."

He still looked confused—then his eyes widened, and he turned to Tsauderei, who nodded and chuckled softly. It was as if I could watch Peitar working it all out.

Atan put a few spoonfuls into a pot and poured in boiling water, sending a wonderful fresh scent through the room. She said, "We were just talking about the breakup of the empire. I hadn't known—had you?—that it wasn't just Sartor, but Colend and the Land of the Venn that broke up, or were broken, at about the same time, and we wondered if it was coincidence. . . ."

And there we were, launched right into history. The talk was way over my head, but I found it interesting to listen as they veered from theories to people—how the Dei family always seemed to be somewhere close by, if not involved in kingdom-changing events—and how personalities could alter the course of entire nations.

Not once did Peitar go distant. In fact, he'd never been so expressive for so long a time. At one point, he and Tsauderei had a long debate about why Norsunder had attacked only certain kingdoms.

"All we truly know about the Norsundrian command is that they exist outside of time, so they have the leisure

220   Sherwood Smith

to watch plans unfold over centuries. And from the old records, I believe they like the hunt, the game, the subtle twist of a dagger, and not the bludgeon."

Atan poured out more steeped leaf. "No," she said. "Sartor was bludgeoned."

"But that was an underling's plan," Tsauderei countered. And then, to Peitar, "Some of my colleagues in Bereth Ferian do not like my pursuit of our enemies through records, but I maintain we're going to have to understand them if we're to defeat them."

"Naturally I agree, since it was you who taught me." Atan laughed.

Peitar put down his cup. "I wish you could talk to Derek. Maybe he'd listen to you."

"Why? I'm full of reading and not a trace of experience. Your friend would probably dismiss me as another hot wind gusting through the eaves."

"No." Peitar hesitated. "At the least, he might consider that slam justice is another form of tyranny."

"Slam justice," she repeated. "I admire the Esalan brothers tremendously, but I don't believe that there really is justice outside the law." Tsauderei glanced from one to the other. Atan went on thoughtfully, "But what if the law doesn't promote justice? Another topic for debate! Are you tired of debate?" She laughed and rose to her feet. "Tsauderei and I sometimes spend half the day in debate when we should be practicing magic—or so he says, if I'm not sufficiently dili-gent. Meanwhile, I seem to have let the pot go dry. Shall I fix some more?"

Peitar stood. "No, thank you. I promised someone I'd go to the lake."

"Do return, if you have the time. I already have a mental list of records with which to arm myself against our next attempt to solve the world's problems."

Tsauderei said to me, "Hold him to that swim." He pointed at Peitar. "Then you come visit me."

We didn't talk at all on the flight back. When we landed outside Irad House, I saw the old lines and pain in Peitar's face again, and blurted out, "Isn't Atan wonderful? Don't you like her?"

"Very much," he said. And that was all—though usually he had a lot more to say, and even a few quotes to throw in.

eleven

S till, even if Peitar hadn't said much, he had meant every word. I was delighted when he offered to accompany me on my next visit, and those visits soon became a habit. The two of them talked about magic, and about history, and what it meant to lead a kingdom, quoting back and forth from Adamas Dei and other famous writers. I started reading those books, looking for ideas. And I wasn't the only one. Innon began *Our Provident Careers*.

Another thing Peitar and I began to do together was fly late at night, before bed, just to talk. We had years to make up for. I soaked up his stories about his time in the valley with Mother—any stories about Mother, really. We went on to Selenna family history—and, finally, Father. To my surprise, Peitar had some good memories.

He had seen how much Father loved our mother—how he delighted in trying to surprise her, with her favorite foods, with gifts. Selenna House had been filled with music. The garden was her kingdom, and she made it into the paradise I remembered. "You have to realize," Peitar said, "our father wouldn't look at anyone else after he met our mother. Even though she had no interest in him at all."

And he talked about his accident for the first time. "You

cannot blame Father for this wreck of a knee, no matter what anyone says," Peitar said, gazing at the scattered stars. "He agreed to postpone my riding and sword lessons to please Mother. And when it happened . . . well, you know how our uncle feels about mages, and withstanding pain. Father would have sent for a healer had I asked, but I lied and said I felt fine. That's what I'd been taught to do, and I could see it made things easier for him. But Mother could see the difference between what I was saying and how I was feeling, and she thought—well, that I was turning into another version of our uncle."

"No! She couldn't!"

"But she did. I understand it now. It was that mistaken impression, when I was trying so hard to please them all, that drove her out into the garden during that sleet storm when she was already sick." That final illness had killed her.

A sob wrenched me, and Peitar gripped my arm. "That's why it's important for us always to speak freely to one another," he said, looking into my eyes. "Not to hide and second guess. There's already been too much damage because of that."

I thought of my promise. "I'll try."

Back at Irad House, I wrestled with Adamas Dei's memoirs until my eyes burned. When I went to bed at last, a square of light from Peitar's window painted the trees outside.

⌣ ⌣ ⌣

A WEEK OR so later came a hot, breathless morning. "Thunder on the way," Lizana commented at breakfast. "We'll clean the house."

"Now, how did the one thing lead to the other?" Bren asked, chin in hand.

"You may contemplate it," she said, "as you mop the upstairs floors. Innon, you will dust. Lilah, you get the floors down here."

"Foogh," I grumbled.

"And you," Lizana said, pointing to Peitar, "are to drop the studies and go swimming before the weather changes."

"Yes, Lizana," Peitar said meekly.

"No books," she added.

"No books," he echoed, raising his hands.

And so it was. Innon finished first, then joined Peitar. I was mopping near the front door when a knock startled me. I don't know if it was the foreboding weather or Peitar's increasing concentration on unnamed studies or Lizana's flat voice or all of them, but somehow I knew who it was before I opened the door.

And I was right.

Derek stood there, nearly as thin as Peitar, his face just as weary. His hair had gotten longer, but he clearly hadn't noticed, because he would have been the first to condemn himself for looking like a noble. "May I come in?" he finally asked.

"Oh! Sorry." I held the door open. "But step carefully. I just mopped."

He remained where he was. "Is Peitar about?"

"Down at the lake."

"No, he isn't," came Peitar's voice, as he landed on the porch behind Derek, who turned with a wary quickness that alarmed me. But then he saw Peitar and relaxed, and so did I.

"You," he said without preamble, "were right. You were right all along, and I've been a fool. No, worse, for the consequences are worse. . . ."

"Later," Peitar said in a gentle voice. "Later. Come in." He led him into the sitting room. Innon followed.

"From the lake we saw someone flying in," Innon whispered. "I don't know how Peitar guessed it was Derek. Never thought your brother could move so fast. He shot out of the water, straight into the sky!"

Peitar said, "Lilah, I apologize for marking up the floor."

Just then Bren came hurtling down the stairs. "Derek!"

"Bren, I can't believe how fat you are! This life suits you."

"Fat?" Bren looked down at his bony self, amazed and pleased. *"Fat?"*

"Are you hungry?" I asked Derek, who was laughing. "Thirsty?"

"Nothing right now," he replied. "But thanks, Lilah."

Bren fidgeted impatiently. "What about Deon? And

Dirty—" He looked around guiltily, but Lizana was nowhere in sight.

"I don't know about Deon," Derek said, "which I consider good news, unless I hear otherwise. As for Darian Irad, he still controls Sarendan, for which I have my own lack of control to blame. Leaders of riots don't bring stability."

"Not everyone turned against you, Derek, " Bren said, looking appalled. "Not everyone, surely."

"No, but enough. The farmers are angry that the weavers' guild still exists. Why should the weavers continue to get paid for each piece of work when crop prices rise and fall, and the farmers can't even buy clothes? And the weavers are angry because they can't afford bread. I almost got everyone to agree on a wine tax for rebuilding—everyone except the vintners, the barrel-makers, and the wagoneers." He rubbed his forehead. "And that was only the beginning."

"But you did have a plan. You did! The nobles were to pay the taxes, because they're rich. We all agreed to that!"

Peitar said quietly, "Except how can they pay when they're dead, or their holdings looted, their land and homes destroyed, or they've run off to the army at Obrin?"

"So our people are fighting each other?" Bren looked sick at the news of betrayal.

"Not all," said Derek. "We've still got loyal followers. In fact, many of them are training themselves into a semblance of an army. They learned something, watching Darian's forces carve their way through rioters."

"So there's going to be a lot more fighting."

"And they want you as the figurehead," Peitar said, rather than asked.

Derek shrugged. "I'm on the condemned list anyway. Why not make one more try? Irad has his best commanders spread thin in order to reestablish control. And they have as much trouble as we do trying to find out what's truth, what's false, and who's where." Then he turned to Peitar. "Help me make a plan for afterward."

"Why?"

"Because the only one in all this nightmare who made sense was you. I have come to listen for once, and not to argue."

My brother did not reply. Bren stared at Derek with that betrayed expression, and Innon looked down at his hands. Nobody spoke until Lizana appeared in the doorway. She took Derek's appearance in stride. "I think we might as well begin the midday meal, Innon. Peitar, get out of those damp clothes."

As we ate, the low sound of thunder got louder. Any time the talk seemed to veer toward Sarendan or Derek's problems, Lizana firmly changed the subject. Bren and I had to clean up, and Derek and Peitar were gone when we finished. "They're planning," he said angrily. "They're out somewhere making plans, and we're not a part of them."

"You don't know that," I replied, but I sensed that it was true.

Before Bren could answer, Innon burst into the room, *Our Provident Careers* in hand. "Listen, I think we need to talk about—"

"They're meeting without us. They don't want our help!" And Bren slammed out.

"Well, I tried," Innon said.

"I know. And Peitar keeps saying that's he afraid for me—I'm not prepared for war, and all that."

"Well, you aren't. Neither am I," Innon said reasonably. "I thought I was, after all those years of fencing lessons, and I thought I'd go for training, but then I heard what happens to the new cadets at Obrin. They have to be foxes for the seniors to hunt—and beat with canes, if they catch you—and you have to endure it over and over until you get tough enough for the real training. And I heard that *before* the revolution."

"So when we made that promise, you never meant to keep it?"

"No. No, no." Innon pushed his hair back. "It's just that if we're going to help, we need a way that uses our strengths. It's stupid to think we can help with fighting. It's clearer since I've been reading the brothers. They were always learning what the other side would do. And they didn't use force, they used wit—like the time they discovered that evil baron behind all those attacks on the road."

I grinned. "You mean we should disguise ourselves as foreign cooks, so we can overhear the secret plans while some baron and his guards believe we're making a fancy dinner? I don't think we'd be very convincing, and even if we were, how would that help Peitar and Derek?"

Innon made a face. "I know, I know. But it's the *idea*, see? They keep talking about using wit instead of strength, and they managed it without anybody getting hurt."

"I see what you mean—and I'm thinking about ways to help, too. I just haven't figured out how, yet."

"Neither have I," he admitted. "Anyway, since there's no stopping Bren from flailing around in that storm looking for Derek and Peitar, I'm going back to the brothers. At least they make me laugh."

"And we'll keep on thinking," I said.

I went upstairs to record Derek's arrival—and realized how long it had been since I'd written in my book. Lightning flared outside, and rain drummed against the roof as I wrote. Afterward, I stretched out on my bed and wondered what Peitar and Derek were talking about, and fell asleep watching the silvery runnels on the windowpanes.

twelve

I woke to find a note on my desk in Peitar's slanting hand, and ran downstairs. The boys were in the kitchen.

Bren didn't even look up. "You know, then."

"They're gone."

"Sneaked out without letting anyone know. So what now?" Innon asked.

Wit instead of strength.

Bren was rubbing his thumb back and forth along the edge of the table. Chalk made a moon-sliver under his nail. Bits of dreams and old ideas and my talk with Innon flitted through my mind, gathering like moths to a light.

And there it was.

"We can use wit," I said slowly. "Because we don't have strength. Just like Innon said. Slam justice can work." I looked at the boys. "I know what to do." Wonder—excitement—anticipation—it all came spilling in. "I *know* what we can do!"

Bren hunched his shoulders. "Don't say we ought to mind our own business."

"Not going to. What we are going to do," I said, unable to sit still because I couldn't contain my excitement, "we—we are going to become . . ." I took a deep breath. "We are going to become the Esalan brothers."

The boys stared at me like I'd sprouted antlers.

"Hoo!" Innon gave a sudden laugh. "That's it. That's the kind of thing I was trying to think up!"

"We're going to become men?" Bren asked, looking skeptical.

"Not men, thieves!"

"Thieves?"

"Yes," I said. "Thieves of *information*. Remember what Derek said, that both sides have trouble finding out what's really going on? He and Peitar need to know my uncle's plans so *they* can plan. And we're going to find out, because nobody ever pays attention to kids. We'll go to Miraleste. . . and we'll become spies."

"Spies," Bren whispered. "It's perfect. But I don't see how."

"You haven't read the book," Innon said. "They lay it all out—we could practice some of their tricks. Use their tools. See if it works. We'll have to be extra careful, because we can't be discovered by *either* side, but I have an idea." He lowered his voice. "If we get in trouble we can't get out of, because none of us are good at swords, we knock 'em out with Lure."

Bren asked. "What good is that? There's no Lure flowers anywhere in Sarendan."

"We can harvest the ones here at the lake, and take them along with us."

"We'd knock ourselves out, too," Bren said. "That stuff is dangerous."

"Here's something I never told anyone. I know that I promised Lizana to stay away from the Lure. And I meant to! But I kept using the smell as the place to turn around when I was swimming, and guess what? I was able to get closer to that end of the lake each day. You *can* get used to Lure, at least a little bit. I think I could hold my breath, grab some flowers, and put them into something where the smell doesn't get out. We'll take that along."

"I think it might work," I interrupted. "Listen! We'll *be* brothers! Innon, you cut your hair. With old clothes, nobody would recognize you. As for me, no more Lilah Selenna. I'll cut this off." I held up my braid. "And turn into Larei."

Bren jumped up.

"Where are you going?" I asked.

"To read that book!" he yelled, and pounded off to the library.

THE FIRST PERSON we needed to fool was Lizana, and the easiest way was to pretend that everything was a big game.

We tried to catch one another sneaking in and out of the house, using the Esalans' tricks of observing from a distance how much you could or could not see from a window or door, and how to keep people from noticing you.

Innon got his friends to help, and I recruited Dawn, and we used their houses, too. After all, we'd have to go to a lot of unfamiliar places.

We made sure to discuss our plans only while flying, or at the lake, or the far end of the garden, and we started making up code words and signs in case we had to communicate in public.

At the end of the first week, Bren had gotten to the part in *Our Provident Careers* where the brothers came up with their name. There were three of them, and they signed their "work" with their initials, *SLN*, which became "Esalan." He wondered aloud what we'd call ourselves.

"I've been thinking about it ever since I read the book," said Innon. "How about the Sharadan brothers?"

"I *hate* my stupid name!" Bren protested. "Why not our initials?"

"Our initials sound stupid, too." Innon waved him off. "You just don't like being named after a noble family. But it points the finger away from us."

"It might get the Sharadan family into trouble," I said.

"So? They were terrible governors as well as snobs. If King Darian sends spies after them—if any Sharadans are even still alive—so much the better, because then the king's spies won't be searching for *us*."

"It sounds good, but you'll have to decide, Bren, since it's your name."

"Well, put that way, it's a slam."

Innon said, "If that's decided, our next job is to get tools, and practice."

"And learn our way around the city. Derek told me and Deon to do that, but I wasn't there long enough." He turned expectantly to me.

"I don't know Miraleste. All I ever did was ride the coach in and out."

"I know some of it," Innon said. "We can learn our way around when we get there."

"As for tools, I'll ask Tsauderei," I said. "I'll tell him it's for a game."

First I went to visit Atan, because I hadn't seen her all week—and it gave me time to work on what I'd say to the mage. I hadn't meant to tell her anything, but when she asked how I felt about Peitar going back to Miraleste—Tsauderei had told her—out it all came.

She listened closely, and at the end said, "I do wish there'd been a chance to meet Derek. He sounds fascinating."

"Oh, he'd probably snarl about your being a noble," I grumbled.

"Yes, I look like such a delicate princess," Atan retorted good-naturedly, flicking the frayed hem of her work shirt. "Oh, Lilah, this is tough. But if I were you, I'd do exactly the same. I think the Sharadan brothers and getting information are fine ideas—and if it becomes dangerous, you can return here, and Derek and Peitar will be none the wiser."

"Except if they actually see us. *That's* what worries me. A disguise will fool other people, maybe even my uncle, but if Peitar saw me, he'd know right away, and Derek would recognize us all. Maybe the boys could become girls, except then they have to worry about climbing in dresses, and if I'm a Sharadan sister, I'm right back to looking like me. . . ."

"Do you think Peitar and Derek will stay in Miraleste, then?" Atan asked.

"Well, won't they? If they've got to spy around and start another government, they'd have to be there, right?"

She looked straight through me, thinking. It was just like Peitar. "Well," she began, "from everything I've read, the easiest way to shipwreck a government is to capture the leaders." She got up and paced, her fingers braiding up her hair with the quick, absent expertise that comes of doing something every day, for years, without a mirror. "Still, I don't think Peitar is going to be in Miraleste. Derek's first plan didn't work. So I think Peitar will want to visit all of Derek's old leaders, one by one, and talk to them about a new plan. He might even take the risk of speaking to those he knows among the loyalists. Yes." She nodded. "He would. I think your brother has more courage than most, because he has to face danger with no weapons but his wits. Just like the famous brothers."

"So you think he'll be traveling around the kingdom?"

She finished braiding her hair. "Yes. Weaving a . . . a tapestry, you might say, of mutual consent, one person at a time. Which gives him authority without ever using force."

"But if he talks to loyalists, they could tell Uncle Darian."

"Yes. It's a big risk. But can't you see him believing it worthwhile to try?"

"Oh, yes." The Sharadan brothers now seemed like a children's game. I said in a rush, "So you don't think *my* idea is stupid?"

Her answer was surprising. "Come."

She led the way outside, and instead of talking did the magic, and we took off.

I had never seen Atan fly before. It was clear she was well practiced. We soared westward, over rocky chasms and gorges so deep their bottoms were lost in shadow, even though the afternoon sun was strong on our backs. The farther west we got, the more desolate the mountain terrain became. There was an intense feeling of brooding ugliness.

Before long, we saw untouched stretches of snow, and the peaks where the great gryphs nested. Magic protected us against what had to be bitter cold. Gray clouds loomed closer and closer, and then we were in them. Atan veered close and took my hand. We landed on rocky ground. Cold fog fingered my clothes and hair with dank thoroughness.

Atan stood motionless. Then she raised her hand and spoke soft words, and wind swept down from the peaks and drove the clouds away in a boiling, ghostly mass. It lifted our hair and made our clothes snap and flap, but Atan stared straight down so I did, too.

The ground fell away toward parched meadowland that

shimmered strangely, vanishing in a grayish haze.

"Sartor," I breathed. The world's most ancient kingdom.

"The very eastern end," she answered. "I'm not much older than you, not in real time, but very soon I am going down into that land to free it."

As we watched, the clouds churned and a shaft of strong golden sunlight struck glints in the rock below. The flash lasted the space of a breath, but Atan smiled in a way that echoed it, and said, "I'm glad we came." The smile turned rueful. "But Tsauderei does not like it, and I have responsibility for you as well. Come."

On our flight back, she said, "You asked if I think you're wrong to try, and I say no. But like I said, I've no experience. Talk to Tsauderei, Lilah. He's very experienced, very smart, and very powerful."

I agreed, though secretly resolving not to *tell* Tsauderei—only to get him to use his magic to procure us our tools.

Gehlei was waiting when we returned. She frowned, seeing the direction from which we had come. The last Landis heir was hedged about by those who loved her most, just as I was, yet she was determined to fulfill her vows.

I flew on to Tsauderei's, but the closer I got, the more scared I felt. I wanted his advice, but what if he forbade us to try our plan? Maybe he'd even use some spell, like Peitar had threatened, to keep us from leaving the valley. I circled overhead, imagining his questions and my answers until I felt ready to face him.

Tsauderei was in his usual seat by the window. When I came in, he eyed me. "What have you done that you shouldn't, or what haven't you done that you should?"

I tried to sound casual. "Oh, we've invented a game that needs tools, and we don't know where to get tools here."

"Tools?"

"Yes." I gave a practiced shrug. "Little hooks, for opening things—"

"Like lock picks?" Tsauderei asked, his brows winging upward.

"Well, I suppose, though I don't know what those look like."

"And you want these tools, kind of like lock picks, for . . . what?"

"This game," I repeated.

His eyes narrowed. "Lilah."

One question, and I'd already ruined everything! "Are you too busy for a visit? If you are—"

"You'd better give it to me straight, or I'll be forced to heed Peitar's rather unnecessary request and tie you three down."

"Unnecessary?" I repeated warily.

"Necessary only if you do something stupid." Tsauderei gave me a grim smile, folded his arms, and sat back. "Convince me that you aren't doing something stupid. Lying to me," he added, "would number among the things I'd consider very, very stupid."

I fingered the scraggly end of my braid. I studied cracks in the paint on the windowsill. Then I addressed the air just beside his ear. "What would be stupider?"

"Let's just set lying as the floor, shall we?"

"Well, I hope that means that you'll listen, then. Because here's our real idea." I laced my fingers together, took a deep breath, and told him everything. When I finished, my heart was pounding.

Tsauderei stroked his beard and looked out the window for a while. "And you have been practicing to be spies?" I described our "games," our hand signals and coded language. He took it in. "How would you get your information to Peitar and Derek?"

"Bren says that there's someone on the kitchen staff who used to be Derek's main contact in Miraleste. If they're still there, we could get messages to Derek."

"That's good thinking. But your uncle is back at the palace, you know. What if he gets his hands on you?"

"I'm going to make sure he doesn't know who I am," I said. "I'm going to be Larei."

"If—I say *if*—you are convincing, and he caught you and didn't realize who you were, he'd condemn you to a common criminal's death. Youth won't stay his hand, not now. He's far too angry."

"I don't care. I mean, I do care—very much. About staying alive, I mean. Not about *him*. And, anyway, that's why we'll have the Lure, in case we do get cornered."

"We'll talk more about the Lure in a moment. Lilah, have you considered the other alternative? That if your uncle sees you, he'll know who you are?"

I shivered. "I'll have to make sure he doesn't." Then I said cautiously, "You're acting as if you might agree with us."

"What I'm attempting to do is discern whether you really know what you face. It's true that you witnessed some terrible things after the revolution, but I don't think you've considered what it all means to those in charge. Peitar and Derek you might understand to an extent, or you wouldn't have come up with this plan—but your uncle has to be factored in, because if you're successful, he's going to be tracking you, and I don't know if you're going to be able to avoid getting caught. And if he sees *you* and does recognize you, what has been a nightmare of humiliation will crystallize into a betrayal by the one person he loved—your mother."

"Humiliation?"

"Lilah. He lost his kingdom—not to another army, but to untrained, badly organized common folk. Can't you see how humiliating that is? Especially to a man who measures himself by the standards of the old king, your great-grandfather. He might have talked himself into thinking that you and Peitar were friends with Derek without actually being part of the revolution, but if he discovers Rana's daughter actively working for his enemies, it would make everything that much worse."

"I don't plan to ever let him see me."

"You keep that goal in mind. Have you told Lizana any of this?"

"No! She didn't even like it when Peitar went back."

"She worries about you all. And I am fairly certain that Peitar extracted a promise from her about your safety. But you may leave Lizana to me." There was a long silence. Finally, he said, "I think . . . with some emendations . . . it might just tip the balance. Yes." He placed his hands on his knees. "These emendations will be safeguards, because a week or two of playing spy games doesn't train you to outwit adults. But I suspect you would go anyway, so I'm going to take my precautions, and you will agree to them."

"I promise!" I said, trying not to jump up and down.

"I will get your tools, once I look again at *Our Provident Careers*. You continue to practice those skills."

I flew home so fast my eyes stung.

The boys nearly strangled trying not to cheer. We raced out into the garden, and Bren let out a whoop that scared birds out of the trees. Then he rubbed his hands. "Let's set up some new plans! Harder ones. We'd better start practicing at night, too. The sooner we're ready—" He stopped when the foliage rustled.

Then came the sound of someone thrashing, and finally a high squawk of annoyance.

Bren's eyes widened. "It can't be . . ." He darted toward the shrubbery, Innon and I close behind. "Deon!"

thirteen

"*I thought* I heard you yelling!" Deon stumbled out of the bushes, her hair in her eyes. "That flying was wonderful—best thing ever happened to me—but then I landed in those blast-nasty shrubs—"

"Never mind that!" Bren cried. "What happened to you!"

"Oh, that's a *long* story." She made a terrible face. "And most of it is so stupid and boring I'll scream if I have to tell any of it before I get something to eat!"

"Lizana's inside," Innon said. "I'll sneak in and grab something without being seen. It's practice!"

Deon glanced from Bren to me, then sat down. "You're up to something. I can tell. And it's something you don't want the grown-ups to know, which means I'll like it."

"We are. You will," I said, thinking that four brothers would be even better than three.

She sighed happily. "I'm so glad that those foresters taught me the magic! All right, here's what happened—and then I'm in on whatever you have planned, got it?"

Bren grinned. "Got it."

"Well, it was stupid. I was cleaning out the big carriage that belongs to your family, Lilah. Derek had signs on it that it was for the revolution. One of the cooks sent me to clean it, but what she *really* wanted me to do was get a love letter that someone left inside for her."

"Ugh!" Bren and I said together.

"Well, I found the letter, and dusted a bit, but I was so tired, and I thought I'd take a nap, and she could think I was scrubbing the whole thing. So I curled up in the storage place under the seat and dropped right off. There was *never* any time for good sleep."

"So the king did get you, then?" Bren asked.

"Oh, did Derek guess?" Deon asked, sounding disappointed, but then Innon appeared, red-faced from running, and handed her some bread and a peach. "Anyway, I woke up with the carriage jolting on the road. I was stuffed inside, holding my dusting rag and that letter. And yes, I opened it, and yes, it *was* a love letter. Ugh!"

The three of us snickered.

"Well, we finally slowed down enough for me to get out. And there was Dirty Hands himself! I don't know who was more surprised! He was a mess—blood on his clothes, face all bruised, his wrists chewed up something frightful. Hadn't had a thing to eat for days, so he looked as starved as one of us at home." She turned to Bren. "I gawked at him, he stared at me, and then he started laughing. He took the letter away, and looked at it like *he* thought it was some spy thing, but after he read a few words, he went like this." Deon curled her lip. "And he said, 'Yours?' I said, 'Yuck! Not a chance!' Then . . . he went on reading it!"

Innon cracked his knuckles. "Yup. See who it was from. If he could."

"Who cares?"

"Maybe one of the guard, or else why would they have to leave letters? He'd want to know who was on whose side."

"Who's telling this story?" Deon demanded. "*Anyway,* after he read the thing he gave it back, and I threw it out the window. We were a long way from Miraleste. Nothing in sight but fields, most of 'em burnt."

"Phew," Bren said. "So then?"

"So then he asked me if I was one of 'Derek Diamagan's rabble,' and *of course* I lied—who wouldn't? But then I had a real bad moment, because he went like this." She narrowed her eyes, and again I could imagine my uncle's face. I must have caught my breath, because she cast me a quick glance. "You know that look, don't you? I used to think you nobles had it easy, but now I'm not so sure. Not around *him.* Anyhow, he said he thought I was one of the people who came to shout at him when he was a prisoner. Well . . . I had. Three times! Because I kept thinking up more insults. I said that Derek had made me do it, and he said, 'You needn't have been so assiduous, then,' or something like that, and I could just feel the noose around my neck, but he had this look like he was about to start laughing again. Then we stopped, the door opened, and a warrior was there."

"And?" Bren prompted.

"The warrior helped him get out. Another warrior took me straight to the cook tents. And that's the end of the stupid part, and here comes the boring part. Days and days and *days* of cooking and cleaning. I was the only girl, at first. The rest were all noble cadets from Obrin. After a week of us bumbling around making terrible meals—and those warriors complain worse than any courtier!—some of the palace staff came. We worked just as hard, but they told us what to do, and the food got better and everything more organized. And that was it. We moved camp, always in the middle of the night, and oh, do they travel fast! All the news we heard was about riots and killings and the king's mood. He made them practice fighting and drilling, and a couple of times they brought in prisoners."

None of us wanted to think about what had happened to them.

"Finally, we got another order to march—right back to Miraleste. Warriors were everywhere cleaning things up, or forcing work parties to do it. Dirty Hands gave us pay, and offered us palace jobs or freedom, and I said I wanted to go home. He said, 'Make sure you do.' I did, just in case he sent someone after me, but after I gave my pay to Gran, she told me Derek left a message: if none of you was in Selenna, I was to go to Diannah, mention your name, Lilah, and do what the robbers told me. Robbers! I hoped I'd get to join them, but flying was even better!" She finished off the peach and licked her fingers. "Phew! So what's the plan?"

I cleared my throat, ready to tell the story of our vow, and what Peitar and Derek said, and the Esalans and our idea, but Bren knew his cousin better.

"We are going back," he said. "In disguise. As thieves, and spies."

Deon rubbed her hands. "When do we start?"

DEON—OR DAEN, HER Sharadan brothers name—fitted right in. She slept in my room and wore Mother's clothes, which fit her much better than they had me. After the army camp, kitchen work was nothing to her; she was the fastest at chores. But she was impatient. All those weeks of drudgery made her crave adventure more than ever, so she threw herself into practice. She was the first up every day and the last to give up each night. Once Bren explained how the brothers learned to hide in plain sight, she invented the game of stalking one another through the village. The only rule was, if any adult noticed us enough to ask what we were doing, we lost and had to start over.

Once each of us had managed a number of successful captures, Deon was ready to leave for Miraleste. But Innon wasn't. Thorough by nature, he insisted on teaching us some rudiments of sword fighting. So we lined up in the far end of the garden, and he handed us sword-length sticks. Deon started right in jabbing and slashing.

"Now, listen. You'll get the basic moves, but don't think

you can defeat anyone who knows how to use a sword, because you can't. *I* can't, and I've been practicing since I was little. There's a huge difference between dueling, which has all these rules, and real fighting, which doesn't have any. What you *can* do is learn to block, giving you time to think of some other way to get something solid between you and the other person's steel."

Deon sighed. But Bren nodded grimly—he'd seen the truth of Innon's words that first night, when Peitar and I were with poor Bernal in the palace garrison.

So each morning before breakfast we sneaked to the far end of the garden to practice with our fake swords.

Tsauderei had gotten us another defense: a brace of throwing knives. After sword practice, we took turns hurling the knives into a dead tree at the edge of the garden, going farther and farther back from the target as our accuracy improved. Bren, with his keen eye, was the best. I was worst. My arms ached. My whole body ached, at first.

I was much better with Tsauderei's picks and locks. Each night, when we had finished cleaning the kitchen, we went up to the roof. The mage had shown us the basics, and we practiced until we could open the locks blindfolded. We learned about all of the different kinds, how to tell them apart by feel, and how to be fast and accurate.

Next came clothes and travel packs. I made the packs out of extra fabric I found in the linen cupboard. Innon worked on the boys' clothes, and Deon adapted a few of Mother's flying outfits for the two of us. The fabric was dark, because the brothers said that dark clothes kept you invisible in shadows. Both she and Innon put in plenty of pockets.

Bren had the steadiest hands, so he was in charge of glass-cutting, with a special tool that was so sharp that one careless touch would make your finger bleed for half a day and hurt for two more. Tsauderei had given it to him, along with a spell that repaired glass, so Bren practiced at his house.

The mage was pleased with our preparations, except for one thing: Deon could read slowly, but she was barely able to write. Even Derek hadn't been able to get her to work on it.

"You might have to send a note," Tsauderei said to her one day. "Or receive one. Why don't you ask Lizana for lessons? She's one of the best teachers I know." Deon didn't say anything, just scowled at her bare toes.

As soon as we left, Bren said, "That's a great idea about Lizana."

"No, it isn't." Deon shot into the air. "It's boring! I want to spend my free time with the village kids. I haven't learned half of their songs yet, and they love the ones I made up."

"Writing lessons might keep Lizana from getting suspicious about everything else," Innon said.

"I'll keep you company," I said to her. "I'm still working on some of Tsauderei's books, but they're slow going. Let's ask her to help after breakfast, if she doesn't mind."

"Why should she mind?" Deon asked, with one of her

sudden changes of mood. "What else does she have to do? *We* do all the housework."

"She writes a lot of letters," Innon said, flying beside her. "And she has one of those magical letter cases that my parents used to have, before all the magic wore out."

"I'll bet you Tsauderei gave it to her," I said. "Maybe she writes to her sister. Or Deveral. Anyway, ask her—then she might think you're spending your afternoons practicing."

Deon did, and Lizana seemed pleased. We added tutoring in the mornings. Everybody joined in, so Deon wouldn't feel alone. I toiled away at Adamas Dei, though I didn't understand half of what I read; Innon worked through some books about guilds and treaties; and Bren finished *Our Provident Careers*.

There was only one bad moment, a morning when Deon was taking a very long time to copy something out, and I puzzled over Adamas Dei's words about how different cultures view the world. *Isn't there one way to view the world*, I was thinking, *the true way?*

Lizana had been watching while she waited for Deon to finish. She said, "That's a difficult book, Lilah. What made you choose it?"

"A friend," I said. Which was the truth.

"You mean a friend who lives in an old cottage?"

"Yes! Did Tsauderei tell you about my visits?"

She gave an approving nod, and I thought, *She sees more than we think she does.*

From then on, the four of us took extra precautions when we went to practice, never leaving through the same door, or at the same time.

The days became weeks and settled into a routine, and although we worked hard, our goal in mind, each of us made sure to save time for what we liked best. I continued to visit Atan, Deon went to the village to trade songs, and Bren drew. Innon not only swam but took flying trips to collect Lure in a waterproof bag. He would hold his breath, swoop down, and pick a blossom or two—but it made him tired, so he could gather only a few each day.

Then he insisted that we all practice getting used to the Lure. We tried. At first breath, we felt invincible, but after the second and third, that quickly turned to silliness, then wooziness, and we barely made it home to fall asleep. The next day, we all had headaches.

"This is taking too much of our time! Why not just let Innon be in charge of the Lure. He knows the most about it, anyway," Deon said.

"I'd rather be practicing lock-picking anyway," added Bren, and I agreed, even though I could tell that cautious Innon was disappointed.

Then after almost a month of hard work came the morning when Bren finally finished *Our Provident Careers*. He returned it to the library and waited until Deon's lesson was over. "Let's all go swimming," he said.

Halfway to the lake, we stopped to talk, hovering in

midair. "I think we're ready. How about the rest of you?"

"Yes!" Deon said, somersaulting happily.

Innon was silent. I had a feeling we could practice for years and it wouldn't be enough for him. "I've been worrying more and more," I said. "Let's go."

He sighed. "All right."

Later, when I told Tsauderei, he gave me that narrow gaze, then nodded shortly. "Come here in the morning. I'll have breakfast waiting, and some other things."

The last person I talked to was Atan. "Fare well," she said, clasping my hands. Gehlei stayed in the background. "When it's over, you'll return and see me, won't you?" And when I'd promised, she said with a wistful smile, "I'll want to hear everything. I can read forever, but there's nothing like experience—someone else's, if I can't yet have my own."

I wanted to say "Your time is coming," but, mindful of Gehlei, I stayed silent.

When I got back, I visited my mother's portrait. I thought, *Tomorrow we go, Mother. And I will try to help Peitar. And I'll try to make sure Uncle Darian doesn't see me. Not because of his feelings. I don't really believe he has any. But because of yours—in the past.*

Mother smiled gently, as she always did.

So watch over us, if you can.

I STILL REMEMBER that last dinner. I'd look at my food and the peaceful kitchen, and I couldn't really believe I was about to leave. My body knew it, because my middle was a wad of knots.

Deon and Bren traded off telling one of Derek's best stories. Even Lizana listened, smiling faintly, as she moved about the kitchen, for it was her turn to cook.

When the evening ended and she'd said nothing at all, despite our behavior (including a million hints that Deon couldn't resist dropping, because she loved having a secret), I wondered if Lizana had her own plan. I hoped it didn't concern us—that we wouldn't wake up and find ourselves turned into potted plants, statues, or something, to keep us from leaving.

I had my Larei clothes and the travel pack with my extra outfit and blankets, my fashion book, and two pens and a bottle of ink I had taken from Mother's desk.

The last thing I did that night was cut Deon's hair. Afterward, she took a bath and combed it back, like the boys'. I left my own until morning, just in case Lizana checked on us. At first I was afraid we wouldn't be able to get to sleep, but excitement had tired me out.

It was dawn before I knew it. Since I was always the first awake, I'd been appointed to rouse everyone. I bathed, dressed in my tunic and knee-pants, and then, instead of brushing out my mane, I used the scissors from the desk to hack it off.

How light my head felt! I ruffled my hair, glorying in the freedom.

Then I looked in the mirror. The Larei staring back was different from the early days. My face seemed a different shape. My skin was tanned, and the brown in my hair had lightened, making the red seem brighter. My eyes and brows seemed more slanted than ever, reminding me of my father, and I felt a pang of sorrow.

I looked little enough like Lilah that I didn't think a glimpse would give me away.

Then I tied my cut-off hair and Deon's into a knot and put it into the pack. I poked Deon, who was up and dressed in an eye-blink. After putting the bedding through the cleaning frame and tidying the room, I went to quietly waken the boys.

As we left for Tsauderei's, I looked down at Irad House through the blue-gray morning shadows, my throat tightening. What would Lizana think when Tsauderei told her? I was tempted to write a note, but what would I say?

But excitement crowded out my grief, for the other three were lively, Deon most of all.

"Breakfast is ready, brats," the old mage said when we arrived.

We hurried through the meal. Then Tsauderei said, "Innon, you should be in charge of this, for you're the least likely to lose it." He held out a small cloth bag. "I'll teach all of you the spell, in case you can't find food. You'll always get a loaf of that nutbread they make in Diannah Forest."

"By magic?" Bren asked. "How does that work?"

"It's a very difficult series of spells, drawing on supplies they keep in Diannah," Tsauderei said. "You've got a dozen uses at most before they wear out. So use it only when you really need it." After we learned the spell, he brought out another precious object. "Now, who wants to carry this glowglobe? I trust you know how to be very careful with it."

"Me! Me!" Deon exclaimed. "I promise I'll take good care of it."

Innon tucked the bag away, Deon carefully wrapped the glowglobe in her spare outfit, while Bren stowed the remains of our breakfast.

"Now, Lilah." Tsauderei handed me a ring on a chain. "This is because it's too big for your finger, and it might call attention to you."

"All right," I said, slipping the chain over my head and dropping the ring down the front of my tunic. The ring was cold against my skin.

"If you are in danger of losing your life, you hold it like so." He demonstrated. "Then repeat this spell." I repeated the words until he was satisfied. "It's what you might call a summons ring. It will alert me and give me a destination to focus on. I can transport you out—just you, if you are alone, but all of you, if you are hand in hand. Guard it well."

"I will," I promised.

He made sure he had our full attention before he continued. "Remember, my Sharadan brothers. There is no such thing as slam justice—not if 'slam' means force. Do what you can to help, but if things come to violence, *get out*."

Before we left, I turned to the mage. "I feel bad about fooling Lizana."

Tsauderei gave me a nod of approval. "I will tell her about our agreement, and also what you just said."

I was a little heartsick as we soared up and up and the valley dwindled below, and I suspected that the boys felt the same.

The magic guided us north, and we winged swiftly over the mountains, talking from time to time. We practiced our signal codes as we flew, and when we reached the highest peak, I tossed the knot of hair down into a crevasse and thought, *Farewell Lilah and Deon, and welcome Larei and Daen!*

Then we saw Diannah Forest. We stayed as high in the air as we could, hoping to fly all the way there. But soon we were being guided gently toward the ground.

"Head up!" Bren yelled, fighting to stay aloft. "Go fast, keep your head up!" Innon, Deon, and I were fine, but Bren struggled so hard that he, the best flyer of all, came down into a thorn bush. He climbed out, exceedingly chagrined.

We started down the trail, Innon teaching us one of the valley work songs. It was new to Deon, but she quickly wound up leading the singing, the distinctive Sartoran triplets echoing through the trees, for we wanted the guardians to find us as soon as possible.

She was in the middle of making new verses—one for each brother—when an old man and a young one emerged from the shadowy forest. They were both dressed like guardians. "I remember you!" she said to the youngest one. "I'm Daen now. We've come straight from Lizana."

The men didn't react.

"We need a horse," she went on.

"Why?"

"Because we have to get to Miraleste."

"Why?"

Before Deon could get us into trouble, I said, "We're going to help Peitar Selenna and Derek Diamagan."

"Four children," the older man said. "Are you by any chance great mages in humble form?" I knew at once that he was teasing, even though his face and tone were serious.

"Laugh if you want," Deon said. "But you'll see. We'll be famous soon."

"Famous." Bren nodded firmly.

"And feared," added Innon. With his sun-bleached hair short, his face looked rounder and less threatening than ever.

"Far and wide," I finished, not to be left out.

"I have a fine mount right at hand," the man said, the corners of his mouth quirking into his gray-and-brown beard. "Recently rescued from an undeserving skinflint."

His companion led out a large draft horse on which we all fit, more or less. Unfortunately, Deon and Bren were fastest, so they got the front. Guess where I was stuck?

As we rode off, Deon turned and yelled, "Remember the Sharadan brothers!"

⌄ ⌄ ⌄

THAT NIGHT, WE camped near a stream. In the low-lands it was still so warm we didn't need our blankets. We ate the rest of our breakfast, taking turns at telling stories— except for Deon, who sang a funny insult song she'd made up in my uncle's camp. Uncle Darian was defeated in some imaginative ways that night, and Derek and Peitar were amazed and grateful.

As we lay under the starry sky, Bren said in a dreamy voice, "If there wasn't any trouble, and you could do what-ever you wanted, what would you do? I think I'd like to travel."

"I *know* I want to travel," said Innon.

"I want to be a pirate." Deon spoke the way you do when you know everyone else disagrees. "A girl pirate that attacks only bad people, like the stories about Dtheldevor and her gang in Everon getting the Norsundrians."

"Her secret base is an island off Wnelder Vee," Innon corrected. "They attack Norsunder's ships along the coast of Everon."

"Oh, who cares exactly where. Maybe none of them even exists. My Gran says it's all a lot of noble hot air. But that's what I'd *like* to do."

"Lilah?" Bren asked. "I mean, Larei?"

I bit my lip. "I've spent so much time thinking of what I *don't* like to do . . . I don't know. Read histories? Travel?

Have adventures?" The truth? Right now I was doing what I really wanted—going to help.

"Well, seems to me we're about to have some adventures soon," Innon commented.

THE TRIP WAS uneventful. We met some patrols as we got closer to Miraleste, but after a few brief questions—we claimed to be looking for work, which was true enough—they let us go.

On the fourth morning we began meeting more road traffic. Mindful of the horse's welfare—we wouldn't be able to keep it, and it wasn't fair to let either rioters or warriors capture it—we let it go and walked the last leg.

"Don't forget the plan," Bren whispered when the city gates came into sight. He spoke to us all, but I had a feeling it was meant especially for his cousin.

Deon's quick smile betrayed her excitement, but she kept a steady pace as Innon hefted his bag over his shoulder. I swallowed and wiped my sweaty hands. Up on the gates, warriors moved back and forth, watching the crowd of slow-moving wagons and people going to and from market. No one paid us the least attention.

The Sharadan brothers had arrived.

PART III

Slam Justice

one

Our first job was to learn the city. Our second, to find a hideout.

Deon knew her way around already, from running messages for Derek, but she contained herself as Innon made us walk the full length of the main street. Before we split up, he said, "If you get lost, head uphill until you can see the palace, and you'll be able to figure out where you are."

Bren took the west side, nearest the palace. If he was recognized, he'd be remembered as kitchen help. Deon took the north, Innon the east. We agreed to meet outside the Three Princes Inn—no longer the Freedom Alehouse—at sunset.

I explored the twisting streets of the south end, marking the turns and landmarks and noting the guardhouses. Masons, bricklayers, carpenters, and glaziers were rebuilding—but not, of course, in the poorer sections.

All the streets had been cleaned. The foul smell was gone, now that the Wand Guild was back at work. Some merchants had tents or makeshift storefronts; others had combined their shops. Patrols moved at a deliberate pace, watching everything.

Almost all of the revolutionary slogans had been whitewashed over, and I imagined Uncle Darian's well-trained
city guard marching with buckets and brushes, their mail-
coats jingling, as they solemnly painted out all the references to "Dirty Hands."

The sun was setting when I returned to the Three
Princes. I found Deon playing a game with a few local kids,
while Innon scouted the big shops nearby.

Bren came rushing down the hill when it was almost too
dark to see and torches were being set out along the main
street. Just as he reached us, a patrol rode into the wide,
three-way intersection, and other riders and pedestrians
scrambled out of the way.

"Curfew!" a warrior shouted. "Return to your homes!
Everyone indoors by evening bells, unless you have a pass!"

"I've got a lot to report," Bren said breathlessly.

"And I found us a place," said Innon. "Come on, we'll
have to leg it."

We sprinted downhill to the east side, the poor area of
Miraleste. Soon I had a stitch in my side. All that flying
had been nice, but I'd gotten out of the habit of running!

By the time he led us into a narrow, deserted alley, the
evening bells were ringing. We skirted broken stone and
burned timbers and stepped in under the warped, smoke-
blackened sign of a candle shop.

Ash and cinder had been swept up against what remained
of the counter. We climbed a set of narrow, rickety stairs to

a loft. Innon lit a candle from his pack, and we were able to study our new home. "The entire alley is deserted," he said. "No one will hear us here."

"It doesn't smell like fire," Bren said.

"I think it happened a long time ago. You can see how the alley ends at the burned-out wagon yard."

"Looks good." Deon nodded. "Nobody around, already been looted. I like it. Let's stay." Bren and I agreed, to Innon's obvious relief.

"I swept downstairs so we won't leave footprints. If we fence off this loft, we can have light, since there are no windows up here."

"So let's use the glowglobe," Deon said, taking it out.

As Innon hesitated, I said, "They're spelled to last for years. I don't think we'll use up the magic that fast."

He snuffed the candle, and we set up the glowglobe on a wooden box. The light made the loft seem almost cozy. Then we unloaded our packs. I picked a spot close to the edge so I could keep an eye on things, then folded my blanket into a makeshift pallet. Better to sleep uncovered than to lie on the hard wooden planking—but I said nothing, because Deon would be sure to make a comment about nobles and weakness.

After we were settled, we divided up the last of our stale bread and dry cheese.

"Water," Bren managed before he started coughing.

"Communal well just up the street," Innon said. "We'll

have to get a bucket with a clean-spell—either steal it or work for it, because they cost a lot."

Bren turned to me. "Can you get one from the palace?"

"Me! I'm not going *near* the palace! I thought *you* would spy there."

"It has to be you." As he talked, he drew idle shapes in the dust. "See, I went to the kitchens, and Mirah-cook is there. She's not Derek's contact, but she's one of us—she was helping Lizana save people. Mirah remembered me. She told me that they need a spit-boy they can trust. I'd do it, Larei, but you know your way around the palace much better than I do. More important, you know some of the secret passages."

"And look where they got me," I said flatly. "Besides, I don't know anything about spits."

Bren pretended to crank one. "All you do is turn the handle until someone tells you to stop."

"You won't be stupid again and walk right into Dirty Hands." Deon leaned forward eagerly. "Look, none of us knows the palace like you—not even Innon." Innon nodded in agreement. "Think of the adventure!"

Bren said, "You'll wear palace gray. And like you told us, no one looks at servants' faces."

I groaned.

Deon gave me a look. "*If,*" she said, "we *really mean* to be the Sharadan brothers—which was *your* idea—and build a reputation, and *help,* then we *have* to take some *risks.*"

The boys waited, Bren still drawing, Innon studying the ladder as if it was about to sprout wings.

I choked down the last of my bread. "First thing in the morning."

Deon nodded, then continued, "Anyway, the servants count everything at the palace, that much I know. I'll find a bucket with the clean-spell on it."

"I'm going to keep exploring," Innon said. "I have an idea."

AT DAWN I trudged up the servants' road into the palace. Barking dogs chased around as I joined a long line of servants and delivery people waiting to pass the guards. I scuffed through the dust covering the old paving stones and tried to look bored.

When it was my turn, I said, "Mirah-cook expects me. New spit-boy."

I was waved in by a big mail-gauntleted fist and sped straight to the kitchens, head down. I was terrified that Uncle Darian was at some window, watching me.

Mirah-cook was a tall, long-nosed woman with hair the same color as mine. As soon as she saw me, she asked, "Who are you?"

"Bren sent me," I said, my heart pounding. "Larei the spit-boy."

She eyed me sternly, then said, "Sit here. Turn the spit slow and even until these chickens are done. I'll tell you when."

I sat on a stool next to a deep-set fireplace with a big wheel of iron spits and cranked the wooden handle, unnoticed in the constant swirl of activity. There was a bucket of fresh water nearby, with a ladle in it, for me. This was thirsty work.

Mirah was one of seven cooks, each overseeing different things, from the delivery and preparation of fish and fowl, baked goods, vegetables, and desserts to the final arrangements of cooked food on fine dishes. Pages arrived and left, carrying the same silver trays I remembered from before the revolution. Someone had managed to hide them.

I kept turning the spit until Mirah appeared and motioned me to stop. As a young man in an apron began to slide the cooked chickens onto serving platters, she led me to a small room. "We'll get you a proper uniform," she said.

She took a gray tunic from the linen closet and sized it against me. "That should fit. Now, what's your name again? Can you come every day?"

"I'm Larei. As for coming every day, I—I don't know," I hedged.

She peered at me closely, as if she wished she could see inside my head. "*Who* sent you, again?"

"Bren."

She eyed me—clearly she wanted something more than Bren's name. "He was vouched for by . . . two people."

"Derek," I said carefully. She nodded, but she still seemed to be waiting. For what? I remembered our arrival at the beginning of summer. Bren was pretending to be the page to . . . "Lord Peitar Selenna," I added, very softly.

Her face cleared. "Good! I hoped so. This is *very* important. I need someone trustworthy to listen to a very important meeting and report back about what they say, but none of us will fit into the hiding place that we managed to put in just last week. You know where the blue dining room is? Not the old formal one, it's still under reconstruction, but the smaller one next to it?" I nodded and pulled the tunic over my clothes. "You do? Good. Under the table, wall end, there's a door hidden in the baseboard carving. Crawl in there and pull it shut. One of us will let you out when it's safe. Take this and scoot."

She indicated a silver tray laden with bowls of nuts and grapes that someone had set on a cart. I hefted it and raced down the servants' corridors, past palace buildings that had been completely cleaned. Most of the walls were still bare; I wondered if artisans were working on new tapestries and statuary.

The blue dining room overlooked the lake and the garrison. Everything was new and smelled of fresh paint. I set down the tray, then ducked under the table and felt along the carved leaves and vines along the baseboard. It was impossible to see, and I had to go over it three times until a section clicked and a small square of wall opened.

I saw what Mirah meant. As small as I was, I just managed to fit inside. With the door shut, tiny holes in the carving gave me bits of view. A short while later, people entered. There was the clink and tinkle of silver, plates, and wine-glasses being set out. Mouthwatering smells came next.

All but one of the servants withdrew. Then the door opened again, and I saw three sets of heavy blackweave military boots, followed by a pair of green court shoes with emerald and diamond clasps.

There was the sound of pouring, and then, "Begone. We can wait upon ourselves." It was a fussy courtier's voice— the owner of the expensive green shoes.

After the servant left, closing the door behind him, Fussy-Voice said, "Benoni. I trust you'll have a better report today." Benoni! I knew who that was—Petran Benoni, the army commander!

"No," came a deep voice. "Same."

Another voice, higher and more sarcastic, observed, "Are you worried about your own report, Flendar?"

Without warning, a pinched, aristocratic face appeared upside-down in front of me. I held my breath. Just as well I couldn't move, or I would have betrayed myself.

The pale gaze swept this way and that, and then the face disappeared.

A snort from Benoni. "Expecting spies under the table, eh? Do you check under your bed at night?"

"It's my job," Fussy-Voice—Flendar—said officiously, "to see to it that the only eavesdropping is done by *us*. If you'd done *your* job, we wouldn't all be sleeping in camp quarters while the rabble that half destroyed the palace laughs behind our backs."

A fourth voice said with good-natured humor, "Oh, give it over. Petran jokes us all—"

He stopped as the door opened. I heard another pair of boots. From the silence, I knew they had to belong to my uncle. I'd planned to stay away from him—and here we were, in the same room, my second day in Miraleste!

Cramped as I was, I wormed my fingers under all those clothes to close comfortingly around Tsauderei's ring as my uncle said, "Sit down. Serve yourselves. Benoni, your report."

"There's trouble all along the east. I'll give you the details when we meet with the couriers. We're pretty certain it's Bernal Diamagan and his old contacts, though everyone we talk to insists they've never heard of him."

"Then you should be executing the town leaders as an example," Flendar cut in.

"No," my uncle said. "At that rate, half the populace will be gone. Anyone you catch, send to me. Anyone you suspect, send to me. No more summary hangings, unless you apprehend them in the act of sabotage. Flendar, your report?"

"I'm up to thirty couriers, but recruitment is necessarily slow. I have to be very careful, I'm certain you'll agree—"

"Your command structure is?" Uncle Darian interrupted.

"All any of them know are two others. They report to me, and I tell Leonos where to send a patrol."

"Have you given their identities to Leonos?"

"No," said the third man, obviously Leonos.

Flendar's tone was ingratiating. "You yourself ordered—very wisely, I might add, Your Majesty—that you wished their identities known to as few as possible. We don't know how many of the city guard have relatives among Diamagan's rabble, for example."

"Yes, yes. So there is an identifier?"

"Everyone outside of my staff here in the palace wears a heron signet, all copies of my own."

"Leonos?"

"Aside from the fact that the loyalty of my guards has never been questioned, it works so far." Leonos sounded slightly hesitant.

"But?" Darian prompted.

"Most haven't the stomach to be putting civs to the question, especially children or the elderly."

"Flendar?" Uncle Darian's voice was sharp.

"It seems more efficient to conduct my own investigation . . ."

"You heard me: hold them. If they have to wait a week—a month—so be it."

"As you wish, Your Majesty. I take it, then, you'll want to make time for the old man we found this morning? He's been positively identified as one of Diamagan's messengers."

"What have you done with him?"

"Well, we used the knouts. His attitude was defiant, and

it was necessary to remind him who holds the whip-hand these days."

"Go. Find out his status. If he's alive, send word to me, and I'll interview him myself."

"But . . . now?"

"Yes. We all agree that the sooner we tie Diamagan by the heels, as well as my enterprising nephew, the sooner we'll have peace, do we not?"

Scrape of a chair, and footsteps. Door shutting.

Benoni said, "I don't like Flendar being able to whistle up our own people whenever he thinks he's flushed some spy—either he or his thirty 'well-trained' minions. He's trying to interfere with our own orders."

Uncle Darian said, "We all know he's a lying, sneaking weasel, but I want such moling done for me, not for Diamagan. Just see to it that he doesn't get an opportunity to exercise his taste for torture. He's to spend his time finding spies. And we need that done, because surely Diamagan has people moling here. There are probably two or three of them in the kitchen or making beds right now." I held my breath. "Let Flendar sniff them out. You, Therian, are to continue trying to find my nephew."

The fourth man said, "Understood, Your Majesty."

The clink of a wineglass.

Then, without any warning; "And what is the progress in locating my little niece, Lilah?"

two

~~~~~~~~~~~~~~~~~~~~~~~~~~~

My heart battered my ribs so hard and fast I was sure they could hear it.

Oh, Bren, Deon, you birdwits! I told you I didn't want to come near the palace, and here's why!

"No trace," said Therian.

"Never mind, then. If she isn't here or in Selenna, then I know precisely where she is. Put someone to watch the Diannah Road. If she appears, I want her brought straight to me. It's the only way to ensure that my nephew will come out of hiding."

The rest of the talk was about the army, Bernal, and the east. Then my uncle wanted to look at a map.

They left, and I stayed where I was, that horrible phrase, "my little niece, Lilah," repeating over and over in my head until the door opened again, and someone said softly, "Mirah sent me. Are you here?"

"Yes," I said, and someone pressed the catch on the baseboard.

I crawled out under the interested gaze of a tall, skinny boy of about fourteen.

"I can't get in there," he said. "My uncle had to work fast, so he made it too small. Here, we'd better clean up."

We were halfway through collecting the half-eaten meal when a girl in a page's tunic came to help. The boy gave me a warning glance, and I wondered if this meant that she was a Flendar spy.

Back in the kitchen, we set down our trays, and he left. Mirah led me back to that little room, then gave me an inquiring look.

My uncle's words still echoed, but I was afraid that if I said my name I would give myself away. "Bernal was almost caught twice; the revolutionaries are now cutting communications; Benoni is to put out more patrols, but they can't kill people. They'll send them to the king for questioning."

"And that horse-dropping, Flendar?"

"He's spying on *everyone*! Even in the kitchen, and his spies outside of the palace all wear heron rings."

"But not the palace spies." She let out her breath slowly. "One of his snoops is on the pastry staff, and another is a page."

I shivered, despite the stuffiness of the room. "Do they meet there often?"

Mirah shook her head. "Only when the king wants the military and Flendar together. It's midway between the garrison and Flendar's office in the south parlor."

The south parlor. The last time I had been there was the night of the revolution, when Peitar and I were thrown into the garrison. I shivered again.

Mirah gave me a look. "Remember. You only talk to me,

or Nina-cook, or her son Lexian—that's who fetched you. Now eat. It's past noon, and food comes with the job. We'll be cooking for dinner before long."

I was already exhausted.

All too soon, it was back to the hot spit. I was anxious to talk to the other Sharadan brothers, but I had a full afternoon of sweaty work ahead first. By late afternoon, when the night staff started to arrive, I felt like I'd been trampled by a herd of horses.

I snitched one of the fine napkins to wrap up my dinner and some rolls and cheese. Evening bells were ringing as I finally slipped inside the hideout.

"It's me," I whispered.

"Larei!" Deon popped her head up. They had hung an old cloth to block the glowglobe light. "Did you bring food?"

"Food and report." I climbed the ladder to the loft.

The other three ate and listened, and when I finished, Deon rocked back and forth in delight. "You're wonderful, Larei!" She rubbed her hands. "We *have* to do something to this Flendar!"

"No," Innon said, in his painstaking manner. "Attacking him won't get the information we need for Peitar and Derek."

Bren snapped his fingers. "You're right. We have to try to find out who those spies are and warn Derek's people. Heron signet—did that Flendar have a ring?"

"I don't know. All I saw were shoes." I rubbed my stiff neck.

"Then that's tomorrow's work."

FOR SEVERAL DAYS the others roamed the city, looking for people with heron rings. Or rather, Innon and Bren did. Deon spent more time with the local kids, learning their songs—and the neighborhood gossip.

I worked in the kitchen, confident that there'd soon be another conversation of importance—that spying was easy. Mirah never asked where I lived. It was clear she thought I was a messenger. I got to know Nina-cook, who was short, round, and friendly, but I scarcely saw Lexian, who was always busy with page duties.

A few nights later, Bren returned with chalk-smudged fingers. "Have you been wasting time wall-drawing again?" Deon accused him.

"Not any more waste than you and your songs."

"Some of those songs are *revolutionary* songs," she said. "I notice the guards listening."

"And chasing anybody singing them," Innon said.

"But they get heard! I want to make up a good one that *everybody* will sing."

Bren said, "Well, the drawings get seen, too. I made a good one of Dirty Hands crushing a lot of people with his boot. You should have heard the squawking! And I signed it 'Sharadan Brothers.'"

"I don't *just* sing, either. Remember, I got our bucket."

"True," Bren said, helping himself to a drink.

Deon hugged her knees against her chest. "I stole it from a meanie, like the brothers said—a porcelain seller in Five Points. He won't even let kids near his front window! Says we dirty up his nice glass. So I taught some of them my song about misers, and they went to the shop to sing it, and I ran around back to pinch the bucket."

"Good job," said Bren, and Innon and I agreed.

She sighed. "But it's boring, walking around looking for heron rings, which is why I listen wherever there's music. This bard's come to town with a new song, and it's got the prettiest melody!" She hummed a snatch, then scowled. "Too pretty for silliness about a weaver and her suitors. I think I should turn it into something *interesting*."

"I've been following the patrols and learning their schedule," Innon said, and grinned. "The brothers always made sure to know where the patrols were."

"So? Even *I* wouldn't throw things at a patrol."

"If we know where they are, we can avoid them," Bren said. Deon didn't know Innon yet, but we did. That grin meant he had news. "Talk."

"Well, here's what I discovered. The loyalists mostly live where nobles support them. Like Boatmakers Row, over near the fish market and dock. Who buys lake boats but nobles? And Upper Weaver Street—where most of the good flax and the silk goes. Nobles order cambric and silk and embroidered clothes. Most of *our* people live here, on the east side, so that's where the guards patrol. And the patrols' favorite tavern is here, too. It's called the Red Raven. They stop there between rounds."

"Red? Raven?" I asked, trying to picture one.

Innon laughed. "The owner's name is Raven, and he has red hair—like yours. Anyway, he used to be in the guard, so they like going there. And he makes these crispy potato things. I sneaked one off someone's plate . . ." Innon shut his eyes in remembered delight. "We *have* to get some money. Anyway, when I was there today, I saw three people all wearing the same sort of ring—square, with a bird's head embossed. I figured it had to be the heron signet."

"Were they talking to the patrols?"

"No. Ignoring them. Except for one woman, who flirted." He grimaced. "She told them how safe she felt now, and then asked if they'd arrested any plotters lately, and when that disgusting Diamagan would be hunted down."

"Huh. Spying on the city guard?" Deon curled her lip. "What a fool."

"Not if she's trying to catch people who are secretly on our side," I said.

"That's not all," continued Innon. "Those other two with rings? Well, they talked, and did *they* sneak peeks to make sure no one overheard!"

"Did you hear anything?"

"No. But I watched."

"No one noticed you?" Bren asked. "Sounds like you were there a long time."

"All afternoon. It was crowded. An old man was snoring away in the corner, so I sat at a table with some empty glasses and pretended to be asleep, too."

Bren rocked back and forth, drawing little shapes on the wooden floor. I knew he was thinking hard. "We need money, don't we? I want more chalk without having to steal it."

"I need paper." I held up my book. "I'm running out of pages. I might run out of ink."

"I want good food." Innon gave a deep sigh. "Are you getting paid, Larei?"

"I didn't ask," I said. "And Mirah didn't offer."

"Because then you can come and go," Bren said. "I learned about it when I was a page. Mirah doesn't have to report you to the palace steward if you don't collect wages, and so he isn't going to be paying attention when you come and go. And you're still considered a scullion, even if you're not actually washing, so you get scraps."

"That's why it's so easy to get food," I said.

Bren went on. "We have to get our reputation known, and we need to do something about Dirty Hands' spies. And we need a name for them! Something no one will pay attention to, if we're overheard. So, not 'loyalist,' or even 'enemy,' and definitely not 'villain'. . ."

"Buckets. I thought that when I stole ours," Deon said. "It's such a stupid word! We'll call them Buckets." The boys snickered.

"I won't even have to write it," I said. "All I need to do is draw a little pail."

Bren said, "Let's burgle the Red Raven. First strike against the Buckets."

three

After we changed into our dark clothes and checked our tools, we curled up to get some sleep. I didn't think I could shut my eyes, but suddenly Innon was shaking me, the midnight bells tolling in the distance. We gathered around the glowglobe.

"Just as we practiced," I said. "I check ahead to make sure no one is watching."

"I look inside the windows while Larei's watching the street," Deon added.

"I stand guard over Bren while he cuts glass, and take the piece as he hands it out," Innon said.

"And I do the glass." Bren waved the gloves that Tsauderei had given him. "Let's go!"

"The Sharadan brothers' first caper," Deon whispered. "It'll make a great song."

"Not if we don't carry it off," Bren muttered.

The streets were deserted, and in the dark all the houses looked alike. Innon knew when to listen for patrols, so he took the lead. My night vision helped, too. The Esalans had said, *In darkness, watch for movement in shadows, and listen for sounds out of place.* All I saw were cats on the prowl.

We neared the Red Raven, and I could tell from the

others' quick breathing that they were as excited as I was. Innon and I checked the side streets, avoiding the circle of torchlight from the lamp pole. Then Bren chose his window while Deon and I kept watch. He cut out a pane, quick and silent. Innon set the pane aside and laid the cloth napkin from the palace carefully over the edge of the glass. One by one we slipped in.

Now my heart pounded as loudly as it had in the dining room cubby.

Our only light was from the street and a dim glow at the top of the stairwell. I moved cautiously, not wanting to bump into a table or bench. The room was close in the night heat, smelling of ale, cider, and cooked food.

Bren put a piece of paper on the counter as Deon watched the windows. I kept an eye on the stairway, then moved where I could watch the windows and the stairs while the other three searched the entire room by feel, the way we had practiced. Bren was done first. Then Deon. There was a soft *clink*, and we all stilled. But no one upstairs had heard Innon. He raised his fist, the signal that he was done.

In reverse order we slid back out the window, I snatched the napkin away, and after edging the glass with smelly stuff Tsauderei had given them, the boys fitted it back into place.

We ghosted back to our hideaway, where we collapsed, gasping with pent-up nerves and giggles. For a short time everyone talked and no one listened, then I said, "One at a time! I want to record our first true caper. Now. What did you do, or get? Daen?"

"Paper!" She brandished it in triumph. "Some of these are bills, but too bad."

"I can use the other side," I said, dipping my pen and writing. "Thanks! Bren?"

"First, I got some scraps of apple tart, which I replaced with a fine drawing."

"What?" Deon demanded. "Why didn't you show me?"

"You were looking right *at* me. How should I know what you saw?"

I cut through their squabbling. "What did you draw?"

"A sour face, with mean eyes looking right out at you. I learned that trick in the valley. And it says, *You turned your back on freedom and justice, but those who want it are not turning their backs on you!* Signed by the Sharadan brothers."

"Hoo," Innon said appreciatively. "I should think that'd cause some talk."

"So you got the money?" I asked.

He held up a pouch. "Found it on a shelf behind the crockery, in a wooden box."

Deon snatched it and emptied it onto the floor.

Then Bren made a face. "Um, I think we forgot something." At our blank expressions, he said, "Did anyone remember the Lure?"

We looked at one another. Innon groaned. "I sure didn't.

And after all the trouble I went to gathering it!" It was in the corner of the loft, right where he'd put it when we first arrived.

"Ugh." Bren shook his head. "That might have been nasty. I thought you girls had the Lure, since we were carrying the tools."

"And I thought *you* had it, Innon," Deon said.

"From now on, we should each carry our own," he declared. "I'll buy some little bags tomorrow."

Deon swept up the coins and dropped them back into the pouch. "Most of it's copper flivs, scarcely worth a pinch of honey or hay, as my granny says. But! There are four silver squares, and *two* six-siders. Here's for the bags." She handed him a silver. "That should get four, if you bargain. We can hide the money under the table. All we've had to eat were the scraps that Lilah brought, and two bites of apple tart each. I'm hungry."

"I'll bring more food tomorrow," I promised.

"In that case, I think we ought to have a nutbread. What say?" Innon did the magic and Tsauderei's bag plumped out with a soft *paff*. The bread was even fresh and warm. We washed it down with water—"We bucketed the Buckets!" Deon chortled—and settled down to sleep.

IN THE MORNING, Deon wanted to go back to see what had happened—and, of course, to have a private gloat. "Get those potato things," Innon said. "A plate of them costs five flivs. Gives you a reason to be there. But bring some back for us."

As usual, my day was spent in the palace kitchen. It was hot, and everyone seemed irritable. I had nothing to report, but at least I managed to get half a leftover chicken pie as well as a loaf of bread and greens.

Innon handed out the bags of Lure after we ate. They were cleverly constructed of two layers of waterproof fabric. "Be careful—making these put me to sleep all day. And hoo, did my head hurt when I woke." He rubbed his forehead.

I said, "If it does that to *you* . . ."

"We'll only use them if we're desperate," Innon said. "Good thing is, Lure works fast and you can use it more than once. Here's what Tsauderei told me. If you throw it into a room with the windows closed, all you need is three or four blossoms to knock everyone out. You need more if the room is bigger."

"But won't it knock us out too?"

"Not if we wait until we hear everyone fall down. Then we hold our breath and collect the Lure, put it back in the bag, and open the windows to air out the room. The smell goes away fast. There's a little water in the bags to keep the Lure fresh, and we can use the Lure again, but each time it'll be a little weaker. Lure loses its magic when the blossoms dry out."

Deon had been barely containing herself through his

explanation. "My turn!" she burst out. "Raven was so angry! He was *boiling* over your drawing, Bren. I heard him talking to another shopkeeper—she kept going on about how it must be Diamagan, or his worthless, murdering peasants. Then his wife went to the money box and screamed!" She waited until we'd finished laughing. "I just sat there, eating potato crisps—and you were *right*, Innon. They cook 'em in garlic and onion and olive oil, and—"

Bren groaned, interrupting her. "Did you think to save any?"

"Ate 'em all. Couldn't help it. So *you* go next! That woman—I want to get her good. 'Diamagan and his murdering peasants.' *Faugh! Fheg!*"

"Does she have anything we would want?" he asked.

She shook her head. "A quilter. I went to see. She has kids our age working there. Working *hard*, too, and they looked hungry. We could go set her place on fire."

Innon sent her a quick, worried look. Deon often talked wildly, but I didn't believe she would actually set fire to anyone's house, especially if they were in it.

"No, that's just the sort of thing that will make us look rotten, and what good does it do?" Bren said. "If she has money, we could do what we did at Raven's. How's that?"

Sure enough, Deon shrugged. "I suppose. But *you* didn't hear the nastiness in her voice."

I said, "Well, we don't know what the rioters might have done to her shop. Derek said himself he couldn't stop the worst of them."

Deon rubbed her hands, ready to get started. "Why are we blabbing? We'll steal the money. Leave a note."

And so, that night, we did.

OVER THE NEXT week, we burgled three shops either belonging or catering to people whom Bren or Deon had seen wearing the heron signet at the Red Raven. We took all their money and left notes from the Sharadan brothers, thanking them for their donation to Diamagan's cause. Each time we were faster, and even though we carried Lure, we didn't need it.

Bren not only got his potato crisps—and brought some back—he was delighted to overhear complaining from one of the patrol leaders. "He kept cursing, saying that Captain Leonos is being pestered daily for justice by the 'king of weasels.'"

"Flendar!" Deon chortled.

"And! They think the burglars were 'some noble family.' Raven pulled out my note!"

Innon had been thinking. "What about all this money? We can go and spend it, but then we're liars. We aren't helping Derek and Peitar, except to make Flendar's Buckets mad."

"We've got to find out where Derek is and get the money to him," Deon said. "That cook might know."

As usual, when it came to the palace, everyone looked at me.

"All right," I grumped. "I'll ask Mirah. But I have an idea, too. If we come across anyone who's really desperate, we leave them money with a note that it's from Peitar and Derek, delivered by the Sharadan brothers. Maybe it's not information gathering, but it's still helping the people they want to protect."

"That's really smart," Innon said. "I can think of a dozen places."

"Me, too," Deon said. "Starting with some of those kids at Five Points who can't get jobs. They look so skinny, they can't be eating much."

"I'll go back to the Red Raven, and find some more donors," Bren said. We all laughed.

"Rich ones *and* mean ones. And while I'm at Five Points, I'm going to work on my new song. It's going to be about Dirty Hands and his Buckets!"

THREE DAYS IN a row I turned spits while the others spied and left coins and notes in Bren's best handwriting, saying, *Donated by the Sharadan brothers, in Derek Diamagan's and Peitar Selenna's cause of freedom!* I tried to get Bren to put Peitar's name first at least half the time, but he refused, saying, "The revolution was Derek's idea."

Two of those nights, we went out and thieved, first from the porcelain seller who hated kids, then from a rich land-owner who put his tenants out in the street because they couldn't get work to pay rent.

I hadn't yet been able to catch Mirah alone and ask her if she knew how to contact Derek.

On the fourth morning I left before dawn, hoping to reach the palace before it became too hot.

The sun was up and broiling by the time I reached the kitchens, and things were in the usual controlled chaos. Mirah hailed me with relief. "You're here early. Good. Everyone has bespoken cold dishes, and just as well," she said. "We'll be putting out the fires by noon, or none of us can live in here." She muttered, as so many had over the past few days, "A far cry from my youth, when we still had the cooling spell during summer."

Here was my moment. "I have a question."

She gave me a sharp look, but just finished loading chickens onto the spit.

And so I did five rounds left hand, five rounds right, left, right . . . As I cranked the handle, I became aware that most people were working in complete silence. My first few days, everyone had been talking so much the kitchen was a roar of noise. Today, all I heard was chopping, scraping, mixing, sizzling.

When the chickens were done, Mirah said, "Kessah will have a turn now, and you will make a delivery, Larei. Come along." I followed her to a small room where silver trays, decanters, and bowls filled the shelves. "What?" she asked, hands on hips.

"Do you know how to find Derek's and—and Peitar's people?"

She let her breath out in a rush. "I thought you were one of their messengers."

"I'm a runner for other people, who are trying to help them." I looked at her with hope.

"I'll see," she said, and then it was back to work.

Even though the sun had gone down by the time I left the palace, the paving stones were still warm under my feet. Everyone around me looked weary and glum.

But not Deon. When I reached the hideout, the first thing I saw was a flush in her cheeks and an extra curl to her grin. "Two of Flendar's spies are meeting a patrol tonight. At the Red Raven, after it closes. And Flendar wants to be there, too."

"Because?" Bren prompted.

"Because the patrol is going to be taken to where Derek and Peitar are hiding!"

"You mean they're *here*?" I gasped. "In Miraleste?"

Innon frowned. "Really? Then why aren't there more patrols and a worse curfew?"

"Because the patrollers don't know yet." And she sat back, grinning in triumph.

"Now, that's nacky," said Bren. "How'd you find out?"

"Remember that flirty woman? You know, the one with the ring? Her name's Liseon Alafio. And I've been following her all week."

"Wait, wait!" I scrabbled for my fashion book, as Deon fidgeted, but I knew she loved having her deeds recorded. "All right, go on."

"Well, most of the time she went to stupid places—like the dressmaker's. But I kept at it, hiding in plain sight, and working on my song so I wouldn't fall asleep on my feet. This morning she went to a baker's, and when he saw her, he went like this." Deon peered around so obviously that a tree would be suspicious. "I ducked down behind a rain barrel. At first I didn't get every word. Then I heard her say she'd sent a report to Flendar last night, and *knew* he was going to steal their credit. The baker thought they shouldn't tell him where Derek and Peitar were until he arrived with the patrol. Liseon agreed, but there was something slimy about the way she said it."

"We've got to find out where and act fast!" Bren exclaimed.

"We'll follow the Buckets to where Derek and Peitar are hiding, and use Lure on everybody," I said. "And then we'll carry out Peitar and Derek and their friends and put them somewhere safe. We'll leave a note that they were saved by us!"

"Except, how do we carry people twice our size?" Deon asked.

"And where do we put them?" from Innon.

I threw down my quill. "We need another plan."

"Let's just get to the Red Raven," Deon said, in an agony of impatience. "We can figure it out on the way."

"Not all four of us. That's a waste." We all stared at Innon. "Three go to the Red Raven. One watches, the second Lures everyone, and the third is there in case the second doesn't get out in time. That takes care of all the villains—and saves Derek and Peitar. But," he finished, "only for tonight."

I gasped. "We have to find where they are so we can warn them before the Buckets wake up!"

"How?" Bren asked. "Neither spy said where they were."

"I think that Liseon is going to cheat the baker and claim the credit," Deon said. "You should have seen the way she was acting."

Innon said, "We'll find out, because one of us is going to Flendar's office to raid it. Something," he added, "we should have done long before. Since he won't be there, maybe it will be safe."

"Who?" I asked, but I already knew. Who else was able to get in and out of the south parlor?

"Why bother going to the office?" Deon asked. "Since Flendar doesn't know where Derek is."

Innon hugged his knees. "No, but I bet you that spy's report says where she got her information. We have to find that out if we can—we need to find out *everything* Flendar knows, in case it can help Peitar and Derek. And since we know where Flendar will be tonight, this is the best time to look in his office."

I started packing my tools as Deon said, "Since I found tonight's caper, you have to tell me if you like the beginning of my song. You've all heard 'The Weaver Maid and the Suitors' by now, right?"

"Everyone is singing it," Bren said.

Deon clasped her hands. "You know how it goes, then.

"I knew a merry weaver,
Who liked a handsome lad.
'Twas the season of spring fever,
When love makes all run mad. . . ."

Bren made a face. I crawled into our changing corner to put on my dark clothes. Deon said, "I want to describe the Buckets in a funny way that will make them mad, and make our people want to sing it. Beginning with 'King Dirty Hands the Beanpole . . .'"

Her verse described how scrawny he was, his mud-colored hair, and his chin like a garden spade. After she finished, I said, "Did you *mean* that to sound like Peitar?"

Her eyes widened. "What?"

"I thought so, too," said Bren. "Daen, you'd only have to add a line about a crooked leg—and you know that some-one on the Buckets' side will."

She groaned. "I *didn't*! So how can I make it clear my insults are about the Buckets?"

I thought back to something Adamas Dei and Lasva had both said: *Bind people with a need, and the binding is strong. Bind them with a cause greater than immediate need, and the bond is the strongest.* "Can't it be about freedom, instead of insults?"

"But insults are fun," she protested. "Freedom? What do you say about freedom outside of 'I want it'? It's a good thing to have, but it's boring to sing about. People *remember* insults."

"You can say a lot," Innon began.

I pulled my kitchen tunic over my dark clothes, grabbed my tools—including a candle and sparker—and left them arguing.

four

This time, I was determined not to blunder ahead without thinking.

On the way to the palace, I rehearsed what I'd say. I would be confronted by guards, and my only hope was to rely on being known as the spit-boy. When I got to the gates, I tried to act confident, though I was so scared my knees wobbled.

"Who are you?" came a woman's voice, deep and unfriendly.

I quavered, "I'm the day spit-boy. Mirah-cook wanted me back. For the night. For early morning cooking. Because the fires get put out on account of the heat, but when I got home, I was so tired I fell asleep."

My interrogators were in shadow while I stood in the light of many torches, feeling horribly exposed. How could they not see the dark clothes under my tunic, and my tools? Surely they knew I was lying.

After what felt like a thousand years, a man said, "Yes, that's the spit-boy. Let him through."

The gate creaked open. "Don't be out after curfew again," he continued, not unkindly. "We might think you're leading a pack of rebels." He shook his longbow as the other guards chuckled.

I hurried to the kitchen staff quarters, listening at each window until I heard Mirah's voice, and whispered her name.

She opened the curtains. "What? You'd better have a good reason—"

"I do, but I must be fast."

I climbed in her window. Nina was there, too. "I have to get in and out of Flendar's office as quick as I can." Mirah gave me a hard look, until I told her what we'd found out.

Nina pressed her hands together. "Oh, child, how can we—"

"Quiet!" Mirah said fiercely. "Let me think. I take it you know how to get in?" When I nodded, she said, "Come back here as soon as you are done."

I left my tunic with her, cat-footed through the dark halls to the archive room, slipped in, and sprang the fireplace catch. Then I felt my way along the narrow passage until I reached the end: the south parlor.

I remembered what Peitar had said, and listened.

Nothing. Flendar should have been on his way to meet his spies at the Red Raven, but I no longer trusted "should have been." I peered through a tiny slit into an empty, dark room.

Gone. I let myself in, closed the curtains, then lit my candle.

There was little on the desk, so I turned to the bureau. Locked.

My hands shook as I pulled out my lock pick and eased

the mechanism open. The clicks seemed too loud, and sweat prickled under my arms.

Still no one came. The bureau shelves held neatly stacked papers. I took one stack at a time and read as fast as I could.

Then I found one from earlier today.

> *Liseon Alafio's report. I do not trust Jonah-baker, so here is what I discovered on my own. Fionah Blereus, who owns the stable off Spinners Row, sends stable boys as messengers. I followed one and once I was sure of his destination, intercepted the boy, killing the messenger without witness.*

Liseon had found out where they were going to be, and hadn't thought twice about killing a kid to keep her secret.

Anger made my actions quick and precise. I replaced everything as it had been and retraced my steps back to Mirah's room. She'd gotten dressed, and in silence led the way to the kitchen, her candle flaring, which made the shadows jitter, close in, and jump away.

When we reached the chamber where they kept the crockery, she closed the door, bolted it, did something I couldn't see—and half of the wall slid out.

"It was deemed appropriate for you to know about this tunnel. It leads to the basement of Athaeus House. The new family there does not know it exists. Lexian will let you out and back in again. Go. I'll be here waiting," she added grimly.

And that, more than anything else, hammered home how serious it all was.

The tunnel smelled of damp soil and was lit by glow-globes. It seemed I'd run half the night when I reached a wooden door. I tapped lightly. The door opened into a neglected garden, where Lexian waited. In the distance, the midnight bell tolled. The rest of the Sharadan brothers would be at the Red Raven now.

I squeezed past bushes, and then began another long, frightening run, dodging more patrols before I arrived, dry-throated and panting, at the Red Raven.

It was dark and silent. I felt my way to a window—

"Oh, it's Larei!" Deon!

Trembling in relief, I fumbled my way inside to find the other Brothers standing over a lot of adults slumped in chairs, or on the floor. At first it looked unpleasantly like they were all dead, but then I heard snoring. The air smelled gloriously sweet, making me feel brave and invincible.

Innon was leaning woozily against a chair. "He almost dropped, too," Deon whispered. "But it worked."

Bren said, "Another patrol due soon. What's news?"

"I know who sent the message—it's someone named Fionah, on Spinners Row."

"I know who that is," Bren whispered. "We've got to warn her. If it's not too late already."

"I'll do it. I bet she's all right. I bet they wouldn't do anything to her until they snabbled up Derek and Peitar. And we just stopped that!"

"We'll both go, because Flendar probably put a spy there to watch her house. We'll take our Lure."

"I have to return to the palace," I said. "Let's get going."

While we held this quick exchange, Innon muttered to himself. Deon took charge and guided him to the window.

As they climbed out, I inspected the adults. Flendar slumped at a table. I found Liseon by the heron signet on her finger. She was a small blonde woman who looked harmless. I thought about her killing someone not much older than me, and not caring, and I hated her.

"Larei." Bren beckoned from the window.

There was still a trace of Lure in the air. As soon as I had climbed out, I took a deep breath, and my head cleared. Innon leaned against the wall as the cousins replaced the glass, leaving a fine lettered sign from Bren:

> Your rest was guarded by the ever-vigilant Sharadan brothers.

Then the four of us raced to our hideout, where Bren— dictated to by all of us—wrote the following:

> Fionah, Flendar's spies have found out that you sent a message about Derek and Peitar. The people who

betrayed you are Jonah-baker and Liseon Alafio, who
killed your messenger. We stopped Flendar tonight,
but by morning, they will be after you.

> Your friends in freedom,
> the Sharadan brothers

Innon lay down to sleep off the Lure, and the rest of
us left—Deon and Bren with the note to Spinners Row,
and I to Athaeus House, where Lexian was waiting. We
returned to the palace by tunnel, and at the very end Mirah
and Nina waited in company with an older man—Master
Halbrek, one of my uncle's stewards!

"Did you see them safe?" he asked.

"We don't know where they are, but the capture patrol
was stopped," I said, hesitant to reveal anything about the
brothers.

The grown-ups exchanged glances. Lexian looked down
at his hands. "Who are you?" Mirah finally asked.

"Larei."

Halbrek said in Sartoran, "This child is a spy and must
be put to death."

"No! Wait!" I yelped.

"Ah," Mirah said. "So he *does* speak Sartoran, then.
What did you say to him?"

Halbrek stepped into the light and looked into my
face—and gave an astonished laugh. "Doesn't matter." He

had recognized me, just as I had recognized him. "But I think you had better tell the truth, young lady."

The others' gazes snapped my way. "Young *lady*?" Nina repeated.

"Starting with who you are," Halbrek finished.

Trapped! If Deon had been there, she would have been able to think of some good lie—and look convincing while she told it. But I couldn't think of a thing. And he knew me.

"Lilah Selenna," I said.

Nina covered her face. Mirah let out a long breath. "I hope you realize the desperate danger you are in. Your uncle has dispatched people to find you."

"I know. So he can threaten me and force my brother to surrender himself. I heard him say it when I was in the blue room, but I didn't tell you." The adults accepted this, and, surprisingly, no one looked angry. Did this mean they thought I was good at my job after all—not as spit-boy, but as spy? I turned to Halbrek. "I didn't know you were on Derek's side."

They exchanged looks again, and Nina said in a low voice, "We are actually part of an older group. Much older. But only since this trouble have we become active."

"Older?" I repeated, confused.

Mirah gave a short nod. "There are many of us—more each day, truth be told—who believe that the one we once wanted proclaimed as heir should become the new king."

"But . . . the only one I ever heard about who might be heir was—"

"Your brother. The one we believe should be king," Nina said. "Lord Peitar, the new Prince of Selenna."

five

W̲e all had things to think about now.

The good thing was, they fed me and let me sleep as long as I wanted. The bad thing was, they started treating me differently, beginning with Mirah's saying how I had to remember my disguise—something I'd gotten so used to I didn't *have* to remember. And they made Lexian sleep on Nina's floor, while I got his bed.

The sun was already slanting through the window when I woke.

I hurriedly pulled on the dark clothes and the gray tunic and promptly felt sticky and damp. It was going to be a nasty day.

As soon as I reached the kitchens, I could tell that something was very wrong. Mirah gripped my arm and thrust me toward one of the tables. "Get busy," she whispered desperately.

I had just picked up a knife and a carrot when total silence fell. And I looked up—straight into the face of my uncle. Followed by Flendar!

They were across the kitchen, but Uncle Darian's eyes seemed to pick me right out, and he frowned slightly. "Bow," someone muttered, and I almost hit my head on the table, my short hair flopping in my face.

I felt that cold, emotionless gaze pass over me, and away. Flendar smirked at us all, his mouth twisted unpleasantly. He was dressed more like a king than my uncle was.

They began talking in low voices—and then they were gone.

"We have work to do," Mirah snapped.

As if released from springs, everyone returned to their tasks. For a time the only sounds were from the chopping blocks, the hissing slide of baked goods going into the oven or coming out, and the creak of the spit.

Tension made the hot air seem even hotter. I felt like I was boiling as I chopped my way through the vegetables piled before me. I dared not look up.

No one came near me, either, for an endless time, until: "Come along," Mirah said, and we went into the storage closet. "They're furious about last night's failure," she told me quickly. "Flendar seems to be looking for someone to blame. We think you'd better lie low for a time."

They sent me to stack clean dishes in the crockery room, which took the rest of the day. There were many sets, ranging from hand-painted porcelain to the plain cream-colored clayware used for the servants. Late in the afternoon, Mirah and Lexian joined me. When we opened the secret cupboard, there was Steward Halbrek, a woman in weaver's garb—and a guard.

Lexian whispered, "On our side."

In the half-dark, the three adults bowed to me. I felt like

laughing. After all, there I was, barefoot, grubby, dressed like a spit-boy. But they did not smile. Maybe those bows were really meant for Peitar.

"Lady Lilah," Halbrek began.

"Call me Larei," I interrupted. "You have to think of me as Larei the spit-boy." I spoke with all the assurance of the Esalan brothers' experience. *Live your disguise, don't just wear it,* they had said.

Again, to my surprise, the adults all seemed to approve. "Very well," Halbrek said. "First, a request. Will you show Lexian how you entered Flendar's office? A guard is stationed outside at all times."

I was glad that I'd been as careful as I had. "It's a secret passage," I said, and then remembered that first horrible morning, when Uncle Darian summoned Peitar and me. "The king knows about it, too. Do you think he told Flendar?"

"No," Steward Halbrek said. "I am almost certain he did not. He might feel it necessary to have someone listening to Flendar from time to time. So Lexian, you will have to be extra careful."

"I'll be glad to show him. But you have to be able to unlock the bureau."

"I'll see about the lock. Lexian, your new duty is to copy every day's dispatches and get them to Timeos here." He nodded to the guard. "Or to his sister Pirlivah, on the night watch."

"What's going to happen?" I asked.

"We will identify all his spies," said the weaver. "And we will take care to let those spies overhear what *we* want them to learn."

I knew Bren and Innon would be delighted—and Deon would be mad that she hadn't thought of it first.

"You must act quickly," Halbrek said to Lexian. "So that Lady—Larei here can leave with the rest of the staff, and remain unnoticed."

BACK IN THE stifling hideout, I had to take a big drink of water before I could report.

Deon groaned when I was finished talking. "You get all the fun, Lilah. All we did was make a bunch of spies snore. I didn't even get to throw the message through Fionah's window."

Bren grinned. "You know I've the best aim of us all."

"Bren wouldn't let us talk to Fionah's people when they took the horses through the back of the ironmonger's yard and away. Boring!"

"At least Peiter and Derek must be safe now," I said. "I'd rather be bored watching than turning spits, or seeing my uncle!"

"Ugh!" She made a terrible face. "True! I just wish we could have told Fionah who we were. We don't even get to see people's surprise when they find the money."

"We hear about it," Innon said. "It's all over the city."

"But *that's* not fun, either. I'm not even getting my song done! And if you don't want it to be about how ugly Dirty Hands and his commanders are, you three have to help me." She grinned wickedly. "Or else . . . why don't we go to the palace?"

"Sounds like that Lexian has taken over spying on Flendar," Bren grumped.

"No," I said. "Remember what the weaver said? *We* can spread false information, too."

Deon flopped onto the dusty floor. "So, what, we wait for them to tell us what to do?"

"No," Innon said. "Don't you see? It's *fake* information they want spread. . . ."

Deon bolted upright as I added, "That means we can write a lot of false reports, with code words, references to meetings—"

"Always at midnight, or just before dawn bells, so the spies won't get a wink of sleep."

"And held in terrible places, like the bottom of a quarry at midnight, the far side of the lake just before sunup . . ."

Deon crowed. "Or at the fish market at noon, and carry a basket of old fish as a sign!"

Bren smacked his forehead. "I got an idea! You two can write those up, Innon and Larei, while Daen and I plant false signs. Three stacked bricks, a rock on a fence post. You write them into the reports."

"And we'll leave more mysterious signs." Deon rubbed her hands together.

"And coded messages," Innon suggested. "I can make up a code that's easy to break."

"With lots of sinister hints, and fake names of members of the Sharadan brothers—"

"The sinister secret society of the Sharadan brothers." I could hardly get the words out, I was laughing so hard. "Code names. Leader Hawk Eye. Assassin Twisted Nose . . ."

"Blood Knife and Sharp Fangs and Dead-Aim and—"

"Skunk Stench!"

"He's the brother at the fish market!"

After that, it was impossible to stay serious, and I didn't give a second thought to the real enemies or their real tasks.

THAT WEEK WAS the most fun we'd had since we left Delfina. One of Deon's friends at Five Points was a cousin of Fionah Blereus, so we were able to find out that she and her family had gotten away safely. And we finished Deon's song.

> *I knew a merry weaver,*
> *Who liked a handsome lad.*
> *'Twas the season of spring fever,*
> *When love makes all run mad!*

Became:

I am a freedom seeker.
'Tis nowhere to be found.
From king to common speaker
The words of war resound.

Of course, the last verse was about ourselves, ending with, *And the poor get gold and silver / from the Brothers Sharadan!*

Deon loved that line the best of all. The next morning she took the song to Five Points and sang it to the kids there. Bren soon heard it down at the docks, and Innon from two carters at the north gate. By the end of the week, it was all over the city.

Our codes and signs worked, too. Deon spied a Bucket waiting at the fish market. She laughed until she choked as she described the man waving a basket of rotten fish and being cursed by passersby.

None of us wanted to go to the quarry at midnight, but we hoped Flendar had sent Buckets, especially when there were fierce thunderstorms the two nights after Innon laid his false trail.

We had a wonderful time, and we were helping the cause by keeping Flendar's spies busy. The weather was so hot that I was glad Mirah had told me to lie low and stay away from the kitchens.

Then, one morning, we were aware of a change.

Some of the histories say things like, *The entire city was gripped by one mood*. I don't know if that's true, but here's what I can tell you. All four of us knew something was wrong as soon as we reached the main street.

Innon said, "I think we'd better forget the messages and just scout today."

"It's the weather," said Deon. "This has to be the hottest day we've had yet."

Bren shook his head. "Something's not right. Did a patrol ride through our alley last night? I kept dreaming about being chased by horses."

"Maybe I'd better go back to the kitchens for news," I said, and everyone agreed.

The closer I got to the palace, the more knots of whispering people I saw. A patrol rode along, swords out, the steel reflecting the sun. I kept my head down to avoid the dazzle, as well as any attention. The palace sentries had been doubled, and even they were head-bent in low-voiced conversations.

I walked into the busy kitchen. Mirah's lips pressed into a pale line when she saw me.

She pushed me straight into the crockery storage room. "Oh, child, I had rather be in prison myself than have to tell you, but your brother and Derek Diamagan were captured just before dawn."

six

~~~✦~~~

H er words came through a haze of shock.

"Right now they're being brought from the city keep to the palace garrison. They'll be held here until the trial."

"How?" I croaked. "What happened?"

Mirah shook her head. "We were busy with the wrong mole. The king had another one, Halbrek said. Someone smarter than Flendar, by the name of Therian."

Therian.

"I—I heard that name." I thought back to that awful first day, squeezed into the wall in the blue room. "He was *there*. And I forgot about him when my uncle talked about me—*it's my fault.*"

Mirah said with quick sympathy, "You're just a child. How could you—"

"I should have remembered," I said in a fierce, wavering voice. "No matter *what* age I am."

It's strange how you can recall every detail of one memory, but other parts are gone. I remember the exact pattern of the embroidery on the cushions in my father's parlor, but I wouldn't be able to tell you how I got down to the garrison courtyard.

But somehow I did, and no one noticed me.

By standing on tiptoe, I caught a glimpse of the carriage as it arrived. In desperation, I dropped to the ground and crawled through the crowd until I reached the front.

The guards kept the onlookers back as the carriage door opened. First Derek appeared, his clothes torn and blood-splattered. His hands had been tightly bound behind him, and his ankles were chained. His mouth was puffy; one eye was swollen shut. Guards twice his size force-marched him through the archway into the garrison prison.

Then came Peitar. He was unshackled, and though he was guarded, no one touched him. There were no bruises, no signs of violence.

The biggest guard offered his arm, and if there was a kind of irony in the gesture, there was none in Peitar's weary smile, his quiet word of gratitude, which everyone heard because, though the garrison court was packed, no one spoke. They started toward the prison, and my inability to do anything to help him made me furious.

Then Peitar paused. He lifted his head and scanned the crowd.

And our eyes met.

I knew our eyes met because his expression changed. Did he recognize me? Or was he not sure? Instinct, and my fear for us both, made me do what I did next.

I brought my hand up in the crook-leg sign.

Peitar's face shuttered, and the guards closed in, blocking him from view.

Just after the heavy doors clanged shut, the whispers began. Fierce, low whispers, like a wind through a forest— guards, servants, nobles, merchants.

I stared at that iron door, still on my hands and knees, my eyes blurring with tears of shame for making that awful sign, self-hatred for having forgotten all about Therian, and above all, grief.

WHEN I REACHED the street below ours, someone grabbed my arm, and I whirled around.

Bren glared at me. "Why are you blubbing? Do you want everybody in the city to hear you?"

"It's my fault," I cried. "The Buckets got—"

"Shut up," he whispered. "Shut *up*." A few adults turned to look at us. "Quiet. We heard. We *know*."

I tried to get control of myself as we returned by a tortuous route to the hideout, where Deon was silent, for once, her lips white with rage.

"It's all over the city," Innon said. "Everyone knows they got them during the night."

"It's my fault. It wasn't Flendar who was the danger, but someone called Therian. I heard my uncle say it, that Therian was to keep track of Flendar, but I forgot."

"None of the adults knew, either."

"But I *heard* it. I should have *told* them, but I *forgot*."

Innon shrugged. "Who says they would have done any-thing different? Look. It happened. We just have to figure out what to do. That's why we formed the brothers."

"That's right." Bren smacked his fist into his hand. "We've got to rescue them."

Deon turned on her cousin. "How?" Her lip quivered.

"We can't do it alone. . . ." he began.

"So we get Deveral to help," Innon said. "Remember what he told us?"

"Deveral," Deon breathed.

I gave a great, shuddering sigh. "I forgot about Deveral."

"So did I," Bren admitted. "But Innon didn't. That's why there's four of us. We're all good at something. Look. Me'n Innon are the best riders. We'll find horses and go to Diannah Forest. You two keep watch on things here."

"But they're going to *kill* them tomorrow!" wailed Deon.

Innon said, "I overheard at least three separate rumors that there'd be a trial first."

"That's what Mirah said, too. They're being kept in the palace garrison until the trial."

"Then we have time. But not much." Innon started stuff-ing things into his pack.

"So let's get going." Bren rose. "Our first problem is find-ing horses."

Deon said, "How about Fionah Blereus? Ask Camos,

who's always at Five Points, selling his mother's pies. Tell him I sent you, and you're a messenger for the Sharadan brothers. He'll tell you where she lives now."

"You two take the magic bread bag," I said. "I can get food from the kitchens."

Innon's voice was calm, but his hands were shaking. "We'll go through the gate with the market crowd."

"Stay safe," Deon called as they descended the ladder, at the same time I said, "Be careful."

"Maybe I'd better make sure Camos believes Bren. Then I'll start my spying with the Red Raven." And, after giving me a measuring look, she raced off.

I was alone with my guilt. I knew what Deon's look meant: she was trying not to blame me for Derek's being caught. I kicked the wall—and Tsauderei's ring knocked against my ribs. The ring! Why hadn't I remembered it when the boys were there? We could all have gone to Delfina for help.

Since I've ruined everything, maybe I'd better use it, I thought miserably.

I pulled it out, held it as I'd been shown, and said the words.

A TERRIFYING WHIRLWIND took hold of me, then abruptly let me go. When the dizziness passed, I found myself sitting on a hassock.

The cool, clean air, the windows overlooking the lake—I was in Tsauderei's house!

"Lilah." The mage sat in his chair.

"Uncle Dirty Hands got Peitar," I said. And then the tears came again.

Tsauderei waited until I got the worst of it out, then said, "Talk. Fast."

I told him everything—from when we'd first arrived in Miraleste to the boys going to Deveral. It all came out in a jumble full of hiccupping and backtracking. "So you have to use your magic and go get him out! Get them both! You can do that, can't you?"

"I can," he said. "But I don't think I should."

"Why?" I cried.

Tsauderei gazed out his window at the serene blue lake. "I've lived a long time," he said in a musing tone. "A very long time. But I suspect this is going to be one of the most difficult decisions I will ever have to make."

He faced me. "But I've made it. I am going to send you back, because your brother would never forgive me if I pulled him out now—and I could." He smiled at my expression. "Oh, yes. A relatively easy spell, for there are no wards over the palace—and that's the main reason I must not. Your uncle would redouble his efforts to block mages from returning to Sarendan, even if he had to give in at last to Norsunder to do it."

"No," I cried. "You can't. You have to save Peitar!"

"Lilah. Consider this. While your brother was here, I offered to perform some spells to ease his hip joint and repair his fractured knee. Yes. I can also do that," he added wryly, at my noise of surprise. "It's complicated magic, and it would take time. Given enough time, in fact, I might be able to restore the knee. But he refused."

I sniffled. "He did?"

"Twelve years he's endured those mis-healed joints, but he refused. He did not want to risk having Darian see him whole and remember us mages. We will have to let that trial go on. And your brother will face your uncle."

I was crying again. "But he'll *kill* Peitar. I know he will."

Tsauderei shook his head slowly. "Perhaps he'll consider . . . No," he said somberly, "it's likely he'll make the decision to do so. Oh, Lilah, can't you see how terrible it is for each of them? But we have to let them talk it out, even if that has to happen at a public trial, because they both follow the law as they see it: one the literal law, and the other the spirit of the law."

I jumped to my feet. "So you're just going to let Uncle Darian kill Peitar!"

"No. You didn't listen." Tsauderei jabbed a finger at me. "We have to stand aside—for both their sakes. However. There are things I *can* do. You say the boys are on their way to Deveral?"

"Yes." Hope gave me the strength to stop crying.

"Well, then. Let me think, and do some covert checking around. In the meantime, the plans you four made are good. Stick to them. I think you are doing a fine job. In fact, an excellent one."

Before I could say anything more, he added, "And if we do manage to get through this . . . mess, you will be a great aid to your brother. Yes, yes, you made mistakes, but you've learned from them. I fear Peitar inherited far too much of the Irad passion and vision, and he needs a good dose of the practicality that you got from your Selenna forebears."

And then he sent me back.

seven

⟫⟪

I didn't tell Deon what had happened. I could imagine her saying, *So what's the powerful mage going to do? Nothing?* And she'd get angry all over again.

In the long, weary days before the trial we roamed the streets listening, but all the rumors contradicted one another.

Many were about the Sharadan brothers. Gossip had made us into a great gang, spilling out gold like water, especially because Deon and I also kept ourselves busy by working our way down the list of people who needed help. The only other thing that cheered her up was when she heard someone whistling "The Weaver Maid" as a patrol rode by.

The rest of what I overheard was about the trial, and Derek and Peitar. They had been killed already; they were being tortured each day; they had surrendered and revealed all their supporters; they had escaped. How I wished that the last was true.

We were able to fill our days with activity, but the nights were restless, and we often wondered when Bren and Innon would return. On the fifth night, when there was no sign of them and we were wild with exhaustion, we deliberately did what Innon had done by accident—we dosed ourselves with Lure. One flower was enough to put us both out.

It seemed like a good idea until we woke with upset stomachs, dry mouths, and pounding headaches. As I crushed the spent blossom to dust, I felt sorry for our victims—except that horrible Liseon Alafio, whom, at least, we'd never seen again.

Two days later, I went to the palace.

As soon as we were safely alone, Mirah said, "You shouldn't be here!"

"Everyone thinks I'm Larei the spit-boy," I said. "And I need to know what's going on."

"The trial is tomorrow."

"I have to see it. I have to."

Mirah was clearly unhappy, but said, "All right. But as a page, you understand? With someone safe. And you must stay here tonight."

"The entire city will be under close guard," Lexian added. "The guards have orders to arrest anyone carrying weapons. The criers are spreading the word this afternoon."

The tension in the kitchen was worse, with people arguing in fierce whispers, then breaking apart if anyone else walked by.

Thankfully, Mirah made sure that Lexian and I worked far from the other help. We polished silver, and he tried to distract me with talk of how he wanted to apprentice as a silversmith, the different types of silver and the patterns along the handles, and how the pieces were made. He meant well, but it didn't work.

The horrible day finally ended. I had supper in Nina's room, where I was to sleep.

A thunderstorm struck very late. I thought of Deon, alone, waiting for the boys. What if they were lost in that weather? I couldn't stay in bed and went to Mirah's room, where she was talking quietly, urgently, with Nina, Lexian, and Halbrek.

The steward was saying, ". . . no one's permitted near them, outside of the king's personal guard and Captain Leonos. He spoke to Lord Peitar when they were first brought in, but hasn't mentioned what they talked about. None of us dares ask, lest we make him suspicious."

"They haven't done anything to Peitar, have they?" I remembered what had happened to Bernal the day the revolution began. And Peitar's voice, *A reminder of the price of high politics.*

"Timeos reports they haven't," Halbrek said quickly.

Mirah pressed the heels of her hands against her eyes. "We all must get rest."

IN THE MORNING, the heat was worse than ever.

"Eat, Larei," Mirah said as soon as I had stepped through

the cleaning frame. She indicated Halbrek, busy at his breakfast. "You are assigned page duty today. You'll go early to
learn what must be done." *Early to get into place for the trial.*

But I couldn't eat. Instead, I waited for Halbrek. After he
had finished, he led me not to the great judiciary chamber,
but to a servants' corridor outside the throne room.

"Here?" I asked, confused. "The trial is here?"

He spoke softly as he handed me a royal page's tunic.
"The king said that it's easier to guard, which is true, but
that might be only one reason. You have read your history.
Think about the past." I guessed that this was his way of
telling me that he was as worried about the trial as I was.
"Your duty station is up here."

I followed him up the narrow stairs to the second of
the wall alcoves. Halbrek looked down at the assembling
guards, and the servants sweeping and arranging chairs on
the throne dais. I had not been here since the days after the
revolution. "The original purpose of the throne room was
for the king or queen to sit in judgment over the nobles, the
monarch's oath-sworn representatives. As the years went
by, and the balance of power swung back and forth, these
alcoves were sometimes used by the guard to keep control
over those below. At other times, they belonged to this
or that great house, whose leader sat here with a private
guard, a kind of check on each other and on the crown."

Why was he telling me this? I listened, hoping to hear
about some law that would keep Peitar safe.

"Your brother and Diamagan will be there," Halbrek said, pointing to the alcove closest to the dais. Four sentries stood alert and ready where my brother would soon stand, arguing for his life. "Arrows will be trained on them. And on the crowd below. But none will be on us up here."

His voice was flat, as though his words carried special meaning.

Anguish cramped my middle as I looked at the rest of the great chamber. Most of the old banners had been restored. Otherwise the room was bare, except for the dais, now lined with fifteen high-backed, cushioned chairs a step below the throne.

"The king decided against a military trial," Halbrek continued "There will be a jury added to the three judiciaries: three army commanders, three guild representatives, and six nobles, all chosen by the king."

"Chosen to judge against Peitar and Derek."

"Probably true. Yet it could have been just the military, which would be a harsher process. His army leaders certainly clamored, but the king stood against it."

I was thinking, *Derek started a war, but Peitar didn't. He never lifted a sword. And Uncle Darian knows it.*

A step and a faint *ching!* made us turn. Timeos entered, tall and imposing in his war gear, complete with helmet, bow, and gauntlets. He didn't even seem to see me. His face was pale. "Pirlivah guards the access," he whispered, so quietly Halbrek had to lean forward. I remembered Timeos's sister was a guard, too.

"And?"

"Galtos got the message to him, and he said no." That "he" couldn't be my uncle. I suspected it did not mean Derek, either. "He said if we commit treachery, he will not take the throne."

Halbrek winced as if he'd been struck. "I wish I knew what was in his mind. Both their minds." And then he hurried out.

Timeos looked down at me, his expression kindly. "You're here as runner. The other three guards assigned here are not partisans. If they send you to fetch food or drink, you must obey instantly. Can you do that?"

"Of course." I swallowed. "Timeos. What was Halbrek talking about? Did someone talk to my brother?"

Timeos stared downward, his expression bleak. "Our plan was for me to shoot the king if the trial is declared against us. I would have done it, had Lord Peitar said yes."

I was stunned, thinking, *How easy! Why hadn't I thought of that?*

My fierce triumph lasted about a heartbeat, because I knew what would happen afterward: another riot, maybe even worse than the revolution. And Timeos certainly would not have survived.

But Peitar had refused to allow it. He was sending a

message that his life was less important than the law. Tsauderei was right—not that it gave me any comfort. Because there was one thing I was sure of: the adults were just as scared, and felt as helpless, as I.

And they were just as ready to do something desperate.

eight

The three guards crowded in, and after one glance ignored me. I crouched down so I could see through the railings. Timeos stood next to me, purposely blocking me from their view.

The oldest one said to Timeos, "Stinking mob! You should see 'em. Crowds outside the city gates going clear down to the lake road. Selah and her troops drew riding duty. All day in the hot sun, poor mutts."

"Just as bad on the palace gates," said the second. "Half the city is standing outside the walls."

"Other half ran off to the countryside to hide," said the last.

"Or to join Diamagan's soul-rotted brother. I heard they're forming up somewhere out there. They mean to attack us."

"Well, if he tries to get his rabble to torch the city a second time, that's the last thing they'll do before eternity. Orders are to shoot anyone who busts a window or picks up a rock."

"Not a good day for thieves," Timeos remarked dryly. They all laughed.

Below, a double line of armed guards marched in. "Hoo. There's Captain Leonos," said the oldest. "That's the signal."

As the guards moved out in a ring before the dais, I heard behind me the scrape of swords drawn from scabbards, and the creak and hum of bows being strung and tested.

People began to enter in small groups. Guild members and merchants and countless others shuffled forward, some gaping at the huge banners, others giving fearful glances at the armed warriors in the alcoves. More guards took up position along the lower walls. Soon the huge room was entirely full.

On another invisible signal, the jury entered through the archway behind the dais. First were three military men, all carrying commanders' helms. Then came six courtiers in dark mourning dress, followed by three guild leaders. Finally, three figures in black and white, their faces masked—judiciaries, supplied by the heralds. No one would know who they were.

Except for my uncle.

And then he, too, mounted the dais. From my vantage I could see his face clearly. Timeos had gotten himself stationed here to have the perfect shot.

Uncle Darian moved to the old carven throne and sat down.

The people in the front bowed, as did those behind them, and those behind them. It was as though a wind swept through the crowd. The whispers faded.

The jury settled into their chairs, their manner nervous—even the nobles.

There were no flourishes or fanfares. The Grand Herald stepped forward, struck his staff on the marble floor three times, and announced in a sonorous voice, "Bring forth the accused."

A surge of movement in the next alcove, and Derek and Peitar stood side by side at the railing, guards hemming them in, their drawn swords held points skyward.

The herald addressed them: "Lord Peitar Selenna and Derek Diamagan. You have been indicted for acts of sedition—conspiring against the government and the law with individuals of all degrees. And for acts of treason—the fostering of armed rebellion. Your response?"

"I admit guilt," Peitar said in a clear, steady voice. A moment later Derek echoed him, sounding angry.

The herald looked briefly at the military commanders, then again at Peitar and Derek. "The civilians who have requested their right to face you with their accusations will speak first. Because of your admission of guilt, the military has waived the right to enumerate the acts that your followers have perpetrated in your names. You will then be permitted to speak in your own defense."

Derek said, in a loud, derisive voice, "No one to speak *for* us, I notice."

A swift murmur rose from the crowd. Behind me, one of the guards muttered, "Not at a treason trial when you already admitted guilt, you ignorant peasant."

The herald raised his voice. "Cease! You will speak only

at the time appointed." He motioned, and a vaguely familiar courtly woman about my father's age walked forward
and bowed before my uncle.

Then she turned sharply, so her skirt of mourning gray
belled out, and glared up at where my brother stood. "I
hold you to blame, Lord Peitar Selenna," she said in a hard
voice, "for the deaths of two of my children, and their families. I blame you for the destruction of Corente, my home,
my land. . . ."

She bowed her head. Her shoulders shook, but then she
straightened and went on, telling how many people had
been killed and what houses and lands had been put to the
torch.

After she finished, she turned her back and walked
proudly through the archway. She was followed by a man
who said much the same. Peitar watched, his profile tense
and closed. Derek fidgeted as though he wished to speak,
or to be pacing.

Five or six more nobles came out, accusing either Peitar
or Derek, sometimes both. Most gave them angry stares.
Some spoke quickly, gazing straight ahead, and a few
seemed uneasy.

The palace bell tolled, echoed in the distance by the city
bell.

One of the guards behind me stirred. "Blast and blister,
it's only noon. This'll take an eternity. Send the boy for
something wet and cold."

Timeos nudged me, and I ran. Black spots danced before my eyes, and I remembered that I had not eaten any breakfast.

At the bottom of the stairs, a bored guard asked where I was going, and motioned me through one of the archways into a dusty courtyard.

More guards were gathered round a table of pitchers, goblets, glasses, mugs, and trays, with a few barrels underneath. "How many?" asked one of the kitchen pages, yawning. "And what?"

"Four. Whatever's coldest."

"That'll be the ale," she said. "Just brought up from the cellar."

As she filled goblets, one of the adults addressed me. "How's it sounding?"

"Nobles. Destruction of land," I croaked.

"That's going to take all day, maybe all night, too," someone else said.

"Days!" a lounging footman exclaimed. "They haven't even gotten to Master Gasbag of the Guild. You watch. If *he* gets up there, he'll drone on for four bells, all on his own."

I picked up the loaded tray and walked carefully to the inner hall, paused, and had a quick sip of ale to kill my thirst before I started up.

The guards took the goblets, and once again I crouched down. A pretty young woman came out, her golden hair done in the latest court style. She began in a high, hard voice.

"I accuse you traitors of the deaths of my dear cousins—"

"You lie." Derek's voice echoed off the opposite walls. "That's a lie, Lady Farleon! You and your slithering lover—"

"Cease!" the herald roared above the sudden hisses of the crowd. "If you speak again before your turn, you forfeit the right to defense!"

Derek lifted a fist, not in threat, but in frustration. The guards stepped close. The woman scowled at him, put her nose in the air, and told how his people had killed everyone in her cousins' holding, finishing quickly when the hissing started.

After her came someone I recognized—Great-Aunt Tislah, who'd tried the hardest to force me to be my uncle's pet so many years ago.

Now she said in a shaking, venomous voice, "I speak in the name of my kin by marriage, the Selennas. And on behalf of Lady Lilah, who is a mere child. In her name I accuse you of causing the murder of your father. And where is your sister, I ask you, *Lord Peitar Selenna*? Have you done away with her, too?"

I almost cried out. Timeos's leg pressed against my back in warning, but I had already bitten my lip, hard. I felt my heart would break in pieces and fall smoking to the floor.

Aunt Tislah cawed on, describing the destruction of Selenna lands, and finished by accusing Peitar of wanting to take our father's princedom as a step toward challenging the crown.

She was the last of the nobles. There was a pause, and then a huge man dressed in brocade and velvet, wearing a great gold chain, strutted importantly onto the dais.

"Guild Chief," one of the guards whispered. "That fool will keep us broiling here a week."

So this was Master Gasbag. He unrolled a great scroll, harrumphed, and began a slow string of compliments to Uncle Darian and the courtiers on the jury. They looked restless, and the people below rustled and whispered.

Uncle Darian shifted in his seat, and when the man stopped for breath, he cut in. "Guild Chief. Please. Get to your accusations."

A subdued laugh rippled through the audience. The chief coughed as he hastily unrolled more of his scroll and began reciting the names of dead guild members. From that, he droned on and on, without pause, to damage done against guild buildings. The sun had moved appreciably when he stepped down.

Others came forward. Some said little; others read great lists. The crowd grew more restless, especially in the back, and a scuffle began. Two guards strode forward to break it up. The accusers labored on. Derek stood motionless, and Peitar leaned on the railing, tense with the effort it took to stand so long.

Once the guilds were finished, there were two representatives for the farmers. From his tight grip on the rail, it was clear that these accusations hurt Derek the most.

Through it all, Uncle Darian sat unmoving on the throne, almost completely in shadow.

When the last farmer finished, the herald said, "Accused! You now have the opportunity to speak in your defense."

Derek sent a quick look at Peitar, then leaned forward. "People of Sarendan. I have spent years traveling the kingdom listening to the stories of cruelty and injustice perpetrated by you nobles. You accuse me of destroying your lands, but I say to you: all I did was enable your own people to visit their own form of justice for generations of bad government, unfair taxes, and neglect of rights that once were considered basic—and still are, in other kingdoms."

A murmur, and again the *shush!* like wind through trees.

"In addition, I saw what you did to one another. I say again, Lady Farleon, that you conspired with your lover to kill your own cousins so that you could inherit Helasda—"

"You are not permitted counteraccusations," the herald cut in.

"Let him talk!" came from the back of the crowd.

"He's telling the truth!" a woman shouted.

The guards at the back sprang forward, and again the crowd roiled.

Uncle Darian sat, silent and unmoving.

One of the military commanders leaned toward the herald, who shouted, above the rising voices, "Diamagan! You will confine yourself to the charges or forfeit your right to speak!"

"Proving that this is no trial, and there is no justice, not until you are brought down!" A guard jabbed him warningly in the shoulder, and Derek shook his head. "Never mind that. I have no defense, because though I made no such commands, neither did I halt the acts. Perhaps I was wrong to believe that free people would band together to benefit everyone. My very first command—to torch the city and destroy its rulers—was obeyed. My next command, to halt the riots and destruction, was ignored, and if one must stand the blame for the actions of many, then I am that one. I, and not Peitar Selenna."

The crowd murmured, then shushed each other, as Derek said again, louder, "I repeat. Peitar Selenna is not to blame. He was under arrest, in fact—closeted with the king—when I gave the command to strike."

He paused to clear his throat. "Further, he, unlike me, was against the use of violence from the outset—and the king knows it, for he read a letter in which Peitar warned me against exactly what happened. And when Peitar joined me, after his father was murdered by a mob, it was to try to bring the violence to a halt, not to encourage it.

"One final thing. And this is for you, King Darian Irad." Derek's voice harshened. "Lady Farleon sat in her pretty parlor and swore that she'd help the commoners in her cousins' lands if my people killed those cousins for her—and, were I on the dais, she'd be fawning on me just as she fawns on you. I advise you, when you dance with these smiling liars in celebration of our deaths, you had better watch your back."

He turned away.

A roar surged up from the crowd. Some of the noble jurors whispered behind their hands, two or three looking toward the great throne.

Uncle Darian was silent and still.

Then came the herald's voice. "Lord Peitar Selenna. Do you speak in your defense?"

Peitar had been leaning against the rail, his head bowed. Now he straightened, and a profound silence fell, so intense I could feel it, despite the heat-haze and the smells of close-pressed humanity rising from below.

"Send the boy for something more to drink?" one of the guards behind asked.

I couldn't breathe. *No! Not now!*

Timeos whispered, "Hold. I think it's nearly over."

And my brother said, clear and steady, "I admit freely to having committed treason."

nine

❦

"That is," he said, "if you define treason as the attempt to overthrow the government. If you define treason as I do—the attempted overthrow of our ancient laws—then I don't believe I've committed treason."

He looked intently at the throne.

"I want to go back to those laws, which have been set aside in the name of military strength. That was the king's abiding goal, and it harmed the kingdom. Many of my fellow nobles paid lip service to that goal, but they were using the tax laws to build wealth and power at the expense of those people they once swore to protect.

"The inability to halt the riots and destruction condemns Derek's and my skills as leaders, but the fact that civil war happened at all is telling. Had the old laws been upheld, our efforts would have been met with scorn and disbelief." I could feel his effort to make his quiet voice heard. "People destroy everything when they feel they have nothing to lose."

He spoke to the crowd, and to the jury, but I knew whom he was really talking to. Uncle Darian watched with an expression so like Peitar's that they seemed two versions of the same man—because Peitar *was* a man. Sometime since the day we'd escaped from the garrison cells, he had grown up. I couldn't say how I knew, or what being adult really meant, except it had only partly to do with age.

I blinked against the slanting afternoon light and saw the same tight control, the tension, in Peitar's profile. He was hating this trial.

And now I understood why my uncle hadn't moved or spoken. It had always been this way, at social events that he saw as his duty. I'd always believed he had no feelings, but I was wrong. Uncle Darian hated the trial just as much as Peitar did. Their reasons were different, but their emotions were the same.

Sweat rolled down my face and soaked my clothing. I gripped the carved marble rails and looked at what was left of my close family as I struggled for insight, which seemed to hover just outside my understanding, like the winged spirits of the visionaries in our ancient past.

Peitar had never disliked our uncle. They respected one another, a respect that had made it worse when they disagreed. Then they got angry at one another because neither would budge from his principles.

Was that why my relatives had tried to make me into a semblance of my mother? Some might have wanted a king's pet so they could get me to ask for favors, but other people, like Tsauderei, and Lizana, had hinted that Uncle Darian's own life might have been better if there had been a person like my mother in it. But I'd pushed him away.

What might have changed if I'd managed to take her place in his heart?

Pay attention!

I'd missed some of Peitar's words, but I recognized his tone. He was trying to provoke Uncle Darian to speech. It was the last chance for them to talk, just as Tsauderei said—just as Peitar himself had said in the Valley of Delfina.

". . . one of our mistakes was our belief that people ought not to need leaders, that each should govern him- or herself. I've learned that the idea of what's good for all is not as easy to define as 'what's good for me and mine.' We need education first."

Peitar drew his sleeve over his face, his voice hoarsening. "Last, my admission of guilt. I made it partly to protect those who would have felt it necessary to risk their lives to come forward and speak on my behalf."

Another pause. The room was soundless. The jurors seemed tense, the nobles looking at one another for clues.

"But dissent will not be silenced. Our execution will only make resistance covert, because the true reasons for civil war remain. Despite what some of my accusers said, you yourself know—probably better than anyone else here—that my motivation was never ambition."

Uncle Darian spoke at last. "Your motivation was idealism."

"Yes. And so, what is truly on trial here are the ideals

of justice, of basic liberties—including being able to speak one's mind without fear of royal retribution."

"High-minded words," our uncle replied. "But without meaning. The truth lies in your earlier admission of your own lack of leadership." His voice took on that sardonic edge that used to scare me. "Had your skills been equal to your lofty goals, our positions would be reversed—and I wonder how much talk there would be about 'speaking one's mind' and 'basic liberties' before you had me put to death."

Peitar replied in the very same tone. "Not so much a lack of skills as self-doubt. I couldn't convince myself I'd be a good leader. I was still debating that when events overtook me, and I found myself in the position I am now."

"So you did *not* intend to take my place?"

"Correct."

A brief outburst of comments was quickly silenced. "Then who would? Your hotheaded friend there, whose ignorance outstrips his ambitions?"

"Derek Diamagan didn't embark on this quest in order to make himself into a king," Peitar replied.

"So what you are saying is that you two high-minded revolutionaries ripped apart this realm in order to put who on the throne—his horse-coper brother? Your little sister, whose single goal in life appears to be the escape of her social duties in order to climb trees?" A murmur of laughter. My face burned. "Or did you intend to select one of the kitchen staff, or perhaps a bricklayer, as sufficiently humble to rule a kingdom?"

More laughter, some of it derisive. The noble jurors were the loudest.

Darian said, "Do you consider yourself to be a good prospect for a king?"

"No." A pause. "But I believe I would be better for the kingdom than you are. As would countless others, including some of your servants."

This time the laughter was so loud that the herald had to bang his staff on the floor. The sharp sound echoed up the stone walls, and the voices died away.

Peitar addressed the crowd. "It grieves me," he said in a tone of rebuke, "that my words are perceived as insult. Why can't we value those whose hearts and minds are gifted with insight, whose wisdom might otherwise benefit everyone, just because they've been born to the wrong family? How many potential leaders have been forced to become shoemakers or wagoneers because their families owned no land? There are many, I can tell you, because I've talked to them." Now he turned to our uncle. "Some agreed with me, others did not. The debate of ideas can lead to better ideas. When it doesn't—well, one thing I've begun to learn is what many of your servants have been forced to learn, which is compromise."

His choice of word—*servants*, not *subjects*—sharpened my attention.

"You think," Darian said, his voice hard, "that there is no compromise in ruling?"

Peitar said swiftly, "I know I lack experience. But I've spent my whole life observing, and I say that *your* compromises are only with yourself, not with the people you govern. You ceased to respect the needs of your subjects years ago—the day that you forbade your truest and most loyal servant to interfere, because she had dared to voice a protest." He had to be talking about Lizana!

"Your chief priority has been to build a powerful military defense against Norsunder, but the price has been paid by the people, not the crown. I believe the threat is real, but I also believe that when the infamous Norsundrian commander Detlev does turn his eyes this way, he will not have to come with armies and death-dealing magic, because he'll find his own lack of ideals and an angry populace ready for recruitment. We have managed to make ourselves part of Norsunder all on our own."

Which was just what Mother had said in her diary.

Uncle Darian tightened his hands on the arms of the throne. "All this commentary circles the real question: would you take my place, had you the chance?"

Peitar seemed to look past our uncle, past the throne room's walls, and I knew he was making up his mind. Then the moment passed, and I could see in his stillness that the inner debate was over.

"Yes," he said.

The king addressed Derek. "And you, Diamagan. Were you to have the chance to take my throne, would you?"

"Only if Peitar were dead." Derek came forward to stand beside my brother. "Because I swear that there is none better suited in this entire kingdom than he."

"Then there is nothing more to be said, is there?"

At a gesture from my uncle, the herald again brought down his staff and announced, "The jury will withdraw to determine judgment."

In the prisoners' alcove, the guards moved toward Peitar and Derek, but Uncle Darian stopped them. "A moment," he said.

The guards halted, and so did the judges. The king waved them on, and when the last had passed, he looked up and asked conversationally, as if everyone stood around in a garden and there was no trial or guards or threats of executions, "Have you been masking some of your efforts under the alias Sharadan brothers?"

Peitar's reply was just as casual. He smiled. "No. I wish I knew who they were."

"As do I." Uncle Darian nodded at the guards, and they took Peitar and Derek out. And then my uncle, too, was gone.

Timeos gave me a strained look. "Can you nip out and get something cold?"

Down in the courtyard, I took a long drink of water. Then I loaded my tray and started back, my head throbbing

344 ஐ *Sherwood Smith*

counterpoint to my steps. Where were the boys and Deveral? If ever Peitar needed help, it was now.

The guards were quick to relieve me of my burden. One said, annoyed, "No one is going to get a wink until those two are dead. We'll be on day-and-night watches."

The oldest refreshed himself before he replied. "Guard duty is better than marching in the heat, looking for Diamagan's rabble."

"That'll be next," the last said dourly. "You wait." He glowered down at the waiting crowd. Some had gathered in small groups, and others munched away, having come prepared with provisions. The light shafts were now weak ochre lances against the walls opposite the dais. It was almost sunset.

I wanted to be here, I thought, clenching my fist. Peitar had tried to talk me out of it. Tsauderei, too. Only Atan hadn't, because she recognized a kindred spirit, although her task—the freeing of Sartor from Norsunder—was worlds beyond mine.

And I was unable to protect my one brother from our own uncle.

Then the herald came out, and the guards brought Derek and Peitar back in. Every warrior in the throne room stood with sword at the ready.

There was a tense, expectant silence as the jury returned. They remained standing until my uncle emerged. After they were all seated, the herald announced, "The judiciaries have finished polling the jury. They will now pass judgment."

The three masked judiciaries all raised their hands and touched the black sides of their masks.

The herald struck his staff—this time it seemed to crack inside my skull. "Lord Peitar Selenna and Derek Diamagan. The judgment is that you have committed treason, for which the sentence is death. The sentence is to be carried out at dawn."

ten

Deon cried with noisy, angry abandon. "Stupid, cursed Innon! *Stupid, rotten Bren!* Why can't they be here! I'll kick them all around the city!" She buried her face in her arms.

After the other guards had left the alcove, Timeos had seen my face. His expression echoed my own. "Go," he said, and I ran.

Now I was crouched over my fashion book, staring down at the most recent entry, the day before Derek and Peitar were taken. My description of our "secret" messages was no longer funny, and I hated the sight of the last note from the Sharadan brothers.

I wanted to destroy it all, but that wouldn't change the triumph we'd felt in fooling the Buckets any more than it would change the helpless anger and sorrow we felt now. And Peitar had called it a valuable record. *What's valuable are the words he spoke*, I thought. *Those should be in the record.*

The ink blotched and my letters scrawled and skittered over the paper. I wrote as quickly as I could, ignoring code words and secret symbols. I had to get it all down— the heat, the sound of the crowd—the way the speakers accused Peitar and Derek. How Timeos's knee had pressed into my back when my name was mentioned. Most of all, Peitar's words, and his determination—so like our uncle's. I set down every detail because I knew the story behind Peitar's and Derek's unjust deaths would vanish from the version of history my uncle's scribes would write.

When I finished, my hand aching, it was full dark. I looked up, and the glowglobe picked out the gleam of tears in Deon's eyes. "We have to be there," she said.

I took the book along with my tools and my bag of Lure. Having Peitar's words close to me was a small comfort.

We hurried to Athaeus House, hiding when we had to. Deon tried to distract me by asking about the trial. I got to Uncle Darian's mention of the Sharadan brothers, and she gave a watery laugh. "*We're* the brothers," she said with resolve. "We have to think of something."

I used my lock pick to open the basement door, and we hurried through the tunnel to the dark, empty palace kitchen and crept through the hall to the servants' wing. A sliver of light no wider than a nail trimming glowed at the base of Nina's door. I tapped softly.

"Who wakens me?"

"Larei," I whispered. The door opened. They were all there. "This is my friend Daen. We couldn't sleep."

We'd just found a place to sit when there was another tap at the door. The newcomer was a familiar guard in full uniform—Pirlivah, Timeos's sister.

"Though you'd want a report," she said abruptly. "Bernal Diamagan's just sent a threat to the king—if he goes through with the execution, Bernal will torch the city and leave nothing standing."

"Now the king will *have* to let Derek and Peitar go," Deon whispered.

"Not Uncle Darian," I said bitterly. "Threats would just make him madder than he is already."

"Lady Lilah is right." Pirlivah sighed. "The city guard is to oversee the execution and hold the city. Bernal's people plan to attack on the east side—they hope the poor will join them. After the execution, the king is going to ride there, meet up with the assembling army, and personally take command. The orders are to put all Bernal's people to the sword." She looked miserable. "The only one who's been able to get near the prisoners is Captain Leonos. And Flendar has been bragging about how Therian knew where Derek and Lord Peitar were a week before their capture. The king wanted the army here before they grabbed them."

"Then we have lost." Halbrek was bleak. "We've lost."

"But people are out there, beyond the city gates, keeping watch," Lexian said. "Hundreds and hundreds of them."

Pirlivah said, "More. We're on double duty, no one to get any rest."

After she left, the adults began a whispered conversation

about what the military might do, what they should have done, what had gone wrong. Nobody was able to sleep. My head hurt so much I put my head down. . . .

AND JERKED AWAKE, my mouth dry. The room was dark. I started up, but Deon whispered, "Wait. They just left. They think it's better for you not to know it's almost sunup. I pretended to be asleep." Her voice wavered. "Should we go, too?"

"We—we have to."

I heard her inhale. "Derek's got to have one friend there."

"Here." I stripped off the purple-edged tunic and gave it to her.

As we raced through the empty servants' halls toward the garrison, we heard the faint sound of voices rising and falling in unison—singing. We got to the outside door, which was propped open, and a blue-white glare stopped us short. Deon ran into me.

"L-lightning," she squeaked. "Close."

"Real close." The lack of rain made it the more frightening.

As the thunder rumbled away into the distance, the singing became more distinct.

Deon's eyes widened. "That's my song."

I listened in amazement. Somewhere out there, unseen, hundreds of voices sang the freedom verses—no, it sounded like thousands.

Then she tugged at me impatiently. This was the garrison proper, and forbidden territory; we needed an excuse to be there, however flimsy. There it was, on a hall table: a loaded tray. I picked up a half-filled pitcher and handed the tray to Deon.

We reached the big military courtyard at last, just as lightning flared directly overhead, a startling twist of living blue-white light that revealed rows of silent, armed city guards in efficient lines, some glancing skyward, their faces apprehensive.

When the thunder passed, the singing rose.

> "*. . . and all the nobles lied.*
> *Slam justice for the people*
> *When true justice is denied!*"

"No! They left off the verse about us!" cried Deon.

"They made new verses," I said.

"It's not about *us!*"

"But it's the *people* making verses—they've taken our song as theirs!"

Deon paused, cocking her head, and then grinned.

The sound echoed between the stone buildings, and the rolling thunder never quite died away, so we only caught phrases and the occasional word—and then a hand gripped my arm.

I started so violently my pitcher shot into the air, but its crash was lost in a tremendous clap of thunder.

Deon and I stared into Bren's lightning-bleached face. "Come on! I thought you might be here."

The storm broke at last. Rain streamed down as we stumbled into the courtyard behind him and slipped behind a row of tall figures that smelled of wet wool.

In the next flash of light I saw that the enormous yard was full of city guards, and Uncle Darian stood alone on the balcony.

Peitar and Derek were against the far wall, facing a line of guards with bows drawn.

Someone yelled commands. When the sky lit up again, I was stunned. The execution squad was aiming its arrows at the rest of the guards!

The commander shouted, *"Now!"*

And the lightning revealed his face—Deveral from Diannah Forest, in guard uniform!

"We did it!" Bren yelled, jumping up and down. "We did it!"

No one could see the struggle as the foresters attacked the guards, for even torches refused to burn in the downpour, but we could hear clangs and scrapes and grunts.

"Come on!" he screamed. "We've got to follow—"

More lightning flared as a squad of guards burst through the doors and crashed into us kids. I was thrown into the stone wall, landing heavily on my knees as a sword fight began two paces away.

Derek and Peitar were gone. Uncle Darian remained on the balcony, streaming wet, his expression the same one I'd seen at the trial.

eleven

$\mathfrak{S}$omewhere nearby a man roared, "Huzzah the Sharadan brothers!"

A hoarse cheer went up, and the sounds of fighting increased.

"*There* you are!" Bren pulled me to my feet.

The three of us ran back inside, dodging people walking back and forth or standing in knots talking. We didn't stop until we reached the crockery room, and the tunnel.

There we sank down wearily onto the dirt floor, Bren unshouldering his pack. For a short time we just looked at each other, Deon shivering. "They're safe," she said finally. "Aren't they?"

"Yes. Hope so." Bren's lips were purple in the dim light of the glowglobes. "We were supposed to follow. But I guess we can catch up. Innon will know where they're going."

"Where *is* Innon?" I asked, rubbing my throbbing knees.

"He promised to take our horses straight back to Fionah, first thing. I was to find you two."

Everything had taken place so quickly that it felt as if I had imagined it. My head was still spinning. But Deon's wasn't. "What happened?" she asked.

"When we got to the forest, Tsauderei was already at Deveral's camp—they all knew about the trial."

"Already knew!" Deon exclaimed. "I hate that, after all our work. . . ."

"No, listen!" Bren shook his head, spattering us. "Deveral said they'd try to free them if Tsauderei could magic up a diversion. And Tsauderei said, 'You shall have one. There is bad weather coming. When you need it, the storm will break.' So we rode back."

"And so? How did you get into the palace without being caught?"

"Here's the big surprise—Captain Leonos met us outside the gates. He told Deveral that he'd heard from Lizana." I thought about all of those letters she wrote in Delfina. "The important thing is, he got us in, and found those uniforms for Deveral's people *himself*."

"He's on Derek's side now!" Deon clasped her hands. "Did you hear our song? Did you?"

"Captain Leonos is really on our side?" I asked.

Bren looked up at me through his dripping hair. "He seems to have changed his mind after talking to Peitar in prison. A lot of the city guards agree—they're the ones you saw with Deveral's people, fighting the loyalist guards. Let's go back to the hideout. I want to get rid of this." Bren indicated his pack. "And change."

The moment we slipped out of the tunnel into the over-grown garden, we heard the clash and clang of weapons from the street. After a long while it ended, and we crept out.

Daylight had strengthened as the storm moved eastward. The streets were filled with refugees. People had flung belongings onto carts, carriages, wagons—even a wheelbarrow or two. Rich and poor, it looked like they were all trying to get away.

The only time they stopped was when groups of armed guards rode by. But the guards ignored the refugees. They seemed to be searching for something—someone—else.

"Are they looking for us?" Deon wondered. "I heard yelling about the Sharadan brothers when the rescue was going on."

Bren began to scoff, then pulled up short. We were two streets away from the hideout. "Wait. Captain Leonos asked Deveral if he was part of the Sharadan brothers. Deveral had a really clever answer—it could've been yes or no. If I hadn't known, even *I* wouldn't be sure."

"But if that spread around—" I began.

Deon clapped. "That's why everyone yelled, 'Huzzah!' They all think *we* did the rescue!"

"Which means," Bren said grimly, "that they are searching for *us*."

We looked around uneasily. Several refugee carts passed. We slipped around the back of a building and approached our alley—and there were the guards, busy with a search.

"Yes," I whispered to Bren, hating to admit it. "And our packs are there."

"And the glowglobe? And our money?"

I groaned. "With a note, waiting for our next delivery . . ."

Deon was belly-crawling through the mud to the edge of the alley, where she peered around an old fence. "No sign of Innon," she told us when she returned. "But they've got our knapsacks."

Bren made a face, and I knew what he was thinking. The Esalan brothers had said to always have more than one hideout, but it had been so much work to find and set up the one we had that we'd never gotten around to another.

"Innon might have waited out the rain at the stable," he said. "Or maybe he caught up with Derek and them. I'll go find out."

"He's with *Derek*?" Deon said. "Why didn't you *say* so? I'm coming with you!"

I started to say I would, too, but Bren cut me off. "What if Innon's coming from another street? And walks right into the patrol?"

We were silent as rain splashed around us.

"I'll find a spot to spy here," I said. "If he comes, I'll stop him. Then we all meet. . . ."

"Where?" he asked as Deon began to drag him away.

"Athaeus House tunnel at noon?"

"Don't know where that is." Bren was shivering again.

"I do," Deon said, shivering too. "Let's *go*."

∨ ∨ ∨

I FOUND A good hiding place between a ruined stone fence and an old storage shed, from which I could see the alley opening. The rain turned into a torrent as the search party finished, and it was clear that they were definitely looking for us. They moved to the next street.

I waited . . . and waited . . . and was about to move when a pair of guards appeared from another direction. I was afraid that they, too, were going to begin a search. Surely Innon would have been here by now—if he was coming at all. It was time to leave.

As soon as the sound of their horse hooves was lost in the hiss of rain, I left my hiding place and bolted to Athaeus House. Even as I leaped fences and raced up alleys, I couldn't stop looking behind me.

I caught my breath in the garden and let myself into the tunnel, meaning to wait out the worst of the rain. The walls still held the summer heat, and slowly I stopped shivering. I sat down, thinking over and over, *Peitar's escaped! He's free. But where is he?*

He wouldn't run away to safety—that was the problem. Until he either established peace or got caught again, he'd be right in the middle of things. I was so tired that my mind tumbled between worries and plans, and without realizing it, I slid into a fitful sleep.

⌄ ⌄ ⌄

I WOKE ABRUPTLY, a mass of aches. My body seemed bruised all over, especially my knees, where I had fallen. My head throbbed. And I was starving.

I forced myself to stand and let myself out of the tunnel, into the garden. The sun was out, and I could tell that noon had passed a long time ago. A carriage rolled by, piled high with luggage. There was no sign that Bren, Innon, or Deon had been there, no note.

My tunic had gotten twisted as I slept. I adjusted it and felt the transfer ring. I could have gotten all three of us to the valley—but what about Innon? And would Deon have gone? She'd been desperate to catch up with Derek.

At least I could have asked, I thought, more miserable than ever. *How could I forget the ring? And then fall asleep!*

Should I try running all over the city in hopes of finding the others? Or just use the ring? Yes, I'd be safe at last—and Tsauderei would never let me out of the valley. *I've got to find Peitar. And that means finding Bernal's army . . .*

"Need a ride out of town?"

The voice came from a wagon full of prentices. The speaker was a big, strong-looking boy with black hair. He looked about fifteen. "You can ride with us—we can fit in another." He jingled a coin purse. "And even eat, if we run out of supplies. Mistress Platas gave us plenty."

"Where are you going?" I asked, thinking of my bruised knees.

"East Road, on our way to—"

"East Road?" Wasn't Bernal's army somewhere on the east side of the city? "Thanks!"

I boosted myself up. The others hauled me in and made room in the back.

Twice the boy offered the invitation to other kids. The first squeezed into a corner with a sigh of gratitude and promptly fell asleep. The second, a tall girl wearing a long apron over a coarse-weave gown, walked beside the wagon, her face distrustful.

"Why?" she asked. "You don't know me, and you look like guild prentices. I'm a housemaid."

Up on the driver's box sat a young man and woman around Peitar's age. The woman looked back and smiled. "Crowded yet, Landos?"

"We've still got room," Landos replied. Then he said to the girl, "Like they told us Lord Peitar said at the trial: if we don't help each other, then we're no better than the Norsundrians. Come on!"

I was about to cry, "Peitar didn't say that!" but stopped myself just in time.

"Get left behind?" Landos asked as the girl sat down and tucked her apron over her knees.

She grimaced. "The new *Lady* Jalkenna. Said for me to clean the house and lock up. When I finished, the family

360 𝄒 *Sherwood Smith*

was gone—leaving me to get out on my own. Well, I'll get myself out, and to a new job. Lady Jowl is closer with a copper-piece than a dockside innkeeper." She looked around at the others. Most wore the plain brown tunics of guild prentices. Several had blue squares stitched on the front, like Landos. "You all glaziers?"

"Some," Landos said.

"We're gilders," a girl said, indicating the kids on either side of her.

"Stable hands."

A few glances flicked my way. "Spit-boy at the palace."

"I thought that was palace gray." Landos nodded at my tunic. "So you must have seen some of the action, eh?"

"Like what?" I asked cautiously.

He leaned forward. "Kitchen people hear everything. All the rumors yesterday said that the Sharadan brothers got Derek Diamagan and Lord Peitar Selenna free. Is it true?"

"The Sharadan brothers?" the housemaid exclaimed. "They're *thieves*. My cousin's wife is friends with the stable hands at the Red Raven, and she said the Sharadan brothers burgled them and bragged about it."

"They're *not* thieves," countered the little gilder. "They saved my mistress's sister's family from starving. And not just that family, from what I know."

"That's what I heard, too," Landos agreed.

A stocky, red-haired gilder said, "Thieves! Like the Guild Chief said, only criminals would keep that treasonous coward Selenna from justice. Whom we can thank for our being on our way out of the city, leaving our homes to be burned and looted *again*."

"Treasonous?" Landos repeated, his friendly expression hardening.

"Treasonous coward," the gilder boy repeated, arms crossed. "Never touched a sword in his life, but that didn't stop him'n that bandit Diamagan from sending a mob to cut throats."

Landos said in a soft voice, slow with menace, "You think you can sit here in our wagon and yap out those lies?"

"Yes."

Only when they all stared at me did I realize I had spoken.

twelve

"Yes," I said louder. "Though I don't agree. But that's just what Peitar really *did* say at the trial. People should have free speech. Exchange ideas. But it has to be ideas, not threats. Or else we'll be fighting each other for-ever." My eyes stung, and, oh, I missed my brother. "We can't fight each other, we just can't. Or we'll be all ready for Norsunder to come get us. That's what Peitar said. At the trial." My voice broke on the word *trial*.

Everyone was quiet, then Landos said, "How's this. Since none of us knows what really happened, let's call a truce."

"All right with me," the gilder agreed after a pause. "Though no truce is going to bring back my dad and uncle."

"Well." The housemaid squinted up at the sky as cold raindrops spattered our faces. "One thing for sure. No one is going to do much fighting if that storm coming on is as bad as it looks."

The female driver turned around. "You all right back there? Anyone have anything that melts in rain?" Laughter. Surreptitiously I pushed the fashion book down farther into my waistband, until it crowded my bag of thief tools into my hipbones.

The downpour started. I hoped my two layers of clothes

would keep the worst off, and curled myself in as tight a ball as I could. I was glad of the bodies pressed up against me, for they kept me warm, and I was lulled to sleep by the steady jolt of the wagon.

I woke when it stopped. We were in a half-burned barn, moonlight glowing through cracks in the roof. The prentices climbed out, someone saying, "I'll find the lanterns."

Golden light soon illuminated people stretching, others scouting around for fodder, and someone else unpacking baskets. There *had* been a lot of us crammed into that cart. The gilders stood aside in a group until a glazier girl approached them. "We've got bread and cheese. Plenty," she said.

"Thanks," the red-haired boy responded.

Soon everyone was eating. I picked a spot on a fallen timber near the barn door. People talked quietly around me. It seemed that the city guards were fighting each other, so nobody knew who was in control for sure. Some thought the king still was, others that Captain Leonos ("The traitor!" "No, the hero!") was. The two armies were forming up in the land east of the city, but no one was certain where. I'd have to be careful, then, for I was determined to find Derek and Bernal's army, because I knew the foresters would have taken Peitar to them.

After that, the talk turned to friends and families, sleep and shelter. Once I heard the name *Diamagan*, but then the voices dropped into whispers.

"Who are you?" Landos came up to me. Lamplight from

the wagon reflected in his dark eyes and threw his features into high relief.

"I'm Larei," I said.

He sat beside me. "I'm Landos Gilad. You know Lord Peitar Selenna. It was the way you said his name. Like you were friends. Or . . . family."

Oh, no! I stared, trying to put together a convincing lie.

He continued, with a friendly smile, "I like solving puzzles, and you're making more pieces by the moment."

I remembered what he'd said earlier about my brother. I whispered, "Lilah Selenna." He looked baffled. "My name. Larei is my . . . disguise."

He blinked, his brows knit in confusion. "But you're—"

"A girl," I admitted.

"Well, I was going to say a kitchen boy. But . . . there was a rumor, just before we left. About the Sharadan brothers and the rescue. Someone even said that boys were part of the Sharadan brothers."

What did it matter now? "It's true. Well, two boys were Sharadan brothers, and two girls. I'm one of them."

His gaze stayed on my face like he was trying to read a book. "You're Lord Peitar's sister *and* a Sharadan brother? Hoo!"

"Where are we? I didn't mean to fall asleep."

"We're on the East Road. Come morning we'll turn south into Orleos."

"I know that road," I said, thinking out loud. "We're on the border of Selenna. I could go home."

"You can't go up there alone!"

"Aren't we too far east for trouble? Everyone says the armies are right outside the city, and we left Miraleste a long time ago."

"The army might be spread out," Landos said. "We passed several parties of warriors riding around, searching."

Even though Selenna House had been burned and looted, and held such bad memories, all of a sudden I just wanted to go home. I'd figure out my next step from there. "I'm good at hiding," I said.

"I can't stop you," Landos said, looking unhappy. "But even for a Sharadan brother, I think it's dangerous."

"My whole life has been dangerous lately," I said. That came out sounding so pompous my face burned, and I got up. "In fact, seems to me, since the moon's out, the best time for me to go is right now."

"At least let me give you another sandwich."

"Thanks!" I said gratefully.

I stashed it in my tunic next to my book, and was on my way.

THE MOONLIGHT MADE travel easy. I walked until my knees ached so much I couldn't go on. When I spotted a haystack in a nearby field, I crawled into the middle. It was dry and warm, and I slept until dawn, when a snuffling sound woke me. I pushed the hay aside, and there was a loose horse lipping at the hay. When I stood and laid a hand on its neck, it shook its mane and shifted position. Oh! Waiting to be saddled—that meant it was a riding horse.

I found an upturned wheelbarrow to help me mount, and trotted northward, holding on to the horse's mane with both fists.

When I saw more bad weather coming, I gobbled down my flat, stale sandwich and braced myself. The deluge was soon so strong that I could barely see an arm's length ahead. Oddly, the horse seemed to like the rain. The storm moved on near sunset, and there was a familiar line of hills not far ahead. I was near Riveredge.

When the horse began drooping, I slid off. It walked toward the river as I headed for the wall around Selenna House. With the sun gone, the cool air rapidly chilled. My teeth were chattering by the time I spotted the glowing windows of the Riveredge cottages.

I climbed over the wall and made my way through the garden toward Selenna House. I was surprised to see light in Father's rooms and a distant twinkling, like someone swinging a lantern. Had Lizana come back? Or maybe villagers had taken over the house. At least I was dressed as Larei.

I scaled the argan tree to my room and eased through the now-broken window. The floor was covered with dirt, but the glass had fallen outside.

I was home.

What next? I pulled out the fashion book. It was damp but not soaked. I shoved it under my mattress, then headed downstairs, readying my story. But when I got to the bottom of the stairs, two warriors closed in from either side, one carrying a lantern.

They walked me to Father's parlor, which had been swept, the ruined furniture replaced with benches and a rickety table from the barn, on which was spread a large map. A man in velvet and jewels held Peitar's old lap desk, on which he had written so many letters to Derek. He and a burly warrior faced someone by the fire.

It was my uncle in full war gear—a long purple battle tunic over chain mail, gauntlets, sword strapped over his back, knives in the top of each boot. I lurched to a stop, my mouth open.

Uncle Darian gave me a wry glance.

"I am sorry about your father," he said.

thirteen

❧

"I t *is* you, Lilah, is it not?" When I shrugged, Uncle
Darian said, "You look indistinguishable from most of
the urchins thieving on the streets."

"Thieving because they can't get food any other way." I
tried to sound brave.

"Thieving—most of them—because they like theft. But
we will have leisure to discourse on this subject later." He
glanced at my grubby gray tunic and knee pants and bare
feet and shook his head. "It is probably the most effective
disguise in use," he continued, his tone sardonic. "I missed
you once, didn't I? Where was that?"

In the kitchen, I thought.

"Ah, yes. The kitchen. What were you doing there, as
you did not see fit to make your presence known to me?"

The man in velvet spoke up. "Spying for her traitor brother."
It was Flendar! He pointed at me. "I will wager anything that
you've found your missing spy for the Sharadan brothers."

My uncle gave a short laugh, and the big military man
said, "If so, she ran you good, Flendar, you must admit." It
was Benoni.

Those swinging lanterns—those had been sentries. "I
don't understand. Why are you here?"

"We decided to wait out the weather in relative comfort," my uncle said. "And so we set up our command post here. We will rejoin the army when the weather lifts."

"Command post?" I repeated numbly.

"We constitute the east wing of the army." He gestured to Benoni, who returned to the papers he was reading.

"I thought you were all outside Miraleste. You mean Bernal's people are caught between two halves of your army?"

"I'm afraid you're right," Uncle Darian said, but he didn't sound the least bit afraid. "I suppose Diamagan has joined them by now. And your brother?" He didn't wait for an answer. "Now, let me ask you the same question. What are *you* doing here?"

"I don't know where they are," I said. "I came alone. I didn't know where else to go."

"Until I can determine the truth of that, you may stay in a safe place." He addressed the guards in the doorway. "Take my niece to the cellar room I showed you."

The guards each took hold of one of my arms. They were silent as they led me downstairs and locked me in the treasure room—the same one I'd rescued Derek from before the troubles started.

As soon as I heard the guards leave, I began a feverish, fruitless search for a catch to the secret passage. Peitar had told me there wasn't one, but maybe he'd just never found it. Finally, exhausted, near tears, I gave up, and curled up on the stone floor. I was startled awake by the clatter of the lock.

The door opened, someone yanked me to my feet and pushed me out, to where Flendar waited.

"Tie her hands," he said to the guards, then to me, "The weather is not cooperative. We must postpone finishing off Bernal Diamagan's rabble until we can actually see them. So it's time for you to show us your skills, Sharadan brother. Ready for a game of fox and hounds?"

I opened my mouth, but no sounds came out.

"You will now find out how they welcome cadets at Obrin. You are the fox, and we are the hounds. If you can't evade us, you get a thrashing." He brandished a thin wooden cane.

Up the stairs I stumbled, then the tallest of the guards shoved me down the hall into the foyer.

"Trees are off limits. Thus your hands are bound, to remind you of the rules."

As we passed Father's parlor, my uncle looked up from his reading. My fashion book!

Sick with horror, I stared as he said, "You left footprints upstairs leading straight to it." He sat back, as rain poured outside the window. "I do not have the time to peruse all of this remarkable, if ill-written document. It is very difficult to read, but it's obvious that you and three other brats are connected to the Sharadan brothers." He looked at me, waiting for an answer.

I gulped and studied my toes.

"A remarkable achievement, if even half the rumors are correct. Have you anything to say?"

"You were going to kill Peitar."

"I may yet have to," was the answer. "We shall see. As soon as the rain stops, we will put an end to the conflagration you and your friends so blithely set. After which I plan to read your contribution to the family history. And then," he said, "we will talk again."

He waved at Flendar, who gave me a push toward the front door. Did my uncle know what was about to happen? Yes, he knew. No use in begging for leniency, claiming that I was just a kid—the same thing had been done to him, and at a much younger age, by the very adults who were supposed to love and protect him.

"Run," Flendar said as soon as we stepped outside. "You have the count of fifty."

I splashed across the drive toward the garden. The rain was heavy and hard, and lightning and thunder made it worse. The garden was almost unfamiliar in that bluish light—but not quite. They had to be watching me, so I ran northward in a big circle, laying a false trail. My head ached, and my steps were slow. Twice I blundered into branches and fell in the mud.

But terror got me up again, running until my side was stitched with pain. At last I reached the center of the garden, and the thicket of shrubs that Peitar had made me learn.

372   Sherwood Smith

Glad of every single prickle, I burrowed through, dropped to my throbbing knees, and scrabbled about with my feet until I found the oddly-shaped rock and the woven twine rope. I burrowed my toes under the rock, and shoved my foot under the twine. It scraped painfully, but I pulled with all my strength.

The passage opened almost directly under me. I tumbled in and it closed, water cascading around me. I was safe.

Fear still washed through me in waves. I crouched on the stairs until I could breathe again, then rose shakily and felt my way down the tunnel to where we had slept after the revolution. In the pitch dark, backed up against the piles of treasure, I searched carefully until I found what I was looking for—a big, old-fashioned saber—and used it to saw through the sash binding my wrists.

What now? Where could I go?

I leaned down to find the lantern. When I straightened up, Tsauderei's ring bumped my ribs. I'd forgotten it again! I could do the spell—he, Peitar, and Lizana, would want me to do just that.

But I was a Sharadan brother, and this was my home ground.

So I waited until night had well and truly fallen. The storm was unabated; all I could hear was the roar of rain.

I left the passage, making sure the fountain slid shut behind me. Then I faded around the side of the house until I reached the open kitchen window, streaming with light.

Two guards were preparing food and loading it onto trays.

As soon I heard them leave, I climbed inside and slid a shallow bowl and a plate from the crockery shelf. I pulled out my thief tools. I sucked in a deep breath, opened my Lure bag, shook all the blossoms into the bowl, covered it with the plate, and stuck my head out the open window to breathe fresh air until my head cleared.

Then I slipped out into the empty hall. The downstairs guards seemed to have joined my uncle and his commanders in the parlor, judging from the sounds of talk and cutlery.

I heard Benoni's deep laugh, followed by, "Flat disappeared! More fool you, Flendar."

Again taking a deep breath, I removed the plate, cracked open the parlor door, rolled the bowl in, and pulled the door shut.

Someone tried to turn the knob. I held on frantically. Then I heard the thump of someone falling to the floor.

What had Atan said? *The best way to shipwreck a government is to capture all the leaders.* And so I had. But what then?

The Lure would probably lose its virtue by midnight or so, after which my uncle and his commanders and guards would begin waking up. I knew what I ought to do—I ought to use the ring and transfer to Tsauderei and tell him what I'd done, and then he could find Peitar and Derek. But I was crying too hard to do anything but stand there.

Gradually I became aware of lights, voices, the sound of

footsteps. Torches bobbed outside with a sinister, smolder-ing light, just like the night my father was killed.

I poised to run, one hand on the door, the other holding the ring.

The front door opened and several figures hurried in, led by a slender male silhouette limned in golden-red torch-light. A limping silhouette.

"Peitar?" I gasped, and relief made me dizzy.

"There she is!" That was Landos Gilad, holding a lantern.

"Lilah, I'm *sorry*," Deon exclaimed, Innon and Bren at either side. "The bells weren't ringing, and the rain—I tried to guess at noon—I banged on the door, didn't I, Innon? But you didn't answer, and they were waiting to take us to—"

Derek bent close, interrupting Deon's stream of words. "Are you all right, Lilah?"

"Peitar?" I wiped my eyes on my sleeve. "Derek? *Landos?*"

"He risked a lot coming to find us." Derek clapped Landos on the shoulder.

"I left the wagon," Landos said. "And went back alone to find Lord Peitar. I told the king's people I was a messenger, so they passed me through. I have a feeling that some of them are secretly sympathetic, because they didn't ask any questions. And when I reached the sentries on the other side, all I had to mention was 'Lilah Selenna,' and—"

"He told us quite a story about you and the Sharadan brothers," Derek said.

At his shoulder, the other three brothers grinned, Deon hopping up and down in glee. "We're *famous*," she whispered.

But Peitar looked serious. "So we rode straight here. We stopped at Bren's house to change horses, and he said that two of Uncle Darian's personal guard were in Riveredge yesterday, scavenging food, right before the storm hit. I feared the worst. So I came to trade my life for yours. . . ."

"And I came to offer mine for his," Derek said, looking around. "However, no one seems to be here except you."

"Where is our uncle?" Peitar asked.

"Here." I pushed open the door a crack, and the sweet, dreamy, all-conquering scent of Lure drifted out. "Hold your breath."

Peitar looked past me. The parlor was filled with slumbering forms, most prominent of which was Uncle Darian, hand stretched toward the door.

"What?" Derek croaked in flat disbelief, as Riveredge villagers entered and crowded in behind him to take a look. He moved away from the parlor. "How did you do that?" he asked, and everybody stared at me.

I shut the door. "Slam justice," I said.

Afterward

I was sitting on the rim of the palace fountain, feet in the water, as I tossed scraps of bread to the fish, when I heard a familiar voice.

"Lilah!" Innon sauntered up, dressed in riding clothes. I hadn't seen him since the day after Peitar's coronation.

"Just got back." He sat down next to me. "I was going to ask what it felt like to be a princess. I see it's real torture."

"Peitar said I could take my time getting used to it, but Great-Aunt Tislah's still here."

"She is? I thought you said she was at the trial—accusing Peitar!"

"That's because she believed the rumors that he killed Father, and all those other things she said. I wanted him to kick her out, but he insisted we accept her apology, because she's family. *Pheg!* Anyway, it's easier to wear this gown than listen to her mealtime lectures about what a *proper* princess should do. *And* she can't see my bare feet under the table." We both laughed. "So how was your visit home?"

"My parents are busy overseeing improvements in Tasenja."

"Your house got ruined? But the people in Tasenja liked you."

"Yes. My father and the locals got along pretty well, but there were some roving bands from Helasda. They looted us and attacked a couple of our towns. Everybody's trying to rebuild."

"So how is it, being a Roving Eye?" We all liked Peitar's nickname for the trusted people he'd dispatched around the kingdom. They were officially called "Royal Emissaries," and had a signed letter of passage.

"It's great. I get to ride around and stick my nose into things, and no one can chase me away. I like being important." He pretended to throw back lace from his wrists and grinned. "I like being a Tasenja for the nobles who care about rank, and I like being a Sharadan brother for everyone else, especially those who might want to ignore a kid." Another grin. "You should hear some of the rumors! The farther you get from Miraleste, the crazier they are, and your brother said to never confirm or deny the really good ones—like where we three decoyed the rest of the army while you captured King Darian single-handed."

I snorted. "From what I remember, the rain decoyed the army—on both sides."

"Yes, but Peitar said people want to believe the stories. The truth can go in the records, but for now let people talk.

He says Derek was right about how they make everyone feel better."

Yes, but they also had unexpected results. "People who come to see Peitar look at me like I've got magic powers—it's so strange."

"I was about to ask how things are for him."

"He works all the time. Except when visitors come, mostly courtiers, whose first question is, 'When will you summon the nobles to court again?' Or they present daughters who want to flirt with Peitar and try to become queen."

"Flirt! With Peitar!" Innon thought this hilarious. "What does he do? Does he even notice?"

"Oh, he acts as polite as ever. Then he starts asking questions about the repair and rebuilding in their provinces until they give up and go away. He's serious about no formal court until the kingdom is in better order." I sighed. "Great-Aunt Tislah spent our entire breakfast lecturing him about marriage. If he doesn't send her home by tomorrow, I might visit Bren in Riveredge. Deon's already gone—Tsauderei sent her to a mage he knows up north. If Dtheldevor and her pirate kids really exist, she'll find them."

I thought back over the rapid changes since that night at Selenna House. I'd looked at Peitar, wondering, *What now?* Afterward, it seemed like the entire kingdom looked at him and asked the same thing.

And he'd told them, with confidence. Some complained, but what he wanted was slowly coming to pass.

"So the grown-ups listen to you?" I asked.

"They pretty much have to. So I try not to make any mistakes."

"Derek said the same thing, before he set off to inspect the towns. And Halbrek did, too—they are listened to, but they also have to listen."

Innon leaned back on his elbows. "Well, it seems to be working. Out loud I say that I'm there to gather reports and note anything that requires crown help, but every single person I've visited so far seems to know that I'm also there to check up on how *they're* doing."

"Are you done?"

"Oh, no, I've only just finished the western provinces. Peitar was very specific: every single estate, every town and village. I never knew how many there were."

"Sounds awful," I said.

"Well, that's why I'm doing it, and you're not," Innon said. "Fact is, I'm good at lists and patterns and numbers, so I can tell when someone's trying to blinker me. I really like seeing the kingdom being put back together."

"Derek said that, too." I tossed the last of my bread into the pool and watched the golden and silvery fish rise to the surface. "He just left again yesterday."

"Sorry I missed him," Innon said, and then a yawn

caught him by surprise. "Hoo! I'm tired. Long ride, but I wanted to get here and report."

"How about some lunch first—oh, wait. Here he comes."

Peitar crossed the terrace toward us. He'd had only two visits from Tsauderei, but already his walk was much easier. He limped, but he no longer needed a cane.

Peitar came closer, looking worn out. "Problem?" I asked, some of the fear from the bad days squeezing my heart. I hadn't told Innon, but I still had nightmares.

"No." Peitar's lips twitched. "I studied magic texts far too long last night, and I'm feeling the effects. But I'll live."

And you'll do it again, I thought, but I didn't say anything. We'd promised one another: no nagging about what we thought the other's duty to be.

"Innon! Welcome," he said. "Go have some lunch. Reporting can wait."

Innon called a good-bye over his shoulder as he ran off.

As soon as he was gone, Peitar said, "I will keep assuring you that there is no danger." It was easy for him to read my face, too. "Commander Leonos has already discharged most of the army to their homes to work on rebuilding. And Uncle Darian will keep his word."

"I wish I could believe it."

I hadn't been there when Uncle Darian woke up from the Lure sleep. I wanted to be well away, and I was, sound asleep myself at the home of Derek's new Selenna Leader, who turned out to be Deon's grandmother.

Peitar had waited until we were going back to Miraleste to tell me what had happened. *They carried Uncle Darian to my room, and I made certain that I was the only one there. It was bad enough that he woke to find that he'd lost the kingdom once again—all his leaders agreed to the truce when they found out he was in our hands. I could not bear to make it worse.*

But he could have killed you! I protested.

But he didn't, Peitar retorted. *We talked, just the two of us, after I told him what happened. And when we made our agreement, we walked out of the parlor together.*

Uncle Darian and his leaders agreed to exile, which meant leaving Sarendan. Tsauderei transferred them by magic to one of the northern countries.

Peitar looked beyond the fountain—beyond the palace and the kingdom. "After I was sentenced, Darian and I sat up all night talking. Knowing that you have less than a day to live clarifies your thinking," he added dryly.

"Talking?" I cried. "And he wouldn't halt the execution?"

"It was the verdict. Though he admitted he was angry when he chose the jury. Anyway, I think I understand him better now. The terms of our agreement were precise. I trust him to stay beyond the border until I invite him back."

"I know it sounds odd, but I always feel as if he's lurking around, watching."

"I hope he *does* watch from a distance," Peitar said. "That will keep me honest." I groaned, and he gave me a humorous glance.

But I wasn't in a laughing mood. A growing sense of guilt made me say, "And I've been doing exactly nothing to help."

"Most of what needs doing is being done. I don't know if my plan will work. It's a gamble, and unfortunately the risk belongs to us both if I don't win."

He meant using the crown treasury to pay for all the jobs—all the reconstruction and repaving and reseeding—and not collecting taxes until a year had passed, to give everyone else the chance to rebuild, too.

...tar dipped his fingers in the pool and watched the ...wo things you might consider," he finally said, in ...ice.

... I responded. "That's not exactly nagging!"

... I wish you would write up what happened, ...ed and saw it. I think your perspective would ...g as well as important."

...even want to *look* at that fashion book for at least ...s. Twenty!"

...ery well."

You give in too easily," I grumped. "But I'd rather just ...ell you, and *you* can write it down. You're the one who wrote all those letters. All I did was scribble things."

"I don't think I could do the job you would. I didn't see

what you saw. All I did was worry about whether or not I ought to take action, and once I did, I managed to get myself into trouble from which I had to be rescued." He looked sardonic. "Don't waste time denying it."

"I don't see it that way." And when he didn't answer, "So what's your second thing?"

"You must keep your promise to Atan and visit her. Tell her what happened."

I drew in a breath of sheer pleasure. "Of course I want to go back to the valley, but I keep thinking I might be needed here. You know, in case."

"In case I need any more rescuing?"

My face burned, because it was true. Despite every thing, my feelings were unchanged—I had to watch my brother. Even if he *was* a king. But I kept re what Tsauderei had said about passion and p

Peitar said, "For now, life is quiet here, for both things, if you wish. Eventually return to the old ways, though with signifi I've been thinking about something like t page system."

"When the nobles send their kids to some learn manners and governing?"

"Exactly." He turned his face to the sun. "I people to believe the only requirement for inhe and rank is to be ornamental, because then we'll same problems all over again. But change has to be slow."

I didn't know what to say to that. Some didn't like change, truth be told. Others were trying things they'd dreamed about. Bernal was back in Arnathan, starting his horse farm. Bren was helping repair Riveredge, and thinking about Peitar's offer to send him to Colend, which had the best art academies on the continent.

Mirah and Nina went right back to cooking, but now they had magical aids in the kitchen again. Tsauderei oversaw the mages who were traveling throughout the kingdom, renewing spells. Lexian was prenticed to the silversmiths, and Lizana had come back from Delfina to take Master Halbrek's position when he was appointed a Roving Eye. She didn't say anything, but I suspect she had waited until there was peace because she felt the old loyalties to Uncle Darian, despite her allegiance to Peitar.

Peitar's and my lives were forever changed. Father was dead, and here we were, king and princess. We'd known one another's true selves for so short a time, and now he belonged to the kingdom, whereas I . . .

I belong to myself, I thought, looking out over the lake. Peitar had agreed that if Innon and I wanted, we could dissolve our betrothal. And, before he returned to Delfina, Tsauderei had told me, *Remember what I said. He needs you.*

How? I asked. *I can't govern.*

Be yourself. It's the best gift you can give him.

How could I help him, since we'd promised never to nag each other? What was that about perspective? I groaned again.

Peitar laughed. "Now what's wrong?"

"All that writing. I don't know if I can do it!"

But I have!

And here it is.